Ambrose Conway

BEYOND THE RESO
A Seventies Adolescence

KINGS HART BOOKS

First published in 2009 by
Kings Hart Books
An imprint of Publishers UK Ltd
6 Langdale Court
Witney, Oxfordshire
England OX28 6FG
www.kingshartbooks.co.uk

Cover design: Luke Hughes and Ben Overton © 2009

ISBN: 978-1-906154-12-7

A CIP catalogue record for this book is available
from the British Library.

In memoriam

John Ambrose, Howie Williams and Richard Jones

This book is dedicated to:

The Conway and Hughes families of Rhyl, Auntie Beryl and the family
in Tonypandy and Maerdy, Lesley Hayton, Gail Metcalfe, Deborah
Jones, Vanessa Roose, Brian Jones, Mal Jackson, Martin Gane, James
Smith, Karl Lewis, Mike Bailey, Chris Ruane MP, the McGuinness
family (the Holland team of their day—total football),
Colin Shearing, Liz Plant and Emily of Kings Hart Books,
Dafydd Timothy of Siop Y Morfa, the staff and pupils of Ysgol
Emmanuel and Rhyl High School and Reso residents past, present and
future.

About the Author

Ambrose is a former secondary school teacher and educational consultant who has a particular passion for developing positive reading habits among teenage boys who are so often lost to fiction. He has taught in rural, suburban and inner-city schools and has successfully tested out many of the ideas for *The Reso* on his unsuspecting students.

He grew up in the old Welsh storytelling tradition and recalls the ancient tales of the Mabinogi read in school as well as the stories of hardship, poverty and joy recounted by his parents.

Access to educational opportunity has been a decisive influence in his life and the inspiration for *Beyond the Reso* and its prequel, *The Reso*.

Ambrose Conway is a regular contributor to the educational press with articles on e-learning, raising achievement and inclusive learning among his credits. He has spoken at regional, national and international conferences on similar themes.

Married, with two children, the contrast between his children's upbringing and his own prompted the writing of *The Reso* and *Beyond the Reso* as he found himself constantly comparing the quality of his own experiences of childhood with that of his own sons.

He divides his time between schools, military and industrial archaeology, flying, keeping on top of the garden, reminiscing about the past and worrying about the future.

For interactive resources on The Reso please visit

www.the-reso.co.uk

(please note this site is not controlled or owned by Publishers UK Ltd and as such no responsibility is accepted for the website content)

BEYOND THE RESO
A Seventies Adolescence

CONTENTS

"Remember when we were young, we shone like the sun"

Pink Floyd
1973

It is said that youth is wasted on the young. Who, given the chance, would not want to live those golden, frittered days again? It is for this reason that your parents spend most of your teenage years pointing out where you are going wrong. They can't help themselves. For you represent the closest opportunity to the second chance they will never receive.

(quoted from *The Reso*)

BLURB

At the stroke of midnight on December 31st 1969 I had found myself, albeit fleetingly, in the very agreeable position of being attached to the lips of my rather beautiful Auntie Linda. The new decade had certainly got off to an auspicious start and I had heightened, and probably highly unrealistic, expectations of what the next ten teenage years would have in store for me.

Being attached to Auntie Linda turned out to be one of the high points of what became a decade full of change, most of it painful and disappointing. Three pillars supported my life and all I held dear. All three were about to come crashing down.

The first, my happy existence at Emmanuel Primary School dissolved as part of the natural order of things and I made the transit to secondary school with much excitement and some trepidation.

The second, my home on the Reso estate, along with my friends and secret places, was cruelly snatched from me by the unlikeliest person.

The third pillar, my family, was fractured by events both seismic and secret.

As I was about to find out, life was going to be very different beyond the Reso.

Chapter One
DECADE

If the Clinic playing fields formed the gaping, gap-toothed foul mouth of the Reso council estate, my house was located at the tonsils. Events, good and bad, gargled past our house.

It could be a happy place, as on the stroke of midnight on December 31st 1969, or a place of casual or deliberate violence and menace. I had a fierce loyalty to the estate. I wore, as a badge of honour, the contempt and low expectations the rest of the town invested in us. I knew, and even relished, the fact that we were feared and misunderstood.

I'd grown up in a household where a mysterious, disembodied voice, which sounded remarkably like my mum's, had accompanied me in all my scrapes. It was this voice that had urged caution when my fellow warriors went robbing from the pick and mix at Woollies. The voice was so strong and insistent that I always absented myself from these expeditions on some pretext or other—Romanian family visitors, Polish furniture store employees coming to deliver furniture or some such vacuous excuse.

It would be noble and mature to assume I had developed a keen sense of right and wrong, but to be honest it was fear and a too active imagination that kept me on the more or less straight and narrow. My friends assumed they would get away with their wrong-doing. I always assumed I would be caught. I would be presented to my parents as a habitual felon for a brief and sorrowful parting before I embarked upon, as Sergeant Walker so pithily put it when he had caught me riding my bike on the pavement, "A period of penal incarceration to punish me for my crimes and investigate whether I had a soul worth saving."

I did not know what penal incarceration was. It sounded like the sort of thing that the older lads giggled over when they talked in the corner of the clinic field with their new transistor radio turned up high enough so that you could not make out what they were saying.

I did not like Sergeant Walker though and, if he was saying it, I was sure I'd find it disagreeable on principle. Sergeant Walker had that mix of authoritarian bully boy and evangelical religious zealot based on his 'Strict and Particular' Methodism.

I always thought it strange that his Methodist chapel had the words *Strict and Particular* in gold writing on the chapel notice board. It seemed a bit unChristian-like really. They might as well have written, 'and no riff-raff!' I had no recollection of such sentiments being expressed at any church service, Sunday School or R.E. class that I ever attended and I reluctantly attended many of them. Where Jesus had uttered, "Suffer the little children to come unto me", Sergeant Walker would interpret it to mean, "Make the little children suffer!"

For some people, 'Strict and Particular' Methodism inspired them to do great work in the community. In Sergeant Walker, it merely added religious fervour to his niggardly personality.

It was the fear of Sergeant Walker turning up at my house with a long list of charges against my person, horrifying my parents and bringing disgrace on the family that kept me out of the worst of trouble.

The only thing that could shake my resolve was the ultimate challenge on the Reso—the word 'chicken'.

The accusation of 'chickenhood' would compel me to do the most stupid things. Proving I was not a chicken had seen me disconnect the brake shoes of my bike and cycle unwaveringly on the right hand side of the road around the whole estate pretending, as my tormentors had insisted, that I was an American. Chicken had seen me hold a milk bottle whilst four Little Demon bangers had exploded within it. Chicken had seen me heed the suggestion of a 'friend' at Sunday School, who had suggested that of the four three-penny pieces that I had been given as collection money for myself and my brother, two should go in the collection plate and two on ice creams on the way home. It had seemed an equitable arrangement and I carefully explained the plan to my brother. He had eaten his Cornish Mivvi ice-lolly with relish and I had carefully wiped both his and my mouths with the proper linen hankie I was forced to keep in my Sunday trousers. I had carefully explained that, although the fifty per cent commission WE had taken on the collection money had been fine with God and that the ice lolly did taste remarkably good on that long walk home on the hot Sunday afternoon, it would probably be best if we did not share these facts with mum when we got home.

My brother listened carefully to my words, sucking enthusiastically on his Mivvi, which I took to be agreement, and I relaxed in the belief that our little secret was safe. Outside our gate I stopped him and rehearsed the correct answers one more time. I'd checked with God and he was fine with the ice-lolly idea but that we would keep it to ourselves because mum did not realise that I was now old enough to be able to speak to God personally.

My mother greeted us at the door with the glowing look of one whose children had foregone the boredom of a sunny Sunday afternoon playing with friends to attend Sunday School. I'm sure she saw us, as we stood in the doorway, as wreathed in the light of heavenly benevolence. Behind us, an angelic choir was holding a note of perfect pitch heralding our return to the family fold.

My brother immediately announced, "David spent half the collection money on ice lollies." And the vision was broken. As would have been my brother had I been able to get my hands on him.

It was unexpected turns of events like these that had kept me from a career in crime, and in lie-telling more generally. I had the imagination to know I would get found out.

I felt these certainties on the Reso would continue in the time honoured way but, as the new decade of the 1970s dawned, change was in the heady air.

At the stroke of midnight on December 31st 1969 I had found myself in the very agreeable position of being attached to the lips of my young and rather beautiful Auntie Linda. The new decade had certainly got off to an auspicious start and I had heightened, and probably highly unrealistic, expectations of what the next ten years would have in store for me.

However I was conflicted with two alternative visions of this future. On the one hand, I had every expectation that the pattern of my life in the previous decade would continue unabated. The Reso with all its nooks and crannies would remain comfortingly the same, as would my house at the centre of the spider's web of activity.

On the other hand, there would be changes. Secondary school beckoned and that strange unknown world beyond the estate where people spoke and acted differently. I looked forward with great anticipation to more access to books, models of the plastic kind and biscuits, especially chocolate digestive biscuits.

There would still be the gauntlet of casual violence to run on the estate but my advancing years would leave me better able to cope with that. Hopefully, as my frame bulked up to match my height, I would not be such an obvious lanky target and fights that began with the comment, "You think you're dead tall, don't you?" would become an increasingly rare occurrence.

Another consolation for me was that some of my fiercest potential tormentors—the berserkers of the estate who were untrammelled by any sense of morality or fair behaviour and for whom violence was a way of life—would inevitably fall foul of the police and be temporarily removed from the estate through the good offices of the criminal justice system. That had been the pattern of weeding out on the estate since time immemorial, or at least for the twenty years since the estate had been built, which amounted to the same thing in my book.

True, there was the ordeal of the transition to secondary school to overcome. However, I'd suffered much worse indignities than the traditional 'head down the toilet' and 'satchel over the rugby posts' tales in my daily life on the Reso. To one who had known being held head down among the sticklebacks and leeches of the local cut, the toilet was comparative luxury and certainly more hygienic. I'd also have the kudos of being off the Reso as a guarantor of my comparative safety.

It was a common misconception that anyone 'off the Reso' would come unflinchingly to the support of a fellow Apache in much the same way that the Mafia looked after their own. It was a misconception that many of my fellow Reso dwellers encouraged as it allowed us to be untroubled by lairy miscreants from other parts of town.

In truth, if some of the faces from the estate did leap to your defence, it was less to do with the commonwealth of the Reso looking after its own and more to do with your chief tormentors being put out by outsiders breaking their monopoly on giving you a hard time.

All in all, the transition to secondary school was due to be a happy occasion and a positive experience, although leaving the comfort zone of Emmanuel primary school would undoubtedly be a wrench.

I was aware that, like it or not, and I generally liked it, my world would in future be less circumscribed by the confines of the Reso. I'd move from a world where I knew everyone, and was passingly known by everyone, to one where new faces and opportunities would appear.

I'd glimpsed this on the visit to Glyndwr secondary school where pupils from the other Rhyl schools had been on guided tours. It felt like some medieval town with ties of red and yellow and yellow and black competing with the red and grey stripes of the Emmanuel colours. We were shepherded in groups around the corridors. The others seemed so foreign, yet self-assured, and I felt self-conscious and inadequate in their fleeting company.

I resolved to smile at some of my future fellow pupils and snarl at others so as to keep my options open when the first week in September dawned. Being enigmatic would buy me some time to decide how I wanted to play my hand in the new school, and where in the pecking order I could expect to establish myself. Without being aware of it, I found myself smiling at an inordinate number of what appeared to me to be exceptionally good looking girls from the other schools and snarling exclusively at lads.

In the classrooms were the legitimate inhabitants of the secondary school wearing the house ties of blue and gold. Some seemed deep in work with their teachers while others craned their necks to get a glimpse of younger siblings or friends from their primary schools. They all seemed so much more grown-up than me and I hoped the experience of secondary school would bring about a similar transition in my demeanour.

Over and above the change of school, all would remain reassuringly the same I thought.

I had clearly not picked up on a pattern of events that would ensure that the turn of the decade would bring decisive and fast moving changes in my life, not the least of which was to wrench me from the Reso.

Chapter Two
BATHS

One thing I observed on a regular basis was that things that were bitter, unpleasant or painful were always described by adults as 'character building'. Visiting the school dentist, examinations, the first day of a new job and the open air baths out of season were all sold to me as 'character building'.

The Rhyl Open Air Baths on the promenade were a magnificent structure. They were a massive throw of the financial dice by the local council, to entice holiday-makers to the town from the rival resorts of Llandudno and Colwyn Bay. Dressed in white lime and mortar, like an elongated ice cream melting along the beach, the baths shimmered in the sunlight and nestled around the glass and metal structure of the Royal Floral Hall, protecting it from the sea and the chill north wind and nurturing its south facing aspect.

The Royal Floral Hall had the whiff of what Rhyl might have been. If you had a two shilling piece to spare, exchanged it for a ticket to enter the hallowed hall with its tropical plants, ferns, palms and chattering parrots and stood still in the sunlight, disregarded the smell of fried onions and candy floss and the raucous calls of the Brummie day trippers, you could almost believe you were in a different world—twenty miles up the coast in salubrious Llandudno.

It was probably cheaper to go there on the Welsh Dragon train that linked the resorts and enabled the Llandudno crowd to slum it for the day in 'Kiss Me Quick' land and the Rhyl holidaymakers to aspire to more cultural things.

Not that many Rhyl dwellers entered into the Royal Floral Hall more than once in their lifetime. If you were on this stretch of the promenade with its *Fresh Clwyd Ices* and bracing sun-scorched putting greens, you were heading for the Baths.

If you could not afford sixpence, and there were many times when we could not, the disembodied shouts and screams of children, emanating from behind that twenty foot protective wall were the siren sounds of missed delight. The water was always bluer on the other side of that wall.

We would queue at the castellated entrance to the swimming pool like lemmings, trying as long as possible to stay out of the shade where the temperature dropped markedly and brought out goose bumps on even the hottest days. The pool, at one hundred and ten yards long, seemed to have an unlimited capacity, yet there was always a queue to get in. This could be attributed to one of two people, Alice or Walter, who perched on the high chair at the window where we paid and operated the foot pedal mechanism that released the turnstile to click one person through at a time.

Both Alice and Walter were disastrous in this role for different reasons. Alice was too short for the job really and would have to get off the chair to operate the mechanism for every new entrant. We prayed for an adult with six children to pay for them all in one go and for Alice to click them all through at once. Inevitably, the queue would be made up of youngsters, each paying individually. Alice would insist on settling herself back in the chair after each one paid, shuffling her formidable bottom back onto the seat like some nesting seabird. She seemed genuinely surprised when the next child in the queue asked for a ticket and she was forced to climb down to operate the turnstile mechanism again.

Alice knew us all, our parents, where we lived, where our grandparents lived, where our great grandparents were buried, and felt the need to remind us of it every time we passed her. She was amiable enough, probably lonely, but damned annoying to encounter and share your family history with when all you wanted to do was get through the entrance and swim.

Her silvery grey perm, fussily ornate glasses and rouged cheeks were a constant feature of Rhyl summers. Our exchanges, indeed all her exchanges, always ended with her saying, "Remember me to your mother." We promised to do this but rarely did.

My mum once said that when Alice died, she would take over from Saint Peter on the turnstile at the Pearly Gates. Anyone who could cope in the heavenly queue while Alice constantly hopped up and down off her stool to operate the turnstile foot pedal without using any profanities would be allowed in.

For all her failings in the job specification, Alice was at least pleasant and amiable. Walter brought all the charm associated with a municipal car park attendant to the job. Due to some incongruous and hideous misunderstanding, Walter was under the impression that his job description involved him preventing as many people as possible from entering the baths. He operated a ruthless quota system. If you could not proffer the correct money, he would claim he had no change. If you asked what the pool temperature was he would deliberately take ten degrees from the reading to try and discourage you from entering due to the prospect of impending frostbite and hypothermia.

Any show of impatience, verbal muttering, sighing with intent, or tapping coins on his counter would lead to instant dismissal to the back of the queue. Whereas some people of his age would enjoy giving youngsters a 'flea in their ear', Walter unleashed a whole swarm of waspy invective on every miscreant. He'd quite happily halt the progress of the queue for two minutes at a time to berate anyone who had crossed him. Unfortunately for Walter, his 'window of opportunity' through which he had to pour such invective was the six inch circular speaking hole in the glass window so his worst efforts came out as an incoherent hum to all but those directly in his hissing and spitting line of shot.

Among his many lines of attack was the 'fact' that better people than us had been mown down on the Somme and that they would have loved, absolutely loved, the luxury of standing in the queue rather than pushing up the daisies in the fields of France. They'd turn in their graves to think they had died to support as desperate a bunch of ingrates and good for nothings as was in the queue before him with our long hair, our chewing gum—which he took to be an American affectation—and our bad, bloody attitude. If he had his way, and thank the Lord that he would not, he'd sort the queue into borstal and army and send the girls home to learn how to cook properly and get their hair sorted. Quite frankly, the country would be a better place for it as well and in the long run we'd thank him for it. But we wouldn't.

Having exhausted this line of invective, he'd subside and let one potential swimmer through the turnstile and then someone would ask for change and he would be off again like a chained rabid dog, feeding on angry wasp sandwiches.

I knew that he was right and that many a good man and boy had fallen in the battlefields of France. I was grateful that we were still speaking English because I thought German looked very complicated but I just wanted to get in the baths and swim. So I just kept quiet, offered the right money and didn't make eye contact for fear of antagonising him with a look he decided was lairy.

The click of the turnstile when it came was a blessed relief. We now entered the enchanted walled fortress.

Swinging swiftly right, we'd pass the water temperature reading for the day. Anything approaching seventy degrees Fahrenheit was heavenly.

In the summer I left primary school, we had three weeks at the end of June and the beginning of July when the water temperature did not waiver below seventy four degrees. Everyone who was anyone simply decamped straight from school to the baths.

It was a golden time with old friends and new ones all gathered in the water and on the sunbathing concrete. The pool water, despite daily replenishment from the tidal waters, developed a sheen of cheap sunbathing oil and we were happy to be the golden chips frying in it. The sunbathing concrete required two towels on it to be bearable in this heat and the tarmac pathway which ran either side of the pool boiled and coated the soles of our feet with unforgiving tar.

We thought this would be the *Endless Summer* which we had heard the Californian Beach Boys sing about, only to have the weather break on the same day as the school holiday began and for gales and persistent winds to drive us back to our homes for the best part of two weeks.

Despite this, the two weeks had been heavenly. I'd engineered conversations and water fights with the gorgeous and usually aloof Nicola and Elaine and developed a deep all-over tan which really showed off the dark blue satin swimming trunks with the golden eagle motif that I had inherited from Uncle Tony. Unfortunately, my preoccupation with the girls meant that I'd been somewhat remiss in washing and mangling my trunks thoroughly when changing and three weeks worth of low quality sun oil, industrial strength chlorine and salt water did for them.

My mum replaced them with a cheap blue pair from Woolworths with a white stripe around the waistband and I did not feel special any more. My magic, girl-attracting powers disintegrated with those satin trunks never, I felt, to be fully rekindled.

At sixty degrees Fahrenheit and above, the water temperature was challenging and you either worked to expend plenty of energy in speed contests or played Shark with Woody. Woody was the only person I knew who had the full shark monty. Some had a pair of fins, some had a mask and snorkel, but Woody had the lot. Even without the fins he was as fast as an Australian on steroids in the water. He would give us all a forty yard start along the central lanes of the pool before chasing after us. Inevitably, he'd tag all eight of us before we had the chance to touch base at the far end of the pool. We could not have been more excited than if pursued by a Great White. The flurry of Woody's arm strokes and leg kicks would cause general mayhem the length of the pool with some of the younger swimmers screaming and evacuating the pool and their bladders in a single movement.

The pool shelved gradually from three feet to six feet six at its midpoint before shallowing again. Being six feet tall by this stage, I could manage little tip-toe hops and keep my face above water in the middle indefinitely. This was a useful asset. So much so that I could not help but abuse it.

When Robinson, an emerging bully from another school, passed by the pool and insulted me on being "lanky" one balmy evening, I could not resist suggesting that he got in the water, swam up to me and say this to my face, if he thought he was hard enough. I knew Robinson was a poor swimmer and risked the humiliation of backing down or drowning with me holding him down under in the middle if he decided to try and take me on.

It was the heady concoction of the surrounding girls, the satin trunks and the sound of *Good Vibrations* drifting on a grooving wind that drove me on and I took great satisfaction in the pathetic sight of Robinson divesting some nipper of his lightweight polystyrene float, it being the only thing to hand to throw at me. It wafted ineffectively on the breeze and landed ten yards from me. I laughed disdainfully and followed up with, "Sticks and stones may break my bones, but floats will never sink me!" All the girls laughed and I did a celebratory handstand in the deep water and led my harem to the opposite side of the pool like some triumphant bull elephant seal in dapper satin trunks.

I was somewhat less triumphant two hours later when, exiting the baths, I walked into Robinson and four of his closest allies with a special consignment of fists addressed to me which they seemed particularly anxious to deliver. I made a mental note to either develop gills or to keep my mouth shut when in the water next time.

Despite the pummelling, the black eye and cut cheek elicited a lot of sympathy the next day and apart from the excruciating pain, the battering might almost have been worth it.

Adjacent to the middle of the pool was a large square cut-out which formed the diving area. It was nine feet deep and you did not venture there without risking being depth charged from a very great height.

The diving boards were formed into a ladder with steps escalating at two feet intervals to solid and sprung diving boards. Even when my swimming skills developed, I had an intermittent fear of heights which could suddenly envelop me, and too fertile an imagination to plummet the thirty feet from the top board into the unwelcoming water.

Friends older and younger than me shared none of my trepidation and mounted the steps with reckless bravado to launch themselves headlong into the depths. Perhaps if I could practice quietly I could have built up confidence, but having the pool to oneself was out of the question and public humiliation, as I plunged in shrieking panic like a girl, was yet another reason to avoid the diving area.

I had tried on more than a couple of occasions to mount the steps to practice. I naively thought I could always come down again if the vertigo grabbed me, but the endless queue of humanity climbing the steps behind you made turning back impossible and I was shunted onto a higher board than I'd intended. It was all I could do to unclench my fist from the guard rail and jump with a queue of twenty baying for me to, "GET ON WITH IT!"

I managed to mis-time my last hesitant breath as I entered the water. Any time in the previous thirty seconds would have been adequate. I managed to breathe in as my nostrils entered the water. All those who had not had time to register their mirth or disgust on my inelegant entry, were given ample opportunity to make fun of the coughing, spluttering idiot thrashing for the exit steps with eyes chlorine closed.

One did not go in the water when the temperature registered fifty degrees or below. Unless your school had done a deal with the pool, on a particularly inclement spring, to allow you access to the pool for gratis.

The teachers and all the pupils at my school had initially been very enthusiastic when told that for the next six weeks, at the end of every Wednesday afternoon's school, we would be going down to the outdoor baths for swimming lessons. We'd set out in such high spirits on this adventure— it was, after all, a school trip, like the visit to the theatre we had made and the one to Chester Zoo that was planned.

We were made to march in twos all the way over the Vale Road Bridge and along the High Street. We were too embarrassed to acknowledge anyone we knew as we were press-ganged down the main shopping street like prisoners of war. A couple of parents 'coo-ee'd' at their offspring, who resolutely ignored them and stared fixedly forward.

"There's your gran, Ellis!" said one helpful classmate to the red-faced Ellis. "Shut upppp!" was all Ellis could mutter under his breath.

After the first week when Wally and Russ had detached themselves at the top of the High Street and made their way to the amusement arcades to our left, rather than allowing themselves to be shepherded across the road at the belisha beacon near the clock tower, we were always taken down the boringly residential Bath Street with its lack of temptation and twee guest houses named Shangri La and Dun Roamin'. I had thought that Dun Roamin' was some town in Scotland until someone put me straight.

Walter was clearly highly put out when the main door was opened to let us in en-masse without having to register one by one under his glare at the turnstile. But he was to have the last laugh, for as we turned to the changing rooms we glanced up at the water temperature box and saw it registered *Water Temperature 48 Fahrenheit*. Granted it was a sunny day, but it was early April and a stiff sea breeze was blowing from the north. Clearly, the reported temperature was correct.

We all expressed disappointment that the swimming was going to have to be postponed and prepared to pair up again and begin the march back to school from where we would be dismissed. Unperturbed by the temperature, the teachers began shepherding us to the changing rooms. I thought they were getting us out of the wind to announce that the temperature of the water was so low that swimming would be unsafe. But they didn't, they walked us further and further into the changing rooms to the communal areas at the far end. Boys turned one way and girls the other and a teacher was posted at each entrance door with the brief that we changed quickly.

In its sudden horror, it reminded me of the scene in *The Great Escape* when the party of captured prisoners are given a break on the journey and are talking normally only to turn and see that the Germans had turned a machine gun on them.

We were going to be made to swim in water that was sixteen degrees above freezing in a biting wind. We would have to make our way to poolside over freshly laid and razor-sharp gravel. I looked at our teachers, thinking one of them would let us in on the joke but Miss Jeffries with her kindly face and Mrs Carlisle with her homely one, merely got on with encouraging the class to change faster.

The only thing hurrying up my changing at this point was the dank squalor of the changing rooms. Their substantial concrete and mortar construction mirrored that of an air raid shelter. The heavy walls and single row of glass tile windows high up the thick wall meant that little light and no warmth permeated the building. Cold and damp however circulated freely. Where the roof had leaked, a torrent of green fungus had spread down one wall and dirty water was percolating through it and down into a suspiciously brown stain on the floor. Only the duck boarding on the floor prevented us from having to walk in it as it meandered to the rusted drain in the middle of the floor.

As part of the pre-summer season spring clean, part of the block had been painted in an industrial stone colour and we could smell the incongruous combination of fresh paint and terminal decay in a single sniff.

Mozzie the sensitive, loner boy was already crying and mumbling to himself in a monotone whilst picking idly at the flakes of freshly dried paint where they had bubbled on the damp walls. The current trauma meant that we would get no more sense from Mozzie for the rest of the day as he descended into his regular trough of depression and despair. Our expectations of sense from Mozzie were very limited anyway so this, by itself, was an unreliable indicator of the current state of group desperation.

I'd once asked Mozzie if his family came from the capital of Ecuador because then we could call him Mozziequito. I thought he would laugh as he sometimes did at simple jokes. Instead he burst into tears and started to tear his hair out in small clumps. He ended up looking like the definition of a bad hair day and I resolved to give him a wide berth after this, just in case.

A far better indicator of group desperation was the teeth chattering of some of the girls. This was not the mock teeth chattering accompanied by the slapping of arms which was the international symbol for 'It's bloody freezing!' but real uncontrollable teeth chattering with gaunt, tight jaw-line, blue tinged lips, full body shivering and skin as white as alabaster. I felt sorry for the girls, in their one piece swimming suits and red rubber bathing caps. They looked like novelty matchsticks—the Bronco's which burned green and blue on Bonfire night. Yet we were still in the changing block—God knows what havoc would be caused when the wind chill factor hit us outside.

The boys were trying to tough it out, as the boys always did, but the tell-tale signs of hypothermia were beginning to reveal themselves. Some had gone very quiet and seemed to be trying to occupy the smallest space possible so as to conserve heat. All were deathly white and I knew that had I attempted to talk my voice would come out as a chattering shiver—a frost induced stammer.

Davies the Slipper, who had organised the event and was eyeing our discomfort with some satisfaction, had replaced his Arctic style thermal coat, which he had taken off when we entered the changing block, such was the bite of the cold. No doubt he was busily doing a mental arithmetic sum calculating the satisfaction of getting the whole class into such cold water against the hot water of the parental fallout from losing a child to frostbite.

Like a football manager at Wembley, he led us out of the changing block and around to the far, and most exposed, side of the pool at a brisk pace. There was no roar of the crowd, only that of the biting North wind.

How pathetic a sight we must have made, thirty five of us lined up barely conscious on the side of the pool with The Slipper explaining the technical aspects of swimming, "Without your feet touching the pool floor, Bailey!", the twenty five yards to the other side of the pool, and back into the relative warmth of the changing rooms.

He finished with his habitual, "Any questions?" which was really a rhetorical question in itself, seeing as he would berate, for not listening to his original instructions, any child with the temerity to ask one.

Slower than usual, as the cold bit my brain, I thought to ask for the telephone number of the people responsible for the Geneva Convention and whether he had any small change on him for the 'phone as I appeared to have come out without any. That disembodied frozen voice, that sounded like my mum's stuttered, "Thissss issss not the ttttime nor the pppplace." As usual, the voice was right.

The Slipper put his Acme Thunderer whistle to his lips to signal the start of the swim and blew it in that sharp, clipped way of his. At the side of the pool, toes curled over the curved stonework, nobody moved. The Slipper was clearly incensed. A single blow of his Acme Thunderer could clear playgrounds and stop cloakroom fights. Perhaps its power did not extend beyond the school gates?

I had a beautiful vision of him intervening in a Reso fight with his whistle and the painful surgical procedure that would be required to subsequently remove it from his person.

Thwarted in his plan, the Slipper simply moved down the line and pushed in each wobbling pupil, waiting, with satisfaction, for the shocked gasp of breath as the cold water consumed their body before moving on. After four pupils had been dispatched in this way, some decided to jump in of their own volition, the faster to get the ordeal over with. Davies simply made his way briskly round to the other side of the pool, grabbed hold of the metal pole used to help swimmers in distress and began warding off all the boys, insisting they turned and completed a second width.

A second width was duly completed and we found ourselves in need of help and support to exit the pool and make our way back to the changing block.

We found the girls in a huddled mass close to the one powerful, wall-mounted hairdryer, swathed in bath towels like penguins in a blizzard.

Davies the Slipper led us down to the boys' changing area and allowed us to retrieve our towels from our tartan duffle bags. We sat with the wooden slatted seats corrugating our bottoms as he told us how proud he had been of us, how it would have been easier to postpone the swim but that we had all accepted the challenge and overcome it. He said he felt a warm glow inside that we had accepted this 'character building' challenge. I thought the warm glow came from his fleece lined, wind cheating, thermally insulated jacket. Nevertheless, I would have liked to have basked in any warm glow in my frozen state.

Chapter Three
MARKS

Each year of the 1960s had seen me progress along the classrooms of the external quad of Emmanuel School. I moved anti-clockwise around the school's rooms counting off the years of my childhood.

I'd started in the infants with Miss Hughes, next to the small staff room and the cloakroom with brown shiny tiles and roller towels which were always crisp and clean. Here the soap was of industrial strength, and was carbolic green and brick like.

My abiding memories of her room had been the letters of the alphabet around the wall and the pine scented counting sticks with the yellow 'one inch' stick counting as one and the blue ones counting as five.

I remember my surprise on the first day when the caretaker had arrived at morning break with a crate of small bottles of milk and we had been given one without asking. I don't remember that day as recounted by my mother. She insisted that because of my height, I'd convinced everyone that I was already in school. Indeed I'd even been picked up by the school attendance officer in my garden as a potential non-attender the previous year. On the first day of the real term I had locked myself in the outside toilet and resisted all attempts to dislodge me according to my mother.

At morning break we could also buy Cheese Snacks for one penny a bag and we used to pretend that the box carrying 48 packets was really heavy when we were sent to the stock room for a refill. We'd mock struggle up the corridor fired with pride at being chosen as monitors and excitement at our responsibility. We'd pretend to be steam engines or aeroplanes with our savoury cargo and career down the corridors making the appropriate sound effects until someone appeared at an intersection of corridors or the classroom doors to disrupt our play and investigate the unseemly noise we were making.

But all that was six long years ago and I'd progressed through the school to the last year in primary.

It all seemed like an accelerating blur, each year faster than the previous one. There were autumn fairs and carol services, plays in which I always seemed to be the narrator with pages of script to learn, sports days and exams and worst of all, dental inspections with the foul-breathed and foul-tempered school dentist.

I'd gone from chasing the girls round the playground like a dog worrying a rabbit to speculating on what it would be like to actually capture one.

I'd kicked balls around every blade of grass on the field and got up at four in the morning, as excited at the prospect of playing for my house, Dewi, in the inter-house football match as any player in a cup final.

In all that time I had not really experienced failure, although I was unsure whether this was down to my luck or the school's judgment. I enjoyed school and could hold my hand up for hours in class with that insistent and irritating, "Miss, Miss, Miss!" indicating that I believed I knew the answer. If it was an open-ended question, I'd be prepared to speculate for hours based on prior knowledge. I gathered knowledge like a hedgehog gathers fleas, randomly and incessantly. How irritating to my classmates must I have been, although I never saw it myself at the time.

I had achieved many positions of responsibility from my early days as cheese snack monitor. I'd distributed warm milk and writing paper and been allowed to put out the bean bags and hula hoops in the Big Hall. I liked to think that the teachers recognised my organisational abilities but, on reflection, they would probably do anything to get my insistent hissing of "Miss, Miss!" or "Sir, Sir!" out of the classroom.

A key position I held for a year was to set out the dining room for morning assembly. This was a really responsible job when six of us were allowed in from the cold playground before the bell to remove the benches from the tables, stack the latter in the corner and arrange the former to accommodate the whole school for singing.

In timeless fashion we'd celebrate the *Breaking of Morning, Plough the Fields and Scatter, See Three Ships* at Christmas and *There is a Green Hill Far Away* at Easter. I found the words of these hallowed songs somewhat perplexing. Having *Ploughed the Fields* I wondered why the ploughers had scattered—perhaps they were from the Reso and were in fact trespassing on the farmer's field. I never realised that the second line was attached to the first.

Occasionally, we would sing Welsh songs with gusto. There was a rip roarer of a song with a rousing chorus about coloured goats in which we all had to sing about each coloured goat in turn, compiling them in a list in the fashion of *One Man went to Mow*.

There was a song about a little dog who had new shoes called *Dai Ci Bach* [Dai the little dog]. This contained the memorable line *"wedi cochi eniau scintio"* [having lost his shoes]. When we had practised it in class Tommy Lloyd had burst out laughing, not in a measured way but in paroxysms of laughter. His shoulders heaved and his stomach wobbled and I know the teacher was on the eve of intervening in what she considered a medical emergency. Tears streamed from his slitty eyes and, even though we did not know at what he was laughing, we could not stop ourselves from joining in the mass hysteria. Eventually, even Miss Jones joined in, laughing at the laughter.

It was several minutes before we could get any sense from Tommy. He came to in stages, once he crossed the line when something was so funny it actually started you feeling desolately sad. That feeling came over me regularly when I watched Laurel and Hardy and also Norman Wisdom. It was this feeling of pathos that now gripped Tommy and he tried to explain what had set him off. His first half dozen efforts got no further than sharp intakes of breath and blubbering bubbles of mucus but finally he managed, "We said *Colli*." We stood around dumbfounded, "which sounds like cocky!" and he was off again. This explanation was not really worth the wait.

Nevertheless, whenever we sang that song en masse in assembly we would always sing the line *"wedi **colli** eniau scintio"* with great gusto and all turn our heads to view Tommy as he involuntarily convulsed with laughter as if it had been the first time he had made the connection that was a pale apology for a joke. Each time Mr Roberts would berate him for ruining the tune and send him immediately to stand outside his office.

As a room setting-up monitor I was in a position to change the music on the upright piano and I often substituted good old *Dai Ci Bach* from the sheet music in the piano bench for the chosen tune just to set Tommy off. It got to the point that Tommy would be ejected from the Dining Room by a dismissive wave of Mr Roberts' hand in the line before the offending *cochi*. Tommy would rush out like some incontinent Valkyrie, struggling through the door, stomach heaving with laughter at the expectation of the offending word.

Everyone stayed in school and ate the school lunch and, in Emmanuel, there was a ritual to it that was reassuring.

We sat on tables of eight and we were responsible for turning up at the dining room door in a group of eight which had to include at least two pupils from years lower down the school. This ensured that they got to know the ropes but also gave us a reason to socialise with younger pupils and take responsibility for them. It was in our interest to have a full complement of eight if we were to enter the dining room in timely fashion and maximise our football playing time. It was a clever system all round which had Mr Roberts' stamp of genius on it.

All the food was served on aluminium trays and, wherever possible, divided up into eight portions. The cheese flans and puddings were easy to distribute and the eldest person on the table was responsible for ensuring everyone had equal shares. Less equitable was the distribution of the vegetables and the Friday chips. My liking for sprouts was almost ruined by excess as I was allowed and encouraged to eat as many as possible as there would be no seconds until everyone had disposed of the first course and eight clean plates could be produced in evidence.

There was no choice of food, you ate what you were given, and if you did not like something you hoped that someone else on your table would bail you out as I habitually did with the sprouts. I considered myself lucky that the solid 'meat and two veg' diet I had at home was replicated quite faithfully in the menu. There was only the coconut topping on the otherwise palatable sponge cake and the prunes which were served occasionally to which I had a moral objection.

Friday was fish and chip day and the delicious chips were always a source of dispute as everyone wanted more than their fair share, but only the table captain was in a position to abuse his eighth.

I spent hours in the dining room waiting patiently for food and staring at the unchanging posters on the tiled walls. One illustrated the Scots Guards trooping the colour in the Queen's Coronation year; another, a night scene on the Thames looking down towards the Houses of Parliament and a third, Tower Bridge. I longed to see these places and events in person and staring at them with my eyes slightly out of focus almost made them come to life.

When I was younger, I loved to cocoon myself on the table that extended into what once had been a large chimney breast. For one thing, these were the only two seats in the dining room where your back was supported on the benches. For another, there was a small metal plate, partially secured by screws, beneath the level of the table. I made it my business over two years to release those screws and secure the treasure that I believed lay beyond the plate. I never succeeded and it was left to a younger child to complete my handiwork and claim the prize which probably amounted to a handful of ancient soot and some bird droppings.

As I grew older, and could no longer fit in the alcove due to the restricted head height I preferred the table near the window, beyond which people queued on the corridor. Here you could make rude gestures through the frosted glass and your victims could only guess at your identity. You had to make sure that you had vacated your seat before their eight entered so I tended to confine this activity to when we had managed to reach the pudding stage.

Adults seemed to be incessantly reminding us that this was our final year at Emmanuel. The last school play, the last autumn fair and carol service, the last school trip and, above all, the last opportunity to shoe-horn in those gems of knowledge that we would need to survive in secondary school. I was excited by the prospect of the change, but also knew when I was on to a good thing.

Having to sacrifice the certainties, comfort and excitement of our small school for the anonymity of secondary school was a difficult call for me. I was surprised that others could not wait to move on, without any appreciation of what they would leave behind.

Chapter Four
STAR

There were many things to look forward to on the first day of the first term of my career in secondary school.

After six years of heading down the same road to primary school, it seemed very strange turning left out of the estate and heading towards the railway sidings before turning right past the turning into Clwyd Ave, where my cousins lived, and right again into the road on which our new school, which had always been known as Glyndwr School, but had now been renamed Rhyl Junior High School, stood.

I knew only too well, and the starch crispness of my new white shirt and pristine black blazer reminded me, that everything was different now. Unlike some, I secretly resented leaving primary school. I'd enjoyed the pattern of the year, the routines and festivals and the staff who had all, in their various ways, ensured that I had had such a great time growing up secure and happy.

I would have been happy living my whole life in Emmanuel with its comfortable certainties and measured excitement. I did not take for granted that, being bigger, the new school would be better than my old one.

Familiar faces among the staff would be gone, as would the pleasant geography of the school. Each place holding cherished memories, the parquet flooring and glazed tiles. The ropes that opened the curtains on the stage always summoned up the dry throat of a reluctant stage debut in the school play, with expectant parents beaming brightly behind the maroon drapes. The metallic measuring jugs and sand tray in which we used to study 'Capacity'. The huge square metallic tins which held the powder paints, accessible only when you had levered off the circular lid with a penny coin. The astringent chemical smell of the Gestetner copying machine in the secretary's office; which she wound demonically with a handle, like a reluctant car engine. The grainy metal of the climbing frame in the Hall, which was where we would hang upside down until we felt sick. All these would be lost to me now and I wasn't sure I was ready to give them up.

On that early September morning, in shining new shoes that squeaked when I walked, too tight yellow and blue tie, new to school haircut and pained expression, I said goodbye to all that had been Emmanuel School.

Clearly, not everyone felt the same as me. There was unbridled excitement in the eyes of most of the first year pupils. They did not give a thought to the past. Their eyes were firmly on the large secondary school looming in front of us. Some seemed too eager to enter its gates. Some had even forgotten to lose the black caps that had been included in the uniform list, but which only the most pitiful parents would insist their child wore. The boys from the Reso stood out as being bareheaded and brazen-faced.

What had begun as a black trickle off the estate had congealed into hard knots of Reso boys, as always, feeling security in numbers. I'd caught up with James and half a dozen others. Normally James was safe company but, seeing me, he started on a theme that he had played throughout the summer holidays.

"Brave of you to turn up, seeing as Howie is going to sort you out today."

This had been my worst nightmare, and perhaps why I had spent the last few days dwelling in the past rather than relishing the future. James had regaled me over the summer with tales of the legendary Howie, a brute of a lad, whom I only knew by reputation. Howie, according to James, hated tall lads, lads with birthmarks, lads who shouted out, "Sir, sir, sir!" when answering too many questions in class.

I'd laughed things off at first as James had never wound me up like this before, but he returned to this theme so often that I began to believe that Howie would see in me the sum of all he hated.

As we arrived, James indicated a well set boy with dark, curly hair and large white teeth. He seemed to be the centre of everything going on, a tornado in human guise flicking off caps, dribbling footballs and catching tennis balls with fantastic dexterity. No doubt this was Howie and shortly I would be the one with blood tricking down my freshly ironed shirt and over the new brown leather briefcase that I clung to like a life belt.

I knew the briefcase had been a mistake when my parents handed it to me. I found it stuffed with their expectations for my secondary education. A pencil case with new pencils; two ended rubber with pencil and pen deleting properties; pencil sharpener; a ruler; protractor and set square; several biros of various colours and a Platignum cartridge pen with four spare cartridges.

I suddenly realised that this was the opportunity that they had been denied and they were determined that I was not going to be disadvantaged as they had been by circumstance. My dad's grammar school education had been stolen by the Great Depression when his father, employed as a craftsman in the house building trade, had been laid off. My mum had lost a proper secondary education to the Second World War. Suddenly, the battering I was about to take seemed small beer.

Howie strode towards me with an air of menace. He eyed me up and down and I waited for the insult that would precede the violence.

"So you're David are you?"

I tried to think of the right answer and considered saying nothing. Before I could assemble any reply, I felt a mighty whack on the back and a smiling Howie was whisking me off to play football. James collapsed in laughter behind me. Thinking this was the lull before the storm, I treated Howie with suspicion for the first week. However, seeing him in action I realised that I had made a good friend. He intervened to break up fights, ensured that no one in his circle was bullied and was truly merciless with people who picked on the weaker kids.

Whereas most people I knew merely protected what they considered to be their own self-interest, Howie was different. He had a very clear sense of right and wrong and would always intervene and place himself at physical risk to see that right prevailed. It was like being friends with someone who had the presence of Genghis Khan and the morality of Robin Hood and I enjoyed his company. I'd like to think that I shared his outlook and view of fair play but, in truth, I realised I was something of a coward, intervening loudly only when I knew the odds were stacked in my favour. Howie would wade in even when the odds were against him if he thought someone was having a hard time of it.

Howie was afraid of nobody and nothing, or at least gave that impression. He was the first person I had met who was not intimidated by the Reso. In that first week at secondary school, being part of the Reso lost some of its appeal. Ideas that I had grown up with were suddenly challenged or replaced with fresh ones and I felt that, for the first time, I was less of a pack animal and more of an individual. Perhaps secondary school was going to have some benefits after all.

In the coming years of secondary school, I would spend much time in the company of Howie and none of it was wasted. I'd be bemused by his skills at sport where he had phenomenal hand-eye coordination and the speed, strength and agility to turn to any ball sport.

I played in rugby matches where he would break through a line of highly proficient backs with the guile of a safe-picker or the strength of a rampant lion. Sometimes, he would turn back on himself weaving back towards us, trailing bemused opponents in his wake pretending he was scared of them catching him before turning back on his track to accelerate and burst across the try line. We felt we would never lose whilst he played for us.

Living close to the Marine Lake, Howie could find his way into all the rides, even when the fair was closed and we once spent three hours on a bouncy castle until I was too exhausted by somersaults and laughter to move and he was still bouncing and talking his usual gibberish.

He convinced me at one point of the highly unlikely fact that he could speak Swahili and that you could get by in parts of South Africa with the three words 'ewsh', 'bop' and 'gish'. He claimed it was not so much the words as the way you said them that conveyed meaning. Whenever we were in a tight spot or wanted to indicate happiness or despair, one of us would shout, "Ewsh!" to which the other would reply, "Bop!" and we'd both exclaim, "Gish!" Nobody understood us of course, and I had a nagging suspicion that the population of South Africa would have been equally dumbfounded. Still, it kept us amused.

Chapter Five
PIT

For some however, the change to secondary school did not represent a new beginning.

Andy Mottram was a small, bedraggled, moon-faced boy with a permanently running rose. Any conversation with him was always punctuated by copious sniffing. When he was particularly animated or playing football, a snail trail bead of thick mucous would descend from his nose and make an excursion to his upper lip. A sharp sniff would see it defy gravity and retreat back up its path and into the cave of his nostrils.

I'd known him in my primary school, where his name was a byword for mayhem and his luck was not about to change in secondary school.

I know the redoubtable Jones the Adjective, in our primary school, would have heartily approved of the term 'unkempt' for Andy. He could make anything he wore look untidy. Technically, he always wore school uniform, but he wore it in a, and this was another term Jones would have relished, dishevelled way. His grey jumper had punctured sleeves where his bony frame had poked through as he elbowed his way to the ball or through the lunch queue.

In place of a school badge Andy had a singed iron burn where the flat of the iron had been left in contact for too long as his mum dealt with some more pressing domestic crisis. His trousers were always tinged with mud and nobody in the Mottram household had the time or inclination to clean them on a regular basis.

In the dinner queue, Andy was always too eager. When he was made the dinner monitor, by virtue of being in the top year of the primary school, he doled out the food with scrupulous fairness. Everyone received their fair share and he always claimed seconds for his table. Clearly, he had played this role at home with his five younger brothers and one sister. But the relish with which he tucked into his food, the insistent way he scraped the last vestige of gravy from his plate and custard from his bowl, made it clear that school dinner was his main meal of the day.

Andy was never really a close friend. He was always on the edge of my vision, more often than not getting into trouble. He had the unfortunate habit of being the last one lingering at the scene of an incident when the authorities, in the form of teachers or caretaker, arrived.

Where we would say nowt or deny all knowledge of anything untoward happening, he would always argue his case passionately, and often articulately, but always with the same result. He would always end up with the blame and the more he protested, the more teachers felt inclined to punish him. In many cases, I knew he took the blame for others.

"The trouble with you Mottram," declared Mr Jonas in his most magisterial voice, as if he were a some High Court judge passing sentence, "is that you do not know a 'fair cop' when you see one. I predict a life of crime for you, punctuated with spells of incarceration. No doubt, all hope of time off for good behaviour will be lost as you attempt to argue the toss with the prison officers. But at least good people will sleep sound in their beds knowing that your persistent bleating and habitual snotty nose will be off the streets and out of earshot."

This would have been a pretty damning rebuke if delivered personally in the privacy of an empty room. Unfortunately, this was a whole school assembly and we all heard this stinging put-down. Andy was quiet for a moment as, like some barrack room lawyer he considered his options. He drew himself up to his full, meagre height, inhaling copiously as he did so. The mucous rasped upwards into his nose. Gamely, and with his voiced trembling, he proclaimed, "You've got no right to talk to me like that."

Jonas' patience, always a fragile thing, like Chinese porcelain, broke. No more the measured insult, with spittle at his lips he shouted, "Outside the Headmaster's study now!"

It felt like we were living the illustration we had seen in the history book the previous week of the tortures of the Spanish Inquisition. I wanted to implore Andy to recant his accurate but inappropriate words. He walked out as tidily as he had ever done anything, without a flicker of fear in his face. At that moment I envied him his dignity, if not his fate.

I had moments of envying the lives of most people in school. Mike, when he was the first in the class to get a Raleigh Chopper bicycle in racing yellow with black trim; Russ, when his family got a telephone of their own in their house and never had to bother with Button A and Button B again; Dewi when his family went all the way to Bournemouth by train on holiday—every year! I never envied Andy and never wanted to share the series of disasters and the faint smell of sweat, margarine and tobacco which constantly accompanied him.

In the year before we moved up to secondary school, by some effort of will, Andy did particularly well in some examinations and was elevated from the fifteen 'slow' learners who inhabited the cupboard of a room known as 'The Remove' and joined us in the main room.

Like the Football League, the classroom operated on a promotion and relegation basis and Andy replaced Kevin who had occupied the desk nearest the door—a stark reminder that his position in the class was tenuous. This system of two classes has been used as the basis of deciding those pupils who would sit the eleven plus examination. This judged, at eleven years of age, whether they would be clever enough to access the grammar school and the good jobs that lay beyond it. The alternative was the secondary modern which was seen as the option of those destined for craft or manual jobs in factories or shops.

Although the grammar and secondary modern had been abandoned for a comprehensive system two years before, this brutal method of ranking us persisted because it seemed that the teachers did not know how to replace a system with which they, at least, were comfortable.

Kevin had sunk without trace that summer, falling further and further behind in his work and unable to understand explanations when they were offered, and increasingly immune to rebukes when prodded. It was no surprise when he was asked to stand up and empty his desk once the register had been taken on that first day in September. He marched out to 'The Remove' as if court-martialled.

His place was taken by a bemused Andy who eyed the room and us with suspicion, like some wild-eyed Chester Conklin in the Laurel and Hardy films. He entered, animal like, placed his few learning possessions inside his desk and sat uncomfortably as thirty-five pairs of hostile eyes viewed him relentlessly for the first sign of trouble. The feeling was mutual, as we quickly realised that his tongue would inevitably get him into a cycle of trouble in which we did not want to be embroiled. On reflection, he must have felt pretty lonely in our classroom, but we did nothing to accommodate him.

The inevitable came to pass and, despite his best efforts, his isolation meant that he made little progress. From long division to similes, we did things differently in our room and there were glaring gaps in his knowledge and understanding. Jonas the Slipper often stated that, metaphorically, our learning was like a highly detailed road map which would equip us to navigate through life. Andy must have felt that he held nothing more substantial than tissue paper for his journey.

It was exceptionally cruel that Jonas, in a particularly spiteful act of revenge for backchat in the Hall, left it to the half term before we left primary school when we were winding down for the holidays, with examinations done and the prospect of the visit by our class to Chester Zoo, to demote Andy back to 'The Remove'. He chose the last collection of parental contributions for the zoo trip to reimburse Andy the full amount of the trip. He tipped it contemptuously on his desk so that coins rolled onto the floor where Andy would have to lose his dignity and pursue them.

"Your parents, or more accurately, parent, will no doubt have better things to do with this money than finance your visit to see monkeys and apes, Mottram. Collect your things and depart to The Remove. You have no further part to play in this room."

The glare from his eyes showed that Andy was ready to stand and fight. The thought of losing the money held sway though and he forced himself to the floor to collect the coins to return to his mum. At this moment, Andy could not afford the price of dignity which was precisely £1.50 in small denomination coins.

I felt shocked and ashamed that I did not have the courage to speak up at this point. I don't know what I would have said. I did not know how my parents would react when a letter saying that I had been insolent in class duly arrived at their door. They had always backed the school fully and if the school said I had been insolent, that would be good enough for them, I could expect punishment at home as well as in school.

Despite this, I did know that by saying nothing I was on the side of someone who was very wrong to treat another person in this way. It did not feel good to be such a coward and I knew that I should have been on the side of the underdog. But I said and did nothing and comforted myself in thinking there was nothing I could do or say that would have changed things. I thought about my dad's reaction when we were watching *All Our Yesterdays* and pictures of the liberation of Belsen concentration camp came on the screen. Through gritted teeth he told me that he considered that his five years in the army had been wasted time in many ways but seeing what the Nazis had done and were then denying made it worthwhile.

Andy's luck did not change when we got to secondary school.

The secondary school forms were deliberately made up of pupils from all the three main contributory primary schools so you could be sure of no more than a few people from your old class in your new form.

We were now expected to wear blazers for the first time. For those first few weeks we all looked the same and this represented a fresh start to all. For me, moving between lessons was, generally, a liberating experience. I liked the specialist equipment in the science and woodwork rooms, the skeletons and lathes and suspended globes. Once I had mastered the first few weeks of the timetable, and the need to have different books covered in swatches of wallpaper or brown wrapping paper, I settled into the routine.

I particularly liked the fact that P.E. was taken seriously, and, following a series of after school trials, found myself picked to represent the school football team. I could not have been prouder than when I ran home to tell my parents. I knew I was not the most talented footballer in the year but being tall and relatively fast meant that there would always be room for me in the team. I simply had to ensure that the ball came to me infrequently enough for my distinctly average dribbling skills to remain hidden.

I remember saying to Andy just before half term that I had decided that the endless *'ecoutez et repetez'* in the French room was getting me down more than a little. I did not know which town it was but I now knew the proximity of the church to the station and the baker to the library and all the *'gauches'* and *'droites'* required between them.

He did not know what I was talking about. He conceded that he had not attended a single French lesson since the term began. The scale of his absence was such that he had been deleted from the French teacher's register.

The mayhem of the first few weeks of the new timetable and the novelty for the pupils of moving between lessons left plenty of time and space to lose yourself, should you choose. No-one was willing or able to grass him up as only his old Emmanuel pals could put a name and face together and secretly, they admired his enterprise. Officially, Andy did not exist as far as the French Language and its classes were concerned.

Andy had managed to officially disappear within school for two hours a week. I asked him what he did with this time. He said he spent some of it doing any homework that was required, the afternoon sessions sunbathing in the small orchard in the rural studies garden and sometimes he simply sidled off home. Occasionally, he would team up with others who had dodged the odd lesson and they'd play cards quietly, in the toilets if it was raining, or beyond the far wall of the woodwork shed, amongst the debris of past woodworking projects and drama sets.

It seemed like a charmed life until the day we saw him from our French room windows, being propelled by the scruff of the neck by the rugged metalwork teacher with calloused hands, across the field and towards the Head's office. I'd heard the term 'your feet won't touch the ground lad!' many times but this was the first time I'd witnessed it. Andy's feet seemed to be bicycling without making contact with the ground. His feet were certainly moving faster than the two of them were walking.

The metalwork teacher, in his no nonsense tortoiseshell glasses and brown apron of the kind worn by people who worked in hardware shops, was making swift progress across the playing field. His silver grey hair, which looked like it had been filed into place, glinted in the sun at every footstep. He had an air of triumph on his face as if the capture of this truant was the highlight of his career to date.

Andy was ceasing to struggle, like a fish lifted from the water on a hook. No doubt the fact that the teacher also had hold of him by the tie and he was slowly being strangled if he resisted played a part in this.

Andy's mistake this day had been to decide to go home early on a day when the metalwork teachers had decided to hold a departmental meeting in the usually empty workshop on the far side of the field. The glimpse of a bunking pupil passing their windows had alerted all four teachers and they had moved like silent commandos to grab Andy as he climbed the tall iron railings at the locked gate that separated him from freedom. He had one leg over the top of the fence and was in a very compromising position when he felt the grab that alerted him to their presence. Any attempt to continue his climb over the green painted gate, with its blunt iron points would cause serious damage to his undercarriage and he knew the game was up.

"For you Mottram, ze bunk is over!" said one of the teachers who recognised him, and affected the accent of one of the German guards in the prisoner of war films that were a staple of Sunday afternoon television. The teachers all laughed in celebration of the capture and Andy was forced to dismount the fence carefully and present himself to his captors with an uncharacteristic air of resignation.

My classmates, endlessly '*ecoutez*-ing *et repetez*-ing' responded to the monotonous voice on the tape recorder demanding to know when the train was due to leave *la gare*, was it at a quarter to or a quarter past eleven? I was otherwise engaged, imagining Andy's fate in all its gory detail. I heard the substantial wooden door slam with an artillery boom and the distinctive squeak and tread on the wooden block flooring. Then, silence…

To be caught bunking on a single day was one thing. When the attempt to return him to his French class resulted in all the teachers denying knowledge of him, the offence was compounded and his fate was sealed. Furthermore, his absences, by sheer fluke, had coincided with a spate of vandalism in the school, a broken ball-cock in the lavatories, offensive writing on the wall of aforesaid toilets in marker pen (this was a time before it was called graffiti) and the wilful distribution of unused toilet paper across a corridor. As the Head had reminded us from the stage in his weekly address which had the ring of a colonial administrator addressing the natives, "Such incidents might seem insignificant in themselves but they are symptomatic of a slippery slope down which I, the school, and wider society are not prepared to slide."

What had sealed Andy's fate though was not this assembly of offences but the fact that the Head had appealed to the school population in the previous week's assembly, to report 'in confidence' the name of the perpetrator of a particularly nasty act of vandalism. The Head, in his best academic gown, had paused at this point and used his hands to suggest the words 'in confidence' were in quotation marks.

To his, "disappointment, nay chagrin," nobody had come forward to turn in the miscreant. He correctly picked up the fact that we were totally bemused by the word chagrin and his response, in the room of over five hundred pupils was to call out, "You! Tall boy! Find out what the word chagrin means and make sure that this definition is disseminated around this maddening crowd by next week. I shall randomly select a pupil to define it next assembly and, if they cannot, I shall hold you responsible for this collective failure of vocabulary."

How embarrassing I thought, as I turned round to see which unlucky urchin had been picked out amongst all these people and described, like a piece of storage furniture. The punch in the leg from Brian and the sly, smiling wink from Howie on the back row made me realise that I was at the epicentre of everyone's stares.

"You! Tall boy, looking around inanely—the task is yours!"

I was the piece of furniture it transpired.

The Head returned to his task, "I repeat my generous offer to the informant and reiterate the seriousness of the incident—"

The incident in question revolved around the fact that the school was expanding to accommodate us all. There were some builders on site who had brought with them a mobile office and a toilet block on wheels which had been set up in the farthest corner of the playground, next to the construction work.

The Head recapped the misdeed. Standing behind the podium with the school crest emblazoned on it, he drew himself up to his full height and launched again into an account of the heinous incident. "At some time last Tuesday morning, someone in this assembled throng was responsible for crawling underneath the builders' mobile personal rest facility (he could not bring himself to say toilets) and took it upon himself to unscrew the jacks that supported it in the perpendicular plane, thus rendering the facility tottering!"

Brian, next to me, was desperately suppressing all sound of laughter. His shoulders were wobbling, tears were welling in his eyes and he was now biting his knuckles in a vain attempt to stifle the uncontrollable urge to laugh out loud.

There was a general murmur of excited amusement across the hall at the Head's graphic description of the incident. The pupils were joining the dots of what would ensue as a hairy-arsed builder found himself ejected from the collapsing toilets in less than perpendicular fashion and with his trousers around his muddy, wellingtoned ankles.

The staff assembled on the stage had been briefed to see if there was any tell-tale shuffling of potential guilty parties but the general swell of suppressed laughter across the sea of faces had prevented the identification of individuals and risked open mayhem.

Wizened Mr Burton (we called him Gonfera, as in *gone for a Burton*), part of the Head's Praetorian Guard, was left to step in, glaring with contempt from the stage he stood up to quell the mirth and squinted at us, muttering oaths that included such gems as "contemptible imbeciles!" and "unwashed miscreants!" At one point I thought he was going to describe us as 'malignant ne'er do wells!' and he would have used the full set of Dickensian curses to be employed by overbearing characters against the poor, working classes.

The sting of these insults passed me by as I was still reeling from being described so charmlessly, as "Tall boy!"

With the absence of a volunteered name, Andy Mottram had this serious misdemeanour set against him as well. The systematic bunking of lessons had been bad enough but this, according to the teachers, had been the most serious incident in the school in years.

I had witnessed the second most serious incident in the previous week and, surprisingly, it had involved Brian, one of my best mates off the estate.

We had rapidly changed for our afternoon P.E. lesson and were making our way up to the playing field past the mobile classrooms into which had been decanted the science department during the building work. We had already broken our earnest promise to Mr Evans, P.E., to proceed quietly across the concrete playground and past the science lessons in the mobiles without causing a disturbance.

We were bouncing balls, 'headering' balls, playing 'keepie-ups' and generally being noisy. I kicked a ball lazily to Brian, who recognised in its flight the opportunity for that most beloved of football shots, the perfect volley. He steadied himself with a little shuffle of his feet and moved forward to meet the downward path of the ball. Brian was in the habit of providing a commentary to all his most glorious football moments.

The ball met his well dubbined football boot and arced away perfectly, as if to swell the goal net.

"Charlton—smack," announced Brian as we admired his powerful shot, reminiscent of those twenty-five yard hay-balers of B. Charlton of Manchester United and England which nearly broke the goal nets with their force.

We were still admiring it, when Brian, more directly in line with the shot than us, realised the destination of the ball and added "bugger!" to his commentary. With a frightening inevitability the ball, still not decelerating, hit the open Chemistry lab window and exploded into the mobile, knocking over the Leiberg Condenser at the feet of Jones the Smoke, the bull-like chemistry teacher.

In our previous lesson he had assembled the Condenser before our eyes and we had asked the usual question, "How much does one of those condensers cost Sir?"

"This equipment, boy, is priceless," he had said reverently whilst manipulating the glass tubes and rubber hoses and tenderly tightening the clamps as if he was caressing his girlfriend.

This equipment was now lying shattered at his feet as he had been heading to the window to berate us for the noise we were making.

We all looked at Brian to make sure there would be no doubt where the blame lay. An accident was an accident, but a priceless condenser was not something we intended to take the rap for. We needn't have worried though, Brian knew the rules and let us all off the hook by volunteering, "Sorry Sir."

Jones, a man not accustomed to silence, had lost all his bluster. He looked at the shattered condenser, then Brian, and then the shower of glass that had been the condenser again. He finally looked up with a resigned gaze and merely gestured with an outstretched arm to the Head's office.

Brian turned on his heel and like a scolded dog retraced his steps to the door that led to the Head's office. He walked in a curious pigeon-toed gait with hunched shoulders like one who knows a harsh fate awaits him. As Brian's family raced pigeons, his impression now was spot on.

I felt the need to support my best friend in his hour of desperate need, as I hoped that someone would have stepped forward to help me. It was my duty as a friend, the clear playing out of the message of the parables I'd heard so insistently in Sunday school and from my mum. It was my Christian duty.

Immediately though, I felt an even more overwhelming need to go and play football, which I did, leaving poor Brian to his fate.

Brian was able to avoid the perils of the cane, slipper or belt which was the usual tariff for such a serious incident. He apologised fulsomely and sincerely for the accident and even offered to pay for a replacement. I'm not sure how his parents would feel about being saddled for the bill for a 'priceless' piece of chemistry apparatus though.

He capped his apology by an unprompted monologue about how he saw so clearly how he had let both Mr Evans and Mr Jones down in his foolishness and that the incident had given him food for thought about how quickly, if people took the 'law into their own hands', things could escalate to the level of a serious accident.

It was a virtuoso performance which left the Head with very little to say really. Here was a boy who seemed to have taken on board the critical points, fed like pearls before swine from the stage at every assembly. To punish him further would be perverse. Brian and the Head parted as friends with a gentlemanly handshake and the promise from the Head not to mention the unfortunate incident ever again. Brian could not believe his luck, and nor could we.

Andy shared no such luck, his lack of eloquence meant that he was in the frame for all the unsolved incidents of the last half term. The Head meted out the full force of his righteous wrath on poor Andy.

The use of corporal punishments in schools at the time was a given and I considered myself to have been lucky to have avoided such punishment myself to date. Some staff kept a weapon in their classroom to curb the more enthusiastic pupils. A favourite was the slipper. This was not in fact a soft and comfortable bedroom slipper, much beloved of our grandparents, but a black plimsoll. The plimsoll was unused for its original purpose which meant that it was stiff and unyielding and a whack on the bottom instantly imprinted the tread pattern on your backside. Several blows would give your backside the texture of tenderised steak, or so I was told. We didn't eat much steak in our house so I could not comment on the accuracy of the statement. When I say we did not eat much steak, it would be more accurate, in fact totally accurate to say that, if you discounted stewing steak, we didn't eat any steak in our house.

In secondary school, the craft rooms provided ample personal weaponry for the short tempered teacher. Mr Burton favoured a piece of dowelling, specially selected from his wood store. He had more than enough dowelling in stock to cope with any eventuality. He chose the diameter of the dowelling to fit the crime and administered the punishment to the outstretched hand.

That was until Chisholm, a thick set lad who towered above Mr Gonfera Burton, grabbed the dowel on the first downstroke and held it vice-like until the teacher had to relinquish his end of it in what had been a battle of wills that went on for a seemingly endless minute. For a second, I thought Chisholm was going to turn his weapon on the teacher, but instead he snapped it across his knee and dropped the fractured pieces to the floor in what turned out to be a victory for us all.

The alternative woodwork teacher, Mr Shirley, had an altogether different approach to discipline. Unlike Gonfera's lessons, which were endured rather than enjoyed, woodwork in the brick built annexe that looked liked a converted garage was a highlight of the week. We hung on every word uttered by the slightly manic Mr Shirley. He could never remember us by name so individually, or as a class, we were always referred to as 'laddy'.

He would veer from the finer points of the mortice and tenon joint to a discourse about the Arab-Israeli dispute and the importance of righteousness. He was a stickler for tidiness and the return of all tools to the shadow boards at the end of the lesson. Woe betide anyone not bringing an "Apron, Clean, Woodwork for the use of." This habit of describing things was a hangover from his time in the services. All but the youngest male teachers had either fought in the Second World War, like my dad, or had experienced National Service. I thought life must be rather boring nowadays for those who had faced gunfire and active service.

"I don't want to hurt you laddy," was a favourite refrain, "but I will do!" and placing my hand on the workbench, he would take up a chisel and stab it down between my outstretched fingers. He'd build up a rhythm and would look you straight in the eye as he brought the glistening blade of the chisel down again and again. The secret was to look him back in the eye with confidence. Once he knew you had implicit confidence in him things were good.

Although this was a bizarre initiation ceremony, it had its purpose. After the majority had endured the chisel ordeal, he never need raise his voice to us again. Indeed, there was a queue of classmates every new lesson asking to go through the chisel torture so that they could graduate to the elite.

"The punishment for any misdoings from this point forward," Shirley the Dowel declared with religious gravity, "is to endure the lesson with my acute disappointment sitting heavily on your shoulders."

To emphasise the point of the sheer weight of his disappointment he would place you standing bolt upright in the middle of the woodwork room, arms held out at ninety degrees to the side of the body and a heavy, hard-wood cutting board balanced precariously on the back of your outstretched hands. Here we would stand in agony trying to lock our protesting muscles in place so as not to succumb to the tangible weight of his disappointment by dropping the board.

Another practical teacher, who taught rural studies and stood six foot square made a point on our first lesson of introducing us to his colleague, Betsy. Betsy was a substantial wooden bar from the back of a chair. He explained with great elegance that he was a cultured and easygoing man, but that Betsy abhorred indiscipline and that for all our sakes it was best that we behaved and did not make closer acquaintance with her.

He made us all say goodbye to Betsy and replaced her in the desk drawer. If at any time he felt that we were on the edge of bad behaviour, or even if we were being too boisterous, the drawer was silently opened and Betsy appeared on the desk without a word said. A ripple of fear went round the room and we were quickly subdued. It was a highly efficient system.

The legend of Betsy linked whole generations of the school, yet no-one had ever seen her used in anger. The prospect of Mr Edwards, a man who could double dig a trench as fast as a JCB, actually wielding Betsy in anger was too horrible to contemplate. His was the most disciplined class in the school. After all, who was going to argue with a bear of a man who classed among his closest friends a piece of female wood with which, he claimed, he went on holiday every year.

At the top of the punishment order was the strap or the cane which was administered by the Head or deputy and whose lashes were entered in the punishment book. It was this punishment that Andy had to look forward to.

From the French lesson it was on to P.E. and we were quickly changed and up on the far playing field picking teams in the time honoured way.

Having gone to retrieve the ball from an errant shot, I passed the long jump sandpit which would see no use for a further term and a half. Hidden from view at the bottom of the pit in the damp sand was a sobbing Andy Mottram. He was clearly distraught and blubbering and to spare him a crowd of people gathering, I kicked the ball back and pretended to retie my laces at the edge of the pit so that the game would continue without me and I could talk to Andy.

He was in such a state that I first thought that my best bet might be to call an ambulance. Between gasps and tears he managed to piece together what had happened in the Head's study.

He had received what was unjustly called 'twelve of the best'. I noticed he was shivering, not from the day, which was warm and balmy, but from the throbbing pain of the beating. I knew this pulsating pain from when I had fractured my wrist and had to sit for three hours in the casualty department without painkillers in case it needed resetting in an operation. Andy's words followed the pattern of the pain and he inhaled swiftly as the next wave of pain hit.

After some disjointed sentences he managed, "This is what the git did to me."

Still lying down, he dropped his trousers to reveal twelve deep red/blue welts of angry flesh, bloodstained and puckered on his thin legs. At points the welts intersected and the skin had been broken quite deeply. I could see where the blood had stained lines across his trousers.

I was certainly no stranger to violence and had seen blood and broken bones on the estate as the result of fights or accidents but never anything like this. To think a full grown adult had done this as a form of justice or discipline was beyond belief.

Until now I had seen the Head as a well-meaning, well-educated man who was simply out of touch with the modern world. I now regarded him with contempt.

To allow Andy time to settle himself, I stayed with him for a few more minutes then drifted off to rejoin the football match. I did not let on to anyone else that he was there. I could offer no more comfort to him than to leave the fruit flavoured Polo sweets I'd sneaked out to share at half time in the game. It didn't seem to be enough really.

Chapter Six
SHIP

By New Year 1970, I had rather high expectations of my role in the night's celebrations. I'd matured to the point that there was no chance of me falling asleep and missing the whole party as I had done in 1967 when I had first been promised I could stay up for the night. Nor would I repeat the mistake of 1968 when I end up playing Ludo behind the settee by myself because I was too young to understand the significance of the ritual and too shy and intimidated to hold hands with the adults for *Auld Lang Syne* when midnight struck.

I would be a bona fide party regular. Admittedly, I'd have no interest in the Watney's Party Sevens perched on our new twin tub in the kitchen. What adults saw in this foul smelling, evil tasting brew was beyond me. There was a clue, I thought, in the name…'Bitter'. Why go to the trouble of naming something that was designed to bring enjoyment with such a rank name? The alternative was even worse, 'Mild'. It seemed a strange word to use for a drink that regularly left some of our neighbours strident and ready for a fight at the least provocation.

I would stick to my Corona cocktails of Lime, Cream Soda and, if I needed to adopt the airs of one more advanced in age, Dandelion and Burdock which I would pass off as Mild. I would be the perfect host distributing the home-made sausage rolls, cheesy footballs and crisps of many flavours. I'd be particularly careful when distributing the cheese and spam and pickled onion on cocktail sticks, making sure that Auntie Linda always had first choice of the cheeses, for this year we had Cheshire and Wensleydale, as well as Cheddar cheese on offer.

I'd had a strange experience in the summer of this year. One morning I'd gone round to the house of a new friend who lived at the other end of town to collect him for a trainspotting session and found his parents at what they called "The Breakfast Bar" eating grapefruit. It was the first inkling I had that grapefruit was edible. To this point I'd only ever seen it used in our house, wrapped in tin foil and prickled with ham and cheese cocktail sticks on New Year's Eve.

When I realised my mistake, I had a pang of remorse for my Uncle Haydn who, at the end of the war, when confronted with his first ever banana, tried to eat it with the skin still on. How I'd laughed at the recounting of his mistake. Unfortunately, I'd made the mistake of sharing my ignorance of the nutritional value of grapefruit with my friend's parents in their formica breakfast bar. I had the distinct feeling when they burst into laughter that it was one of those occasions where they were laughing at me, rather than with me.

By the end of the year my culinary senses would be assaulted by a range of exotic tastes, few of which were to my liking.

Emboldened by surviving the first term in secondary school, I embarked on one of my long and incessant whines which was my abrasive method of trying to convince my parents to buy me something.

Over four Christmases, I'd waged a campaign for a new bike. Finally, my efforts paid off on the fourth Christmas when a second hand bicycle appeared and I was able to join all my friends on bicycling trips up the valley to the caves at Cefn or the view at Tremeirchion. Until then I'd only seen the single-decker green Crosville buses in the town bus station proclaiming these names. I knew they were exotic and difficult to reach places because a double decker bus could not negotiate the country lanes and inclines to reach them. All these places were now in range of our bicycling excursions.

I knew that a whining campaign could work but it needed to be sustained and subtle to wear my parents down.

The whine in question began with an item in a September school assembly. The Headmaster had drawn himself up to his full height on the stage and, referring to the notes propped on his diary and fiddling with his favourite reading glasses, had announced that there was an outstanding opportunity, not given to many, to embark on a once in a lifetime school visit to no less a place than the Soviet Union, calling at Norway, Sweden and Denmark.

There was a visible intake of breath in the Hall. Such places were beyond the compass of any of the pupils gathered.

I could muster one visit to Blackpool and a solitary but exceptional visit to Ostend as my holiday credentials, other than that there were a number of family visits to the Rhondda Valley in South Wales to stay with Auntie Beryl and her family. To that date I'd considered myself well travelled.

Visits to Tonypandy were always joyous occasions. In the rows of grey houses pitched on the valley sides there seemed to be incessant laughter whenever we gathered.

The extended family, forewarned by 'phone I'm sure, would gather to watch my father find space to park on the steep incline at the front of the house. With no less than twenty family onlookers of four generations, my dad would go backwards and forwards in the red Morris 1100 as we sweated with heat exhaustion and embarrassment on the black vinyl seats, unable to get out of the two door car until my dad was convinced that he was properly parallel parked. Sometimes it would take ten minutes, sometimes twenty.

To be fair to my Dad, he had endured two conflicting navigational systems all the way down from North Wales. On the back seat was my good self with an A.A. map plotting the route and giving my dad ample warning of turnings and alternative routes in the event of traffic jams, just like the navigators in the film *The Dambusters*. In the front seat was my mum navigating by reminiscence of childhood journeys which she had taken. Unfortunately, these had been by train thirty years before, so had very little bearing on current road routes. Nevertheless, she countermanded my instructions on a regular basis, with insistent and last minute instructions to turn right, across the busy traffic, because she recognised a haberdashery shop in Builth Wells that we had passed a decade before and there was a café near to it which made, "Lovely tea and *bara brith* and had spotless tablecloths and toilets, because you can't be too careful!"

Not being a driver herself, she was oblivious to one way streets and pedestrian areas and we'd invariably end up involuntarily having a conversation with a local policeman in the middle of the local market and a hostile crowd. My Mum, babbling on about *bara brith* and toilets, usually meant that we were let on our way without charge. The police officer would helpfully hold up the traffic, pedestrians and livestock as my dad executed a perfect sixteen point turn to exit the street in the correct direction.

There would be a hostile silence for a number of miles. I would resume my navigational commentary and things would relax. At the next big town she'd start again, regaling us with past trips and trying to ingratiate herself to my dad by anticipating which direction I was about to instruct him to take. "That's left here," she'd say with conviction. Then turning to me she'd say, "That's right isn't it, David?"

At which point my Dad would explode with exasperation.

Rhondda holidays were perfect family holidays with trips into Cardiff and Porthcawl and Pontypridd, the home of Tom Jones, as everyone reminded us annually. We'd visit relatives in the next valley, whom I had last seen when I was in my pram, but my mum would expect me to know them all and their life histories.

Much time was spent eating and talking in Auntie Beryl's house and every evening finished late like New Year's Eve.

The South Wales branch of my mum's family was very unlike us. They lived for the day and laughed a lot. We, as North Walians, tended to come across as more reserved and I think they sometimes thought of us as posh. I found this really amusing. I wished we were more free and easy like them. They were perfect company, always glad to see you, easy-going but prone to fits of mock outrage if one of the children got lippy. My cousins were the same, except for Andrea, with whom I shared a long history of rivalry.

Andrea was slim and blonde and with a look of devilment in her eye. She had a habit of tilting her head to one side as she spoke as if weighing you up.

She always took an interest in me, in much the same way that a cat played with a mouse before decapitating it. The fact that I towered over her gave me no advantage as she knew that I could not repay her for all the sly punches, pinches and insults she could throw at me. She was afraid of no-one and was clearly used to getting her way. So, whether it was who was going to have the front seat in the car when we went out for a drive, or which channel we were going to watch on the television, she *always* got her way.

I usually only saw Andrea once a year and always hoped she would be softer and kinder the next time we met. She never was. My home and education on the estate had clearly imprinted on me where to draw the line. I might choose to cross the line but I always knew where it was. Andrea was different. She recognised no limitations, no lines, no boundaries. Andrea just went for it. Each year, I was just pleased to be able to complete the holiday in one piece and this is no exaggeration. One year, in a fit of pique that I had occupied the front seat in the car, she had 'accidentally' knocked the loaded clothes horse into the hearth, starting a fire that required us all, in our pyjamas, to evacuate the house.

Andrea was not to be messed with either in her furious temper or sugar sweet 'can I have' moods. In truth, despite the constant threat of death, decapitation and blunt trauma, I loved her, Aunty Beryl, Uncle Harry, Lorna and Andrew greatly. Aunty Beryl always referred to me as, "our David" and I knew in my heart of hearts that whatever trouble I was in, from a grazed knee to having committed murder, there would always be food, shelter and a welcome for me on their doorstep.

This was the pattern of our summer holidays. Eventful they always were, but they were not exotic compared to those of others.

I knew some of my new found friends from beyond the estate went as far as Bournemouth—every year. Even these posh kids seemed overwhelmed by the holiday destinations on offer by the Headmaster. In that moment, I resolved to be one of the chosen few who would experience these foreign delights.

I knew I had three months to get a commitment out of my parents and began the campaign immediately. I dutifully waited behind at the end of the assembly to collect a letter for my parents about the trip. The Head looked at me in an unusual way and asked whether I really wanted an information sheet as there was only a limited number and he did not want to see any wasted. The embarrassment of him thinking my family could not afford the cost of the trip, which stood at an exorbitant, all inclusive £54, only strengthened my resolve to be involved.

I duly presented the letter at home, declaring the brazen lie that all my friends were going. When pressed about names by my incredulous parents, I deliberately gave a list of names of classmates who did not live on the Reso, and whom they could not cross check as to the accuracy of my claims.

I was clearly developing the adult quality of deviousness as I deliberately included the name of a parent that my mum had grown up with but had now come to despise. Their falling out had come when, according to my mum, Bessie had forgotten where she had come from and developed airs and graces. Bessie now lived in a private bungalow in the select area of town and she drove her mild mannered, 'anything to avoid an incident' husband to ever greater work efforts in order to fund her insatiable appetite for material goods.

According to my mum, Bessie had slave-driven her husband to provide a veritable treasure trove of unnecessary goods, much, my mother sneered with lip curling disgust, "on tick!" Buying things 'on tick' was not done in our house. It was considered the financial arrangement of the Devil. In our house, you either saved until you could afford it or did without. More often than not, we did without.

The one exception was the greengrocer's shop on the estate where my mother had once worked. She was personal friends with Dougie and his wife. They ran the shop which doubled as a chip shop at lunchtime and in the evening.

When I had been much younger, I'd often gone with my Mum and found that she did not part with any money at the end of a fruit and vegetable transaction. Dougie would simply lick the lead of the pencil that usually resided behind his right ear and write in a little order book what my mum had bought, tearing off one sheet and giving it to my mum and carefully moving the sheet of carbon paper one page forward.

I understood that my mum was getting the stuff free so took to venturing in on a regular basis to ask to have an apple or a banana put in the book. I once bought a pomegranate and was then unsure how to eat it. I was shown by an older girl who I had never seen before and who demanded first licks of the succulent orbs inside. It seemed a fair price to pay for the exotic delights of this new fruit and made up for the fact that I could not eat oranges as I reacted badly to the acid within, coming out in a rash within minutes of my first bite. Now, due to Dougie's little book, oranges were not the only fruit.

My inexhaustible free fruit supply lasted all of two weeks, at the end of which my mum was horrified to be confronted with a bill out of all proportion to the usual amount demanded for a regular supply of potatoes and carrots and the occasional cauliflower.

I was sternly lectured never, in any circumstances, to buy fruit or anything else for that matter, 'on tick'. Had my mother been delivering the birds and the bees lecture that some of my friends had warned me about, the two of us could not have been more embarrassed. Living on credit, my mother declared, was like opening a Pandora's box of horrors which would come back to haunt me and Bessie was cited as someone who would lead her family to ruin through her greed and irresponsibility. My mother went on to explain what the little yellow notices with stern black writing that appeared behind the counter in a prominent position in all the shops on the Reso meant. 'Do Not Ask for Credit As a Refusal Often Offends' had always intrigued me as, in school, a credit slip was something given out for a particularly fine piece of work or behaviour. Why adults would ask the greengrocer for a credit slip had always been beyond me.

Bessie, my mother went on to claim, had insisted on having an electric toaster when there was a perfectly serviceable grill located in the gas cooker. She had an incessant stream of workmen and salesmen beating a path to her door to quote her on frivolities. Bessie now had polystyrene tiles up on her kitchen ceiling. Even more unbelievably, she had decorative stone in her front garden.

There was talk, my mother hissed, of central heating, central heating mind! My mother repeated the words "central heating" as if it was an abomination in a world so full of coal. Turning on the central heating with a switch, when honest people slaved over the making of a coal fire was a sign of moral decay. Where would it end?

"She'll be wanting a coloured bath suite next!" my father declared disdainfully, and they both laughed with contempt at such decadence.

Clearly, citing that Bessie's son was going on the trip had struck a nerve, but I feared that we had ventured some way off the point—which had been to secure *me* a place on the trip.

In all honesty, I did not have the faintest hope of them acceding to me going on the trip. However, by asking for the impossible now, I could appear very reasonable when requesting something smaller later. For example, an Ian Allen combined volume of the numbers of all the trains and diesel multiple units running on British Rail. At seventy five pence it was not cheap, but it was the bible of the trainspotter.

Unfortunately, my mention of Bessie's son going on the trip lit a spark in my parents and securing my place on the trip became something of a mission for them.

When they had paid their five pound deposit and were called to the parents' evening to explain more about the trip, it was too late to withdraw and lose their deposit. The fact that everybody, according to me, was going on the trip was belied by the fact that there were only two other parents at the meeting from my year group and three from the year group above. My parents recognised none of them but knew from the Cortinas and Escorts that they arrived in, that they were not from the Reso. These people were surveyors and bank managers, accountants and solicitors.

By now, I was indifferent, if not hostile, to the idea of sharing a two week trip with two people from my year group who I barely knew. I'd have been happy for my parents to withdraw and for me to scale down my demands. However, my parents were now committed financially and, although intimidated by the company they were keeping in this meeting, they were resolved that their son was as good as any and would not be denied this 'marvellous educational opportunity'.

What is more, the whole family had pitched in and I felt like the focus of some graphic sponsored event. I am still unsure how it was achieved but I found myself handing in the Basildon Bond envelope with my final instalment of ten pounds a week before the deadline.

On reflection it had all been a hideous mistake. I was too young and immature to be touring round Europe alone. This was definitely one of those times when the phrase 'be careful what you wish for!' came to mind.

Nevertheless on that hot July day I found myself lying in my sweat-soaked bed wishing I was going to be anywhere other than on that bus to Liverpool to catch the *SS Nevasa* for the cruise of a lifetime.

Driving through the suburbs of Liverpool and out onto the docks was a voyage of delights but when we cornered the last of the warehouses and saw the 21,000 tons of the white *Nevasa* in front of us we were all silent.

Having made our way on board and been directed by a brusque man in a dark blue naval uniform and a host of smiling Indian crew in white uniforms we lay down our carefully packed luggage and surveyed our dormitory. Ours was called Chatfield and dispensed with the unseemly squabble about who was going to sleep in the bunks closest to the portholes by being located below the waterline.

I would spend nights in the terror of knowing that should the ship hit something we would be starting from the comparative disadvantage, safety wise, of being under water from the start. I always made sure that my shoes were kept under my pillow for a fast getaway. Unknown to me, so did every other boy in the dormitory.

Our first activity was an abandon ship drill when we were still tied up to the quay. We were directed to muster stations and shown how to put on the lifejackets in an 'efficient fashion' as the Master at Arms termed it. Clearly the sinking scenario was sufficiently realistic a possibility that they needed to practice for it, I thought.

The Master at Arms had much of Sergeant Walker about him I thought on first acquaintance, a similarity that was to develop on each meeting with the man.

After this, we were left to our own devices for an hour as the ship prepared to sail and I walked hand in hand with my vertigo around the decks staring over the ship's side to the roofs of the warehouses and the old Ocean Terminal railway station or across the other side of the Mersey to Birkenhead and the ferries scuttling in crab-like fashion across the Mersey tide. I was trying to hum *Ferry Across the Mersey* in my head but my brain was busy doing the calculation that we were easily fifty feet above the wharf on this main deck and that the two funnels, all shiny black with two white stripes, towered another one hundred foot above us. At the bow, the ship was so narrow that I convinced myself the moment the hawsers which secured us to the berth were untied, the ship would surely capsize.

With Gareth and Phil, my two school based shipmates in tow, we made our way to the extreme bow where you could stand on a seat and look down at the water many miles below. I envied the way they leapt on to the wooden bench and peered over without a jot of fear of heights. I had to slowly work myself up to look over the bow and down. I immediately had the feeling I was falling and collapsed backwards off the bench, my eyes wide and my heart racing.

There was much scuttling about on the quay now and we were ushered off the foredeck so that the crew could retrieve the ropes. There was a deep bass blast from the funnel and the ship began to nose out into the tide. Slowly at first, with tugs nuzzling her, and then increasingly quickly, the ship sought the centre of the river and the smoke belching from the funnel indicated that the engines were now fully engaged.

With the tide urging us forward we appeared to be leaving the Mersey as fast as a car on the motorway. The wind was now on our faces and, having shot through the mouth of the river and seen the whole of the Liverpool shoreline, we ran to the left or port side of the ship to see our home town of Rhyl glinting on the horizon.

It was a strange sensation to be seeing the town from this perspective and yet to be heading as far away from it as I was ever likely to get. Excitement and worry vied with each other as the three of us stood there speechless like conscripts or convicts heading into an uncertain future.

I would not have classified myself a fussy eater. I ate whatever my mum put in front of me. However, what was put in front of me was of a limited and tried and tested formula so eating aboard ship was always going to be an ordeal.

The galley arrangements on the *Nevasa* betrayed the ship's origins as a Far East troopship. We marched along a cafeteria system, tray and plate in hand, and food was ladled onto our plate. There was no time to peruse and choose; it hit the plate with a resounding clank of the large metal serving spoon or ladle.

The other distinctive trait of the ship was that, true to its name, British India Line, all the crew were Indian. Each group of tables was serviced by an Indian steward. These stewards tended to be of two types. Older men with world weary faces and receding hairlines who made it clear that they had seen enough British schoolchildren to last a lifetime, and young men with longer, silky black hair, flashing smiles and a sense of humour.

One of the latter stood at the head of our table and stated that his name was, and proceeded to roll out a name with many syllables. I caught a 'guru', a 'satya', a 'murthy' and a 'chandra'—but not necessarily in that order. He smiled at our predicament and added helpfully, "But you can call me Charlie Banana. Now, I know your families will be worrying about you as you bravely voyage so far from home so I would feel very bad if you did not eat well and enjoy your time on the *Nevasa*. If you have any problems, you come and see Charlie Banana and he will fix them for you".

His tone was earnest and genuine and his concern for us when he was so far away from his own home and family was greatly appreciated.

The only other Indian I'd ever spoken to was a doctor at the local accident unit and he too, having examined my fractured hand, had been careful and gentle in his tone. I decided then and there that as a nation, Indians were good guys.

Having eaten well at Charlie Banana's insistence, we experienced the novelty of watching a film in the on-board cinema. *Ring of Bright Water* was the film in question and I saw it about six times over the next two weeks. I had my fill of otters in that time.

We inevitably got lost heading back to the dormitory and at one point ended up out on deck. In the stiff breeze and churning water we looked at where Rhyl had last been on the port side only to see an expanse of sea and no light whatsoever as far as the eye could see. We shivered as much at the sight as at the stiffness of the breeze.

Being the youngest in the dormitory, we shot back there, changed for bed and brushed our teeth quickly so as to be in bed and asleep before the older lads arrived back from their nefarious activities. Our last act was to stow our shoes under our pillows for the inevitable evacuation.

Our early night was inevitably punctuated, first by the return of the older lads, intent on mayhem and later by the tour of inspection of the Master at Arms who appeared like Bill Sykes at the door and toured the bunks with menace as we all did our best fast asleep impressions. He spoke under his breath, warning that had he occasion to return again to this dormitory because of noise, then individuals would have bitter cause to regret it. I did not doubt it and screwed up my eyes even more in compliance. Unfortunately, a couple of older lads made the mistake of laughing out loud as the door handle turned shut.

In an instant, the burly petty officer was in and had yanked both of them out of their beds. Through squinting eyes, I saw two more sailors appear at the door and the boys were frogmarched down the corridor and up the stairs in their pyjamas.

It turned out that Wringe and Farndon, for those were the perpetrators' names, spent a couple of rather cold and reflective hours on deck wearing their lifejackets over their pyjamas. The spirit for mucking about was effectively extinguished in our dormitory for two weeks and I was heartily relieved.

I woke up the following morning to a crashing headache and the thump of heavy seas on the ship's side, which also served as the wall of our dormitory. The rolling and pitching motion of the ship was unrelenting and I dressed quickly so that I could get up on deck and sniff some fresh air. The air, when I finally managed to gasp a lungful, was freezing and salty for we were now storming up into the Atlantic proper past the Scottish Islands.

I was not alone in my predicament as every few feet along the side were green featured youths fishing, with strands of mucous, like thick nylon, dangling from their mouths. Their red rimmed eyes pleading for mercy from the incessant motion of the ship. I scuttled off to the toilet, anxious to maintain some dignity should I have to be sick, only to find them awash with vomit. I wished, as if it was my final request, simply to get off the ship.

At this low ebb, a smiling Charlie Banana appeared genie-like. He took me by the hand onto the upper deck and, calling me Sahib, urged me to sit and watch the horizon. He returned a minute later with water, a bucket and paper towels and sat with me for a few minutes explaining that if things got lively at sea the best place to be was high up at the centre of the boat as that moved around least. He explained that by the end of the day I would be a seasoned sailor and that this little unpleasantness would not be repeated. I sat there freezing and zombie like for five hours.

I might have made it through those hours had not a final factor pushed my head and stomach into overload. Either the direction of the boat or the wind changed so that the breeze was now following us. From the crew quarters at the stern of the boat came the pungent richness of curry on the air. I'd never smelt or tasted curry at this point in my life, but the heady richness of this original and authentic Indian brew proved the trigger for me to imitate the wretched and retching lads I'd seen earlier.

The water, the bucket and the paper towels did sterling service over the following hours and, by the time I'd finished, I was convinced I'd halved my body weight.

True to his word, Charlie was right. That evening, ravenously hungry, I took a slice of bread and butter and began to feel a tad better. We docked in Stavanger the following day and I was back to feeling more myself.

The black and white film that my parents supplied with the family Kodak Brownie was beyond its sell by date so my pictures of the voyage were a rather overexposed grey mush. So my memories provided the only more or less reliable record of the voyage.

In my head, I remember the milky greenness of the waters of the fjord and the crash of waterfalls falling from the cliff face over a thousand feet above the ship. I gripped the rail when the ship's horn sounded its characteristic boom which rippled and ricocheted up and down the fjord for over a minute. I felt that, like in a Ray Harryhausen animated film, the walls of the fjord might come together to crush the puny ship.

Stockholm was cleanliness and order and the white hulls of visiting cruise liners.

Leningrad was women with bulging muscles on the road work gangs, an excessive number of people in uniforms saying *"Nyet!"* and students keen to exchange anything of value for lapel badges celebrating Lenin and the Soviet Revolution. We crept into and out of Leningrad harbour in darkness and with a warship escort. We waved to the black uniformed sailors on deck and they stared back at us with contempt as the spawn of capitalism come to pollute their motherland.

Copenhagen was the hugely disappointing little mermaid and the Tivoli Gardens by night and we were now speeding our way home. I had to admit that this was not much to show for my family's heavy investment in the trip.

It was the day before we docked at Tilbury that it finally became our group's turn to have an hour in the ship's 'swimming pool'. Swimming pool was perhaps over egging the metal space full of water. This was a small pool possibly twenty feet square at the front of the ship in what by now we knew as the foc'sle. Holding tank might be more accurate.

After two steamy weeks in the Baltic, the weather had turned nasty again and we were churning through the brown North Sea with the tops of the waves arriving unannounced on the deck. The pool, of course, mimicked the surface of the sea and those who were unwise enough to try to jump into this heaving torrent, risked either breaking their ankles in three inches of water or drowning as they were hit by a fifteen feet tall mini tsunami, depending on the pitch of the ship.

To see Phil, the smallest of our crew, all ginger hair and freckles, one second like Moses as the waters parted, left standing on the floor of the pool only to disappear in an unholy surge as the water returned a second later, reduced us to tears. We bravely saw out the whole hour of our allocation in this deluge before scuttling off the freezing deck trying to vent recalcitrant water from our noses and ears.

Our excitement had been almost hysterical, prompted both by this adventure and the realisation that we were now less than one day from our homes and families.

Something had been rescued from the *Nevasa* adventure after all but I decided I would not push my luck by asking for such ambitious things again. After the past two weeks, I craved only the familiar certainties of home. As things turned out, I might as well have tried to emulate Phil's ginger Canute in holding back the tide of change that was heading my way.

Chapter Seven
MOVE

The forces which led to our move off the Reso had been set in motion more than a year before the event.

My nain had been rushed into hospital with a heart attack, and the first I knew of it was the late night knock on the door heard from the comfort of my wincyetted sheets as I snugly nestled under my green camberwick cotton bedspread. This was a time long before we had a telephone so if my family was to be kept in the loop, someone had to visit us. Uncles and aunties arrived at varying intervals from ten o'clock onwards and, this not being December 31st, could only mean bad news.

I knew that I would not get any straight answers had I made my way downstairs to the snug of our back room and asked outright what was happening, so I lay in bed and tried to work out what was unfolding.

I'd never had anyone die in our family, but the continued hushed tones of the conversation clearly suggested that a crisis point had been reached. I'd determined that my nain had been rushed into hospital and that my uncles and aunties were flitting between the ominous Gothic hospital on the sandswept promenade and reporting her condition to my mum, the eldest of the family. I felt pleased that there was a large family around us to soften whatever blow was about to fall.

There was much brewing of tea; kettle whistling punctuated the conversations. I knew my mum would be making sandwiches. It was her way of dealing with any unpleasant experience—make copious quantities of food and buy some time to think. If she could not solve a problem directly, she could make sure everyone would be able to think with full stomachs.

It was a matter of honour in our house, and the others on the estate, that no visitor was able to leave without at least a cup of tea and welsh cakes or *bara brith*. Most, hungry or not, were forced to leave with a cooked meal and a pudding. Given the quality of my mum's cooking, this was usually no hardship. Of course, the response to this culinary generosity was to clear your plate. This was a moral obligation that has never left me, for as well as the "little children in Africa" whose fate was tied up with me clearing my plate, there was the religious injunction, uttered regularly by my nain that food wasted, particularly bread, was "feeding the Devil". I determined that the old bugger would have no nourishment from me.

Upstairs, cosy and warm, I was also numb and frightened. I was disgusted to find that a part of me was almost eager to experience the grief of a death and to attend a funeral simply to feel what it was like. I was horrified that my mind had drifted in this direction and reminded myself that it was my nain who was being discussed downstairs.

I had to admit that in her Sunday visits to our house she had developed the annoying habit of insisting that the BBC news was on and then falling asleep as soon as it started. "Are we going to watch the news?" she would habitually ask, placing her glasses on in anticipation.

The television channel would be changed by my mother without regard to the cartoon or war film I'd been watching. In an instant, nain would be asleep with her head tilted back and her mouth slowly gaping open as her muscles relaxed. I'd wait a minute to make sure she was fully unconscious and sidle back to change the channel. Instantly, she'd awake from her slumbers and ask, "Is the news over already?" My mother would change the channel again and glare daggers at me. I'd missed the best bits of *Sink the Bismarck, 633 Squadron, The Battle of the River Plate, Ice Cold in Alex* and *Reach for the Sky* in successive weeks in this way. Always one to bear a grudge, I'd made a mental note to find a way to pay back my nain in some way. All in all, this was pretty ungracious of me given my nain's generosity to me. Each birthday and Christmas she'd present me with a crisp ten shilling note from her pension money, a wet kiss and an injunction to spoil myself with it.

My cousin Martin's granddad on his mother's side had died the previous year and he had described in detail going to see the body 'laid out' in the Chapel of Rest. 'Laid out' had sounded like some boxer taking a ten count whilst unconscious and I was keen to experience such a sight at least once. In this quest to satisfy idle curiosity, I had almost forgotten that this was my nain we were talking about.

I though about all the great family times we had experienced, the Christmases gathered around the table with the roaring fire in the grate at our backs and the exotic food set out in front of us. I recalled Easters when snow lay on the ground yet we still went to the fair and Sidoli's Italian Café because nain insisted that it was the family tradition and outvoted the wiser counsel of my mum and her brothers and sisters with her casting vote.

I pictured my nain in her kitchen wearing her pinafore, preparing yet another meal for visiting family members and telling us of the old days and the mining disaster that had taken two uncles and her younger brother in South Wales. I could hear the cheeping of the chicks under the warm lamp in the box on the kitchen table as she built them up ready to join the layers in the chicken coop in the end of the garden. They had been little globes of yellow either collapsed in sleep or noisily climbing aimlessly, but with such energy, over their napping siblings.

I remembered too how my nain had conned us into helping her turn over the waste ground next to the chicken coop looking for snakes. I was both scared and fascinated to find out that real snakes lived so close to us. It turned out that she meant worms, which she fed to the chickens. Whether this was some word lost in translation from the Welsh or an elaborate ploy to get her nephews and nieces to turn over the ground I never knew, but I suspected the latter.

Nevertheless, her harsh upbringing meant that she was not afraid, even in her seventies, to join us in digging. She covered her habitual floral pinafore with a grubby raincoat that she kept on a hook on the back of the door in the wooden shed in the yard. She also changed from her sensible flat, black shoes into a pair of ankle length Wellington boots which had clearly seen hard and extended service over the years since her husband, my *taid*, had died of a heart attack in his forties, leaving her to bring up the family alone. She looked like the picture I had seen in the book *Life in Britain during the War Years of a Land Army Girl*.

That leaning, wooden shed had represented 'old', and nain, to me. It smelt of chicken feed and linseed oil, of dust and mildewed paper, of faded cut flowers and sour milk where the old cat, who was variously referred to as Pushcat (after Puskas the Hungarian master footballer and Real Madrid legend) or Timoshenko (the Russian general of World War II) had neglected to drink his milk in timely fashion.

On the wall was a German helmet which still had its malevolent power some twenty five years after the war. My uncle, who had been a Royal Marine commando, had liberated it soon after D-Day from some poor unfortunate young man like himself but it bore a swastika on one side and the SS runes on the other so we knew its power to do evil. I would never try it on, believing it still to have the power to beguile. Instead, I would always put on the British helmet kept on the top shelf. It was predictably heavy and uncomfortable. The inner lining, dry and brittle, dug into your head and the strap felt too tight.

Replete with an old army service black beret, nain was ready for gardening action and, although she was not a fast mover, she had the stamina and endurance of one familiar with long hours of manual toil. She worked silently and methodically turning over rows of dead vegetation and weeds. My cousin Kath and I fell into the same pattern for a good hour with our garden forks until one of us would be bursting to ask the habitual question, "Nain, what was it like when you were young?"

And she would be off, regaling us with some story of Rhondda Valley life, or service in the big house on the promenade when she had escaped the valleys of the south for the seaside of the north along with her sister. This escape from the valleys of the 1930s felt every bit as epic as any war story I had heard and I hoped I would some day have the same courage to undertake an epic journey.

Without realising it my pillow was by now wet with tears as my initial thoughts about what it would be like to see nain lying cold and dead had been replaced by a full length black and white film starring nain and all the times we had shared. I felt ashamed of my earlier thought and began praying for a full recovery for nain. I tried to reassure God that this really would be my last request for help and that, as it was on someone else's behalf, it held more merit than any of my previous and seemingly frivolous requests for help.

I'd worked myself into quite a panic now as the permanence of separation by death dawned on me. I felt completely unprepared for it and wondered how others coped: the girl running in tears and flames from the Vietnamese village, the babies with the grotesquely inflated bellies which featured so regularly in crisis reports from Africa and, of course, the deadly disaster which I had contributed to in my selfishness, Aberfan. All these horrific encounters with death and destruction had the consolation of having been distanced from me by the television screen. The reality of death had now caught up with me.

I feared the worst when another uncle arrived and overturned the hushed tones of the previous conversation with greater urgency. Then it had all gone quiet. I was left with my grievous thoughts until sleep overtook me.

When I awoke next morning, I found that my nain was still alive but critically ill. My father had departed the family gathering in the middle of the night to join his shift and my mother remained in her clothes of the previous day, having had no sleep and having seen out the last family member less than an hour before.

The pattern of the next weeks upset all our routines with the family taking turns to keep vigil at nain's bedside and contributing to further late night conversations between family members at our house. The rituals of dinner and tea were often overturned with food delivered later or earlier than the allotted anointed hours. Even the tradition of our Sunday lunch, with its roast beef and all the trimmings and rice pudding served piping hot from the oval brown earthenware pot, was disturbed on the second Sunday when things took a turn for the worse and the family rushed to her bedside.

Although I really missed the food, the tang of the mustard in your nose, paralysing your senses for an instant, and the luxury of the roast potatoes and sprouts and rich, brown skinned rice pudding, it was the break in the timeless tradition that really hit hard. It made me realise that the permanence of the 1960s had come to a sudden, abrupt end. I had the horrible sensation that I had been taking far too much for granted.

By the Sunday of the third week, some semblance of the normal order of things had been resumed. It was decided that nain was possibly well enough to receive a short visit from myself and my brother. We were warned not to tire her out which seemed a strange demand. I had no intention of challenging her to a game of table tennis or a snake digging match. I would be more than happy just to see some tangible evidence that she was still alive and that the life that we had led up until her heart attack three weeks before could be restored. I caught myself promising God that if he granted this wish then I really would not trouble him again. Had I been God, I'd really have been increasingly exasperated by this urchin delivering more final demands than the 'leccy man' on the Reso estate.

After a lunch of lamb and mint sauce, Uncle Idris came in his car to pick us up, which marked the seriousness of the event. I decided to forego my usual pleading to sit in the front seat, realising that this was neither the time, nor the place, for such unseemly behaviour. I settled down on the comfy red leather of the back seat of the Austin Cambridge in my best shorts, white school shirt and tie with the elasticated neck that my mother had insisted I wore.

To be leaving the Reso in a car would usually be a cause for celebration and I would ask my uncle if I could dib the horn to any of my friends. I'd wave ostentatiously to them, window down and with my hair, I'd hope, flowing in the wind like one without a care in the world. But not today. I allowed myself to slide down the seat and remain anonymous to ponder the gravity of the situation. I was also anxious not to be seen on the estate wearing my school uniform on a Sunday. Not even my grievously ill nain as an excuse could save me from the ridicule that would ensue.

We parked on the promenade opposite the hospital. As the holiday season was still a few weeks away, there were plenty of parking places.

The sun was up and the breeze was blowing off the sea, whipping up the sand and scouring any exposed skin in a way that would come to be described as 'rejuvenating' but at the time was simply irritating.

The sea, sand and sun made you glad to be alive. To have a hospital with sick people in the middle of this beautiful scene seemed out of place. The hospital, however, had been placed here for precisely that reason, as the convalescent properties of the local climate were seen to be a free gift at a time when people had to pay fully for their medical treatment.

I knew from my dad's family this brutal way of paying for your medicine had hit those who were not well off. Knowing that his family could not afford the medicines on offer, their doctor had suggested bread and milk for a relative with tuberculosis. We'd all agreed that we did not want to go back to those days which, in large part, explained my family's socialist leanings.

The hospital itself was a red brick Victorian affair and was full of foreboding. It had wings and outhouses and took up a considerable area. On the roof, to my surprise, was a weather vane in the form of a running fox. It was quickly explained to me that, apparently, some benefactor had owned a horse called 'Flying Fox' which had won some important race. We'd learned in school that a flying fox was, in fact, a type of bat. I felt that a large, black bat swinging in the wind would be a more appropriate symbol of the emotion this building was evoking in me.

The heavy, dark wood door at the front yielded reluctantly to my mum's shove and we entered a red tiled lobby area. We were prevented from proceeding further by a rotating door. Normally, this would be a novelty and I'd spend time re-enacting the scene in the Laurel and Hardy films when they were spun round, got trapped and caused their usual mayhem, but not today.

The need to wait to enter one at a time meant that I spent more time than I had hoped with a couple sitting forlornly in the lobby area. He was emaciated and yellow of complexion, dressed in a regulation faded dressing gown with *Property of the Area Health Authority* prominently displayed on the front where footballers had their team crest. He was smoking heavily with what seemed to remain of his energy and staring bleakly at the tiled floor. She was crying quietly in her Sunday best with mascara beginning to leech down her cheek. It would soon reach the white fur collar of her coat and I thought I should warn her, but it was not my place.

I was relieved to pass through the doorway and up the steps to the reception area. This too was oak panelled and very dark. The receptionist seemed pleasant enough in her light green cardigan, elaborate spectacles, beehive hair-do and large earrings. She seemed to know my mum and smiled that smile of consolation which intimated 'poor you'. She immediately telephoned the ward to see if we could go up. Apparently, there was some flap on, lunch running late, or bed-baths, or God forbid, someone had died. We were told to wait for no more than a couple of minutes.

We sat in silence on the oak bench which was particularly uncomfortable. My mum did that thing with her handkerchief where she wet it and dragged it across my mouth just in case some persistent rice pudding or mint sauce had lodged on my lip. I thought this was highly unlikely. I think she just did it to pass the time.

Apart from the tick of the clock above the receptionist desk, the hospital was largely quiet. This made the occasional desperate impassioned cries of, "Nurse! Nurse!" all the more disturbing. The nurses' replies always had that same, 'I'm answering you but if you listen carefully you'll pick up on the fact that I'm somewhere else in my head,' tone.

The bench was set back from the main line of the corridor so I heard approaching traffic before seeing it. I quickly picked up on the patients' soft shoe shuffle as their slippers slapped on the cold red stone tiles. The nurses wore sensible shoes with soft soles and walked faster, whilst the doctors and visitors walked fastest of all. A woman in stiletto heels came ricocheting down the corridor at alarming speed before wheeling past us and down to the rotating door with a face like thunder.

When we were eventually called, my mum led the way down the corridor to the stairs that wound themselves around the ancient lift shaft. To the right of me the white, supposedly antiseptic, tiling was cracked and discoloured and to my left the lift shaft headed into the bowels of the building and towards who knew what. I knew that I was now closer than I had ever been to the path taken by dead bodies and I quickened my step.

To my left, there was only a thin lattice of painted metal stopping me from tumbling down the shaft and I reached out to steady myself on the stair rail before thinking better of it. Who knew what germs and infections lay there upon the worn rail and the metal studs driven into it, presumably to prevent the unlikely act of a patient trying to slide down it? Somewhere along its smoothness might be a splinter waiting to deliver infection directly beneath my skin. I decided to breathe lightly and keep my hands to myself which went against my usual approach to new experiences.

On the second floor, having may-poled twice round the lift shaft, we came to the door of my nain's ward. Just outside, in a room with a large white sink set at a low level, a nurse was pouring away a foul smelling and lumpy green liquid. The antiseptic smell that usually reminded me of the horror that was the school dentist, was clearly failing to disguise it. She looked up, brushed away her hair from her face, smiled without conviction and continued with her thankless task. I crossed off anything to do with hospitals from my future employment wish-list.

Our path to the ward was constricted by a number of diabolical contraptions. All were gleaming cream enamel and stainless steel with dials and wheels and tubes and masks. It seemed inhuman to leave such equipment on public view and I could only imagine the havoc they could wreak on the body and the mind.

I sidestepped them and moved into the ward, putting on, as instructed, my happy face to greet nain. The first impression the ward made on me was depressing. I remembered from the interludes on the television daytime schedules the term 'faded opulence' being used to describe one famous country house. The term 'faded squalor' seemed more appropriate here. The paintwork was reduced to muted grey from its original colour and was peeling in places. The curtains drawn around many of the beds were shabby.

We made our way past half a dozen cream metal beds with chipped paintwork, each chip corresponding to dents in the hospital walls and doors, before arriving at my nain's bed. At first I did not recognise her, never having seen her in bed before, and with her stature so visibly shrunk. She and the other patients looked like little caged birds in the ward and it was a disturbing impression which scared me greatly.

Her eyes looked glazed and tearful and it was clear that she did not at first recognise or focus on me. My mum had to introduce me like some long lost relative and slowly her eyes focussed and she mustered up the best, faintest smile she could muster.

"Hello, *cariad bach.*" [dear little one]

This was all she could manage to say and I was pushed to the back of our group as my mum took the only seat and proceeded to update my nain on what had occurred since she last visited. This consisted mostly of a long list of people who had accosted my mum in the street and sent their love to nain, praying for a speedy recovery.

Nain's lips moved to form a smile but she seemed to be making an inordinate amount of effort for so little result and she settled for nodding slightly. This was not my nain of old and I wondered if we were ever to get her back. I certainly had little confidence that the hospital knew where her old bubbly personality had gone and had neither the operating tools nor the medicines to recover it.

This moment of gloom was suddenly punctured by the nurse, whom we had seen emptying the bedpans earlier, entering the ward with said bedpans and slipping on a wet patch on the floor. The metal pans exploded like cymbals and I was about to laugh, as much to dispel the tension as in merriment, when I realised that the nurse was hurt and was groaning in pain on the floor.

A bevy of nurses arrived but the unusual situation meant that their professional expertise momentarily deserted them and they simply flapped around like members of the general public. It took the arrival of a particularly brusque sister with scraped back hair and a sullen lip to restore order. She ordered this and that and the nurse was helped into a wheelchair and moved away. The sister quickly surveyed the ward to ensure that order had indeed been restored. She reminded me of a teacher who had intervened when the cast had forgotten the words in the school play, breaking the enchantment.

I hoped the nurse would be okay. I had even less confidence in the care provided by the hospital now. I remembered how adults falling over always caused me consternation. The only laugh out loud incidents happened in the old silent films. Any other event was deeply suspect. Of the 'adults falling down' incidents I could remember one was fatal, one was embarrassing, and the third I was wrongly accused of causing.

The fatal one had happened in the High Street one hot summer's day the previous year. A middle aged man of ruddy face, dressed in light brown suit trousers and floral shirt, open at the neck, had collapsed in front of me. He toppled like a building demolished, his legs buckling and his body fell vertically until his head flopped backwards, hitting the pavement with the sound of an egg cracking. The ice cream cone he had been eating dropped no more than three inches from his trouser leg. There had been no attempt to discard it or to avoid it staining his clothes.

I knew instinctively he was dead. He had been taken in the middle of the day, in the middle of his holiday, in the middle of his ice cream. There was no dignity, nor fairness, in dying so publicly and so unprepared.

Some years earlier I had seen 'Dai the Post', who had by now been relegated to 'Dai the Limp' by an accident that had led to his leg being amputated, lying on the waste ground near the railway station, whilst out shopping with my mum. He had been very lucky, I thought, that the open bottle he was carrying had not broken in the fall.

I began to move forward to help him up but my mum had stopped me, which seemed very uncharitable. She had insisted that we crossed over to the other side of the road and I felt like the Pharisee in the parable of the Good Samaritan. It appeared that 'Dai the Limp' was not seriously injured though. He was talking in an animated way as if holding a telephone conversation on an invisible telephone, just like Sammy Barker did on his way home from the pub—and then it dawned on me.

I saw Dai in similar circumstances many times over the coming year and then he was gone, dead, pickled in alcohol.

The third falling down incident had been the strangest of all. I had struggled with my mum from the new Kwik Save supermarket in town, laden down with shopping. We had just crossed the Vale Road Bridge and I was thinking that the plastic bag handles cutting into my fingers or the sheer weight of the bags themselves would leave me permanently damaged when my mum, equally laden, pitched forward and fell to her knees.

She did not move for a second and I instinctively asked the stupid question, "Are you all right?" By now she had released her hold on the bags, had scanned all around her and scrambled to her feet as adults always want to contain the embarrassment when they fall over. Equally instinctively, she turned and slapped me on the legs, which was an unusual event in itself. "Why didn't you stop me falling?" she cried out loud. I glanced downwards, trying to give her the non-verbal clue that my arms were full of shopping and that there had been no time to react. But she was having none of it and gathered up her shopping and strode off ahead of me, speaking only the end of sentences, as she did when she was heartily annoyed.

"Show me up in the street!"

On the way home from the hospital in Uncle Idris' car my mum, breaking the silence that had gathered over us, surprised me even more radically by announcing that we were moving house to be nearer nain when she came out of hospital. This was announced, not as an idle musing, but as a fact.

Chapter Eight
PEA

It seemed a sensible and laudable suggestion, to move house to be nearer to nain. Yet it shook the foundation of my world and all I had grown up around. I could tell by the matter of fact way she 'casually' announced it that my mum knew how significant moving house was for the family. I don't know whether she had discussed it with my father but it was certainly beyond discussion now. We were moving and as quickly as it could be arranged. I'd never seen my normally easy-going mum more determined to do anything in her life.

At first I consoled myself with the idea that council houses, being built to a similar specification and design, would be much of a muchness. That being the case, I would be merely exchanging one house for another identical one. I could just about manage that, even if it meant leaving the Reso. All the same rooms and spaces would be there, just in a different location.

For a couple of months, I consoled myself with this thought and went on my way as usual as nain slowly recuperated and was discharged from hospital.

Behind my back, mum had been planning apace. She had filled in the requisite forms for the Council and had even visited and rejected a number of houses. This meant that when she eventually mentioned that she thought she had found us a new house it was already a done deal. Papers were signed and we would be moving in a month. No objections, no appeals. We were off.

I'd kept quiet about the prospect of a move to my friends. I think I was working on the basis that it would never happen just so long as I never spoke of it. This was the verbal equivalent of not stepping on the cracks in the pavement. The fact that nothing had been mentioned for some time had confirmed me in the merits of this approach.

When my mother eventually revealed the exact location of our new home, and she certainly kept quiet about it long enough to arouse the suspicion that she knew how I would react, I was horrified. We were moving to Prince Edward Avenue.

We were exchanging a light and airy 1940s built semi-detached house gleaming in white masonry paint for a smaller 1920s terraced house in grimy, grey pebbledash. We would be near a main road, chip papers would roll like tumbleweed into our garden and the rooms would be dark and airless.

There was nothing about the new house that held any appeal to me. I'd be away from my friends, in a no-man's land. There would be no view of the local hills and the Snowdonian range behind them nor of the trees on the nearest range of hills that always reminded me of a cannon and which had been a reference point when we had gone on cycle rides up the Clwyd Valley to St Asaph, Cefn and beyond. Most of all, there would be no cosy reassurance in each room of the memories and senses shared.

On the final summer morning before we left the Reso, unable to sleep, I'd got up at five in the morning and was met by brilliant sunshine. Alone in the silence of a new day and accompanied only by the milkman, and various cats and dogs, I'd cycled the length and breadth of the estate along every pavement from Arfon Grove to Frederick Street. On each street, there were memories and sensations from times past. Not all were pleasant.

There was the point on Menai Avenue where the Crawford boys, for no other reason than I happened to be passing, had hurled half a house brick at me, which by a fluke, given the speed I was running, had bounced and hit me square in the ankle, downing me as surely as stepping on a landmine.

At the corner of Menai Avenue and Gwynfryn Avenue was the triangle of grass with a crazy paving path intersecting it where we had tested our soap box carts, carefully navigating the sharp turn into the post box, at the foot of which the dogs habitually cocked a leg and the spear grass never grew.

Up past my house was the line of hedges of the Grand National course and I could hear the plummy commentary of the BBC man describing the mayhem of the 1967 event when eleven runners fell at the seventh fence, Sammy Barker's hedge, toppled by the unlikely device of green painted barbed wire hidden in the privet. "They're Orf, they're all Orf!" he intoned as we writhed in agony, mangled in the hedge as a smiling Sammy looked on through his thick glasses with satisfaction.

Here was the corner where lived an important man dressed in full uniform who would perform heroic duties in his work at the local Odeon. And now Gwynfryn Avenue opened up into a rectangle of land heralded by the telephone box which served hundreds of families on the estate and which, we were warned, was only to be used in emergency. This was the stadium of the Flying MacGuinness Family, a tribe of lads who lived for football and could give anyone a battering at five a side. They moved like quicksilver and had an instinctive understanding of what each other would do next. There would be space, then the ball, then a Mac Guinness family member, then a goal. I imagined that they talked only football at their dinner table and at night in their bedroom, such was their mastery of the game.

Where two houses parted at the top of the estate was the old stone bridge over the cut where we netted for eels, leeches and the occasional stickleback. Here, we watched the photosynthesis of the tadpoles into frogs and the metamorphosis of the larvae into dragonflies...or was it the other way round?

At the top of the estate, where I rarely ventured, lived a number of 'aunties' and 'uncles' who had grown up with my mum and dad. From this point, I would turn back towards the shops and past the man who owned a three wheeled car which was really a motor bike with a shed like body strapped to it. The man had long, black combed-back hair and always smoked a pipe. Each year, he would paint the 'car-o-bike' with gloss paint. One year it was sky blue, the next primrose, the following lilac. It was a surprising do-it-yourself approach to motoring, but who was I to sneer as we did not even own a car of any description at this time? The man and his lank-haired family would cruise sedately past us on a Sunday, his wife and children in best clothes and hats on their way to church, a vision of Reso opulence in the latest pastel shade.

I detoured around the back of the four shops in the terrace to catch the first sounds of the day beginning over the concrete wall of the Derbyshire Miners' Camp. Milk crates were being disturbed and the first bacon rashers were hitting the frying pan ready to grease the appetite of the people with strange accents and happy faces who rotated through its gates every week.

I headed west up Rhydwen Drive past Welsh Myfanwy's and thought of the balmy summers' evenings when her voice would ring out over the estate calling in the boys she claimed would be the death of her. "Les-lie, Et-wood!" she would scream breathlessly to summon her brood home from a radius of more than five miles in the still air.

Up past Auntie Lottie's, who was a real auntie, and Uncle Charlie's who could play all manner of musical instruments effortlessly. With a gathering posse of inquisitive dogs, I headed past the house of the family with the shared acne who smelt like margarine.

Ever westwards, I passed the small road that formed the entrance to the playing fields which was the 'Anfield' to the lads from this end of the estate just as the Clinic Field was our 'Old Trafford'. In this short drive of no more than ten houses, lived a lad who looked like Bob Dylan and drove one of the distinctive light blue invalid carriages on account of having polio. Due to a sugar lump, administered behind the green boards that were always used for medical inspections at school, I would not suffer his cruel fate and, thankfully, this terrible illness would be history in a generation.

Turning seawards now, I saw two more grass rectangles badly worn by football and cricketing activities, before turning into Frederick Street where my Uncle Will and cousin Gerald lived. Uncle Will had been in the Royal Engineers in the war. He could hold you spellbound for hours in the living room with the unhurried ticking clock overlooking the expanse of the Cob, the flat flood plain of the River Clwyd, with talk of his adventures in Europe with his mucker 'Big Red', copious amounts of explosives and his trusty Gat.

Back in civvy street, he had resumed his duties at the steam railway engine shed adjacent to Rhyl railway station. It was he who, on a trip with my dad for a 'short back and sides' at the impatient hairdresser's who always yanked my head around whilst attacking me with the clippers, had secreted my dad and me into the sheds to allow us to see the steamy beasts being prepared in their lair.

It was magical to see the engines so close and to see all manner of orifices breathing fire and smoke. The oil and sulphur in the steam had an air of permanence which was an illusion. For in no more than six years, the steam shed had been closed, demolished and replaced by a car park. Uncle Will then made the daily trip over the Cob and along the coast in one of the hateful Diesel Multiple Units which had displaced the beloved steam engines to Llandudno Junction shed where the last dirty and unkempt engines hung on to a precarious existence and premature extinction.

Cousin Gerald led no less a colourful life in my eyes as he was one of a select group of Rhyl men who were summoned by rockets, or more correctly 'maroons', to attend the launch of the Rhyl Lifeboat. We'd hear them across the town at all times of the day and night summoning the crew to attend some seaborne emergency. A deep resonant boom and, if you were fast enough, the flare of the second maroon before a second boom fell insistently on the town.

I was surprised that my cousin Gerald, who was older than me by more than twenty years admitted to not being able to swim. Having spent his lifetime around water, except for his time away on National Service, he knew full well that in the sort of seas that the lifeboat encountered, whether or not you considered yourself a good swimmer was irrelevant, the sea alone would determine if you returned and it was foolish to pretend otherwise.

It was only right that this foray to the furthest end of the estate should pause at the iron bridge that led to the fair and I took stock there for a few moments when I noticed the semaphore signals indicating the arrival of an express from the Holyhead direction. Abandoning my bike at the bottom of the bridge near the animal shelter building, I took the steps two at a time to reach the top of the bridge.

Here, I had spent countless hours in previous years scanning the horizon, like the able seamen in the film *The Battle of the River Plate* for telltale signs of smoke which would herald the approach of my quarry. For me, it would not be the German pocket battleship *Graf Spee* but some equally exotic Royal Scot or Jubilee class locomotive from a distant shed, working her way back home with a rake of exhausted holiday makers towed behind in maroon coaches and moquette luxury.

Today, it was a rattling and dirty English Electric locomotive with a load of ballast from the quarries by the sea at Penmaenmawr scudding along in advance of the stream of passenger trains taking workers and travellers to Chester and points beyond. I stepped aside from its diesel rasp and black exhaust where once I would have relished being enveloped in radiant curling steam. It captured the mood of the day exactly and I barely turned my head to capture its number, old habits dying hard.

Before returning home for the last time, I had resolved to overcome my fear and venture down the most notorious of the estate's cul de sacs, Arfon Grove. In the epicentre of the estate, Arfon Grove had a fearsome reputation, even on the Reso. I'm not sure why, I only knew not to go down there and here I was at six thirty in a late July morning, cycling along the pavement waiting for the sky to fall down on me. Granted, there were some abandoned prams in a few sun-baked un-grassed gardens, but other than that the grove was peaceful and hardly the neighbour of Hades that had been described to me.

I returned home before the rest of the family had risen and negotiated my way upstairs past the tea chests and suitcases full of everything in our life, save a loaf of bread, the tea caddy, milk, cups and saucers and copious amounts of cloths and scrubbing brushes, cleaning and polishing fluids required to complete our tidy and final exit from our home. Between the Domestos, Ajax, Vim and 1001, our reputation as a clean-living family would be maintained.

By the end of the day, the removal van having departed with most of what we held dear, my mother and I were left to struggle with a few additional suitcases which had materialised from the furthest recesses of the loft and the remnants of the cleaning potions and squeegee mops, on a makeshift casing truck cannibalised from a Pedigree pram.

We must have made a pathetic site wending our way off the estate and down Cefndy and Victoria Roads. As a perished tyre disintegrated on its fifth revolution, the pram, with me pushing, made a noisy and unwelcome lurching syncopation as we wandered off the estate, refugees of my mother's making.

I had never felt so embarrassed and desolate.

Our so called 'new' house had been occupied for over forty years by a widow. She was known and respected in the neighbourhood and my mum had known her when she was a child. The terraced house had a side entry to the back garden and a large wooden gate installed as a security device. The gate had clearly previously been the door to the outside toilet. Beyond the gate was a fence of wooden stakes linked together by wire and used by the Council to mark out the limits of gardens in their older properties. The fact that this fence was no more than three feet six inches high rendered the security provided by the gate largely superfluous as anyone of average height could merely step over the stake fence without endangering their dangly bits.

The gate opened out into a small area of fractured concrete which was no more than eight feet wide and then a tall and unkempt privet hedge about ten feet high formed a boundary between the yard and the overgrown back garden. As if trying to contain the encroaching weeds, corrugated iron had been placed at the bottom of this verdant wall of leaves. The corrugated iron bulged, trying to contain the garden growth and it was clear that someone had, for some time, been using this area as some sort of midden as rotting vegetation, spent tea leaves and other discarded kitchen waste had piled up there.

Moses Hughes, our history teacher, had claimed that there is more to discover about ancient civilisations in their middens than in their palaces. He claimed that their health, diet and habits were laid bare there. I had no desire to explore the health, diets and habits of Mrs Goronwy Richards and this view was confirmed when, whilst idly poking about with a stick in the midden area, a broken set of discoloured false teeth came smiling out at me.

As the house faced north–south, unlike our old house which faced east–west and brought sunshine into the bedroom in the morning and the best room in the evening, this privet hedge would have to go as it effectively denied the house any sunlight during the day.

It was with some satisfaction that when we all set to, to clear the corrugated iron, an extended family infestation of mice revealed itself, living a subterranean existence in tunnels where the soil met the corrugated iron. My mother retreated shrieking into the house as mice and rats were her greatest fear. I could not resist following her in and repeating, as a rebuke, the line that she was to hear from me so often in the coming years, "Well, you wanted to move here!"

It was clearly too late to get her to reverse her decision, indeed the family of one of my oldest friends from before primary school had moved into our old house so a return was an impossibility. I found it very hard to hear him referring to my house as his own. However it was important to me to trigger this guilt as often as possible to keep my mother in mind of how much the old house meant to me and the sacrifice I had made to allow her to have her way. I might also have some ammunition in this charge for extra pocket money or special treats.

I remember that the first few months in the house I spent with my nose permanently turned up. This was due to the smells associated with this new environment. It smelt simultaneously of old person and dampness, smells I had never associated with my home before.

The house was a kind of time capsule and it slowly revealed itself as my dad, aided by my uncles, began the process of redecorating. One benefit of this decorating was to expand the dimensions of each of the rooms as the previous occupants had layered wallpaper over wallpaper, robbing each room of several inches of space. Whilst stripping the hall and stairs for redecoration we went through a, reasonably fashionable, sixties' geometric design in orange and brown. A fifties' brown and white stripe then revealed itself followed by a layer of mushroom tinted paint. Beneath this was a thick embossed paper onto which had been painted a heavy lacquer to give a wood effect and beneath this, a dark green crumbly paint. My dad attacked the latter layer with a face mask and a water spray can as he reckoned it was lead paint and he did not want us breathing in the dust. None of these layers was particularly yielding and we were traipsing up and down the stairs and throughout the house with little slivers of ancient wallpaper stuck to our slippers for the best part of three weeks.

I had come off worst of all in the bedroom stakes, having traded a bright and airy, reasonably sized room in the old house for a freezing box room which adjoined next door's bathroom in this one. The ill-fitting windows rattled and leaked warm air, replacing it with a chill breeze and dampness on all but the hottest of days. In the first winter, the glass panes were frosted on the inside and my old green camberwick bedspread was invariably damp in the evening. I was allowed the electric fan heater on for twenty minutes before bedtime and draught excluder was applied, as best as might be, in the gaping window frames. None of this endeared me to the new house.

I kept my old divan and this, along with its winceyette sheets, provided some continuity in my life in these dark, cold days. To placate me, my mum saved up and bought me a small wardrobe from John Brookes', the local furniture shop and post office. It had to be small to negotiate the restricted clearances of the stairs and landing. Once in the room, I only had space for the footstool that I had completed, rather badly, as my first woodwork project in the new secondary school. "Shows promise," was how my woodwork teacher had described it.

"The promise that David will lay down all tools and never darken the door of a workshop again," my dad had quipped. This served as a surface for my evening drink and for my plastic bedside lamp.

So small was the room that a drop-down flap in the wardrobe served as my work surface for homework. I could comfortably sit on my bed and place my knees under the makeshift writing surface.

All in all, the proportions of the room, and the conditions within would not have been out of place in a borstal and I looked out of the window at the night sky divided by wooden bars into twelve panes of darkness and thought of happier times.

This then was my new home, 1 Prince Edward Avenue or, as my dad would always write in his precise and deliberate script on the tickets in the Labour Club Grand Christmas Draw, *1 PEA.*

Chapter Nine
COURT

The air in the County Court was hot and still and if you followed the shafts of sunlight to the windows at the top of the light oak wood panelled walls, you could see dust floating almost motionless in the air. The fact that this was the County Court gave an indication of the gravity of the situation.

From countless television programmes, the court layout scene was familiar. Directly ahead of me was the bench with the high backed leather seats, above it the shield supported by a lion and unicorn with the motto *Dieu et Mon Droit*.

In front of the bench sat the court officials with a copious supply of legal books. To their right were the seats for the jury and, to their left, an area for the press and public. Ahead of them were the counsels for the defence and prosecution and beyond them the holding area for the defendant.

From where we sat in the public gallery, we saw my dad led in by a court usher and directed to a row of austere looking seats. My dad looked slightly incongruous and very ill at ease in his new Burtons' suit which had cost considerably more than fifty shillings. He would have enjoyed a last cigarette outside court and popped a habitual Polo mint into his mouth to freshen his breath.

I hoped, as no doubt he would have hoped at innumerable school plays, that when the time came he would speak slowly and clearly and not fluff his lines.

Glancing around the courtroom I realised that the only time when I had been confined in a scene of such seriousness had been when the death of a much loved teacher had been announced in whole school assembly. There had been stunned silence which lasted for over thirty seconds before the first sobs of the girls were heard. As an emotional release, this sobbing had gathered an earnest momentum until there was not a row in the hall that did not have at least one girl in floods of tears. I saw, two rows down, a girl already red-eyed and bawling who had arrived at school after the departed teacher had left. She had never met the teacher and yet she was carried along in the hysterical crying.

I hoped there would not be any unseemly behaviour in the Crown Court today. The circuit Judge looked rather underdressed for such proceedings in his light grey suit. Here was a man given to dispensing justice which could make or break people's lives and yet he looked relaxed and slightly bored by what, for him, was just another day at the office. It was anything but that for my Dad.

The first official letter had come some months before and had been followed by a succession of ever more urgent communications. My father had been summoned to a series of official interviews and spent a whole weekend incarcerated in a series of police stations, a remand centre and a regional prison.

Early in the process I had been taken into the front room and the situation explained to me. I was sworn to secrecy and definitely knew better than to share this with any one of my friends.

The proceedings were over by lunchtime and my dad had acquitted himself well, speaking clearly and audibly so that we could hear him from our perch in the public gallery. When he was brought to us in the cafeteria, where we had been instructed to wait, he was both a free man and a newly initiated Justice of the Peace.

Had he been facing the most heinous criminal charges, my dad could not have been more relieved that the ceremonial part of the day was over. We all relaxed over pie and chips and spent the afternoon observing a real criminal case being tried, which was both more frightening and more boring than the events portrayed on Crown Court.

My dad was an easy man to underestimate. He was neither tall, nor broad, but possessed a wiry frame ideal for the life of manual work that had become his lot.

Following the war, which had taken him from home and a promising job at the local branch of a national grocery shop chain on a jaunt chasing the enemy across northern Europe with a 3.7 inch anti-aircraft gun, he had missed the opportunity to progress into management and had settled into a manual job to fund his new wife and subsequent family.

He had worked shifts for what felt like forever at the Courtaulds chemical factory down the coast at the ironically named Greenfield plant. In the metal bowels of the plant, he had mixed chemicals and moved bales of the man-made fibres which were to revolutionise clothing with the promise of drip-dry and non-iron shirts and nylon parachutes.

At first sight, his was an unremarkable life patterned by the demands of the shift work, the disrupted sleep patterns and the occasional three weekly treat of a Sunday lunchtime drink at the Labour club. He would return in time to carve the Sunday roast with a bag of *fferins* [sweets] as he referred to them, for the family. Invariably, the treat would be Bluebird chocolate-covered toffees purchased on the way into the club across the road at Frank Knowles the tobacconists and contained in their distinctive white paper bags with pink printing.

Yet below the surface, my Dad had a number of hidden talents. He was an accomplished woodworker and completed any DIY task around the house with a skill bordering on perfectionism. Our house had cupboards, bedside tables, cabinets and a boxed in staircase all constructed meticulously by my father with a minimum of ancient tools he had inherited from his father and which were kept in the shed in pristine order.

Technically then, he was gifted but his talent extended beyond this to sophisticated designs. His bedside tables were so admired that most of the family ordered one at some point. Each was unique in pattern but featured a substantial formica top, inlaid wood of different colours and textures and bamboo and raffia side panels. His was not simply the skill of a jobbing carpenter but of an artist in wood and contemporary design.

I only twice glimpsed another of his physical skills. He sauntered out into the garden on two occasions a couple of years apart when he had arrived home from a morning shift in the middle of the afternoon. I had been idly knocking a plastic football against the shed door, failing miserably to build a keepie-up run that extended to more than four kicks. The ball rolled to him and, still talking to me he managed to keep it up for thirty-five kicks, headers and knees before looping it back to me for a header that I ballooned over the shed roof. I swivelled back to face him but he had already turned on his heel and was heading back to the kitchen door for a cup of tea, a sandwich and a kip.

Following a similar demonstration over two years later, I realised that my dad must have been an accomplished footballer in his day but he had never chosen to tell me about it. I wondered what other secrets he had kept from me, either deliberately or by omission.

My Dad's most frequently revealed gift was for maths and he was a meticulous calculator of bills, measurements and quantities. This gift would have seen him well employed in accountancy or banking, but these professions had never beckoned.

I began to see why having to leave his hard fought for place at grammar school when his father was laid off from the building trade during the Depression of the Thirties, never to develop his potential educationally, had rankled so much with him.

His appointment as a Justice of the Peace was a long postponed reward for him and he threw himself into the training, reading everything methodically and making notes in a series of diaries. He attended the three residential weekends at Bangor University, living the life of the student for no more than three forty-eight hour periods.

He never spoke of the cases that came before the bench at Prestatyn but was happy to discuss the process and his commitment to ensure that everyone had a fair hearing. He would sometimes dismiss, rather magisterially, a comment of mine as 'hearsay' and an unreliable basis on which to mount an argument. I saw this as a little pompous but found that, as we moved through secondary school, the separation of fact from opinion was the basis of historical enquiry and scientific method.

Although I kept the fact that my dad was a JP to myself, I was secretly proud for him that he had become one and felt that he had a valuable contribution to make beyond the drudgery of his workaday life. He looked forward to the days neatly underlined with ruler marked red pen on the court diary on the quiet corner of the living room wall, above the electricity meter cabinet.

Chapter Ten
CORONATION

One of the changes that came about from moving off the Reso was that the Clinic Field was no longer the football field of choice. I could go back there, of course. It was, after all, no more that half a mile from my new house but that would risk lairy comments, or worse, from some of my erstwhile friends or colleagues.

The nearest green space to my new home was the Geufron Square which was no more than a hundred yards down the road. Unfortunately, the designers of this grassed area, which was about fifty yards square, seemed determined to prevent its use as a recreational area for anything other than the elderly.

The border of the Square was outlined by a thick hawthorn hedge, chest high and impenetrable. I'd lost a couple of Frido and World Cup balls to the vicious barbs in that hedge and at three shillings, or fifteen pence in the new money, I had no desire to allow my pitiful savings to be frittered away on punctured footballs.

What was more, the Square was dissected into four smaller squares by two pathways of crazy paving which were used by Council apprentices to develop their path laying technique. These pathways were neither level nor regular and deficiencies in mixing the mortar by the apprentices meant that random, jagged concrete protruded menacingly or just gave way as you tried to run with the ball at your feet.

Where the pathways intersected in the middle of the Square, some bright Council spark had decided to make a further circle of tarmac. Around this circle, four privet hedges, head high and dense were cultivated, each one accommodating a park bench. A less play friendly area could hardly be imagined. Either the designers had worked on the basis that the Square was a recreation area for the older Geufron residents where they could read cobwebbed Victorian novels or they were determined to cow the local children into silent submission.

The final impediment to play in the Geufron Square was Tim. Tim was a dog. You might picture a Jack Russell or some mongrel pooch with an amiable character and a long haired black and white coat who would join in all the games and sit quietly, head on paw, as we gathered to plot new adventures. You would be hopelessly, waywardly wrong.

Tim was the malign hellhound who sat in a concreted yard guarding his owner's vintage Jaguar as it sat on bricks under a tarpaulin, waiting for restoration.

Whilst his owner was away at work, Tim was shackled to a stout chain and was invariably near his kennel at the back of his yard. As you passed the gates, no doubt deep in conversation with a friend, he would launch himself headlong at the gates, his massive muscular back legs giving him tremendous leverage. As the chain was fourteen feet long and the gates fifteen feet from the tethering point, Tim would rise up to your head height, all ivory fangs and saliva and bark himself stupid. You never heard the howling bark until he was upon you which brought you to one of two disturbing conclusions. Either, over this short distance, Tim was moving faster than the speed of sound, which seemed highly possible, or he deliberately chose to stay silent in his attack to give you no warning of his arrival. In either case, it gave you a chilling insight into the personality of this dog.

When walking alone, I always moved away from the fence so as not to be covered in rabid, foaming saliva. I'd always plaintively say, "Hello Tim," in my friendliest voice to try and convince him that I was both a friend and not scared of him. He'd let me pass by for a couple of times and when I had forgotten about his menace he'd launch himself at me again.

One Sunday evening in the previous November, I had walked my nain home, after the nine o'clock news, past Tim's house. There had been no reaction so I'd assumed the dog was in the house watching something cultural on BBC2. Having seen my Nain safely in and with the light on, I set off home.

The week before I'd fractured my wrist playing rugby and was wearing a metal splint and bandaging round my right hand, which I now tucked into my bomber jacket pocket as the night air was particularly cold on my immobilised hand. I passed the yard without a hitch and was passing the door of the house when, from out of the darkness, Tim launched himself at that part of the bandaging that stuck out from my pocket. I was knocked sideways by the attack and gathered my wits to find several stones worth of Alsatian hanging from my arm. For ten seconds at least he shook his head vigorously, trying to separate my hand from my arm. Then he let go and leered at me before turning on his heel and walking back indoors, no doubt pleased with his handiwork.

I had not made a sound in the attack out of shock and not wanting to antagonise the dog further, although, how much further this foaming snarling banshee could be antagonised was a moot point. I now stood with white noise buzzing in my ears, saliva all down the arm and front of my new bomber jacket and a warm sticky liquid drenching my bandages. I hoped this was Alsatian saliva but feared it was blood. I would have complained to the dog's owner, but he was known to have an abrasive character similar to the dog and the idea of walking up to the open front door of the house, along the dog's launchpad, to confront the dog's owner on home turf really did not appeal. So I went home and told my parents, who said I must have irritated the dog in some way. The teeth marks had punctured not just my skin, but also the metal splint and in fact it was only the medical splint that had prevented my hand being severed.

Taken together then, there were better places to play football than in the Geufron Square.

The logical alternative was the Coronation Gardens. This was a large municipal park entered through substantial wrought iron gates with Council crests. An official notice board warned that these gates would be closed at 'dusk' and dusk was determined by the officious, uniformed park warden with a mean, pinched face and a determination to curtail any juvenile high jinks on his watch. Once past the gates, a wide avenue of mature lime trees guided you to where a massive grassed area marked for hockey, football and cricket opened up before you. The field was intimidating in its size and held infinite possibilities.

The Clinic Field was highly territorial and you did not set foot in it if you were not from the Reso, unless invited. The Coronation Gardens were large enough to hold several conflicting activities with ease and did not have one dominant group to control them. They felt safe and inviting. The park keeper, for all his faults, meant that there was always an adult on hand to curb the wilder excesses of the idiots. The downside was that you could not guarantee that, unless you had made a definite arrangement, there would be any of your friends there to play. A brilliant game of cricket on one night might turn into a lonely vigil watching the hockey club training the next night and always, in the background, would be Terry the long distance runner, in his green and white athletics vest and mean sinewy frame, pounding endlessly around the considerable perimeter of the field.

In the farthest corner of the field, where the gardens butted up against the worn corrugated iron sheeting of Rhyl football club, was a selection of children's swings and roundabouts. Whilst parents were in attendance with young children, this was a largely serene haven, but in the evenings as the parents ambled off to make tea, this area took on a different complexion.

In a world untainted by *Health and Safety*, we contrived to test the equipment to breaking point. How high was it possible to soar on the swings? Was it indeed possible to gather sufficient momentum to loop the loop? My growing knowledge of physics suggested that this feat was unlikely but that did not stop us competing on the four adjacent swings until we fell or jumped from the wooden platforms, moulded smooth and shiny by generations of youthful Rhyl backsides.

The witches' hat and the slatted wooden roundabout led to feats of endurance based on running as quickly as possible to give the roundabouts momentum and hanging precariously on them until the weakest began to vomit. A particular favourite game on the spider web roundabout was to cling on like grim death whilst the person who was 'on' fired a leather case ball across your path, hoping to dislodge you.

One evening, I managed to catch an exhausted and disorientated Atherton a direct shot to the back of the head. He rolled off the speeding roundabout like a Red Indian shot whilst on horseback. How we all laughed, well, all except Atherton, that is. He was too busy being sick and nursing a number of bruises and ugly bleeding grazes.

The Coronation playing fields were also a melting pot of cultures. In the quietest corner of the field, one could catch the genteel Evangelical Christians playing catch in what looked to us like their Sunday best clothes, drinking ginger beer and lemonade and eating Penguin biscuits from a wicker basket. They were the Amish of the town and relished their separateness. They were scouting for converts. You knew to accept an invitation to a biscuit or a drink was to barter your soul to a group who seemed to take it all far too seriously and who were convinced that they had an exclusive relationship with God.

Their leader, commonly seen as a prat whilst in school, wore what my mum would have called 'cavalry twill slacks' and not jeans, a starched yellow shirt and brown sandals with black socks and a quietly superior attitude. He had ostentatious wavy brown hair and gave the impression of one who would later find his mark as a Conservative politician. He knew with the absolute certainty of those mentally deluded or totalitarian in outlook that he, personally, had been saved and feared for the fate of the rest of us.

Near the changing pavilion, with its rusty drinking fountain of dubious water quality, could be seen the highly competitive teams of the Rhyl and District Rounders League, all intense and focussed in their ra-ra skirts and garishly coloured tops with hair scraped back and tied in elastic bands, shouting encouragement to each other and celebrating rounders and catches with equal exuberance. They varied in age from their ancient forties to teenagers, some being mothers and daughters, and all seemed to come from some endless conveyor belt of sporty females with bright eyes, flashing teeth and an excess of uncurbed enthusiasm.

Near the hockey posts at the entrance to the ground, Morton lurked. Here the sun seldom reached due to the shade of the lime tree avenue and this suited Morton well. He was a skulker, always between trouble both at school and at home. His crew cut and intense saucer eyes marked him out as different. He was antagonistic to everyone and everything, yet desperate for attention. I'd seen him insult the local hard knock, take a pasting and then insult him again as if to see if the bully would become exhausted before he lost consciousness from the battering. He did not seem to feel pain like the rest of us or perhaps his need to be noticed overrode his pain threshold. I'd known him steal money from his parents simply to give it away to those from whom he wished to curry favour. His unpredictability was both amusing and worrying. So it was with some disdain that one Friday night, as we cooled down from an intense game of football lying on the grass near his part of the field speculating about the shapes we could see in the clouds, we spotted his rapid approach.

He cut across our lazy conversation with the statement that he hated his parents and would probably murder them when he was old enough. We nodded and continued our drifting dialogue. Clearly, we had not paid him sufficient attention as he wandered to the rusty railings which marked the boundary of the playing field and his own back garden and reached in to retrieve some mud and stones and a couple of half bricks. He definitely had our attention now as we were concerned that this ammunition might be heading in our direction. We needn't have worried. He merely mouthed, "I'll show you how much I hate my parents," and began hurling lumps of soil at his father's greenhouse.

From twenty feet away he could hardly miss and each lob resulted in fractured glass. I'd never been a fan of vandalism and destruction, be it Morton or that lunatic in The Who who would smash a perfectly serviceable guitar when people like me were desperate to own one. However, it was quite mesmeric to see such wanton destruction of your own family's property. We thought he would stop after a couple of panes had been shattered but he continued methodically until the roof had disappeared in shards of glass. We saw the curtains move in an upstairs bedroom of his house and started to move away in case we were thought to be implicated in such a mindless act. Morton was unduly devastated when we started to move off. He seemed to be under the impression that this frenzied act had failed to win our friendship and we were all relieved when he wandered off muttering under his breath.

We returned to our rambling conversation about clouds, football and girls only to be disturbed once again by Morton, this time in his own back garden, with a cricket bat under his arm, moving with purpose to the damaged greenhouse like an Australian opening batsman. He had even gone to the trouble of putting on pads and was now busily adjusting one of the straps on his right calf. He took a few practice swings of the bat, checked to see that we were watching and began the systematic demolition of the greenhouse, pane by pane. He continued a manic rant against his parents with every swing. It was both comical and disturbing to watch his antics and I am sure that we all felt happier that there was a set of iron railings between us and the flailing automaton that was Morton.

He was on the final row of glass panes, with no more than half a dozen to complete the destruction, when two bemused police officers appeared in the garden. He turned to face them, bat lifted triumphantly, and, taking no chances, they tackled and cuffed him. Morton said nothing, his face red and sweating from his exertions. They quietly, but firmly, led him away past his crying mum in her floral pinafore dress. The distraught woman looked like she had the weight of the world on her shoulders as she sobbed uncontrollably. That it had come to this, she had needed to call the police to restrain her own child.

We never saw Morton again, or rather, we saw him in rather strange circumstances two years later. Six of the crew who had witnessed the incident were playing rugby for the school at the merchant navy's training school at Menai Bridge. After the game, which we won comprehensively, we were given tea in a grand, wood-panelled hall. We were served by uniformed cadets and there among them, offering us fairy cakes and malt loaf was Morton. He showed no sign of recognising us and studiously did not make eye contact with any of us. Knowing him of old, we did not let on we knew him and he seemed content to remain anonymous. What had happened to him in the intervening years I do not know, but the fire had gone from his eyes and they seemed dull and lifeless. I didn't know if this was a good or a bad thing in Morton's case.

Back at the playground corner, we found some footings had been dug when we arrived one evening after school. Within a week, a climbing frame made of stout trees and rope was erected. The frame had the added bonus on alternate Saturday afternoons of being the ideal perch from which to watch the first half of the matches of Rhyl F.C. as they tackled the might of Oswestry Town, Liverpool Marine, Stalybridge Celtic and Witton Albion. It was a bit demeaning hogging the highest perches of the climbing frame amongst all the toddlers with their parents glowering at us, but finances did not stretch to buying a ticket to watch the Lilywhites play and we knew we could sidle in for nothing once the second half commenced. Once inside the ground, we could take up our regular place on the Kop. We knew with certainty that this place would be available as the Kop, which might hold up to three thousand people, rarely saw more than fifty diehards. One of these was 'Williams the Chant', a perpetual student with ill-fitting woollen jumpers, second-hand shoes, National Health spectacles with the inevitable sticking plaster securing one arm and an acute personal hygiene problem. This accounted for the fact that wherever Williams chose to stand on the Kop, there was always a five yard quarantine area around him. Until he became better acquainted with soap and anti-perspirant, he was always alone in a crowd.

A frustrated commentator, Williams kept up an animated dialogue on the match, weaving in scenes from comedy sketches he'd seen on TV as well as tried and tested chants. If you saw him in action in just one match, he might prove amusing but he trotted out the same stuff every match and his lilting, high-pitched Welsh accent from up the valley in Denbigh, where they spoke at least an octave higher than in Rhyl, carried far and wide.

If an opposing player had encountered a Staziker scything tackle (Staziker being our combative centre half) and a leg injury ensued, he would pipe up, "That winger has a pronounced limp. L-I-M-P, pronounced Limp!" When the on-field action flagged, he attempted to rally the team with the hackneyed, "Give me an R! Give me an H! Give me a Y! Give me an L! What have you got…? RHYL!" Nobody joined in the responses but this did not dishearten him and he would pipe up again a few minutes later, "Give me an R…"

"I'll give you a bloody thick ear if you don't shut up!" came the reply from an exasperated supporter enjoying a piping hot cup of Bovril. Thinking he might be wearing the aforesaid Bovril shortly, Williams the Chant shut up. The following fortnight, the irrepressible Williams came up with, "Give me a T! Give me an M! Give me a V! Give me a J! What have you got? DYSLEXIA!"

It is a little known fact that Rhyl hosted the very first floodlit game of football when Mr Edison demonstrated his electricity generating equipment at the ground in the 1870s. Williams would have known that and thousands of other unremarkable facts about Rhyl Football Club.

The Rhyl team of the 1950s, made up as it was of Scottish footballers barracked at the Army camp at Bodelwyddan no more than five miles away, swept all before them and played under floodlights, but all that remained of the lighting stanchions were the concrete bases to the lights in the four corners of the ground, discoloured concrete like rotten teeth. It was to general excitement that the announcement was made that some new floodlights would be erected at the ground and that night matches would be resumed. When the lights were on, the glow could be seen in the night sky from my bedroom and I was drawn like a moth to the games, no matter how dire.

There was something primal and tribal about standing in the sleeting rain on the Kop on a Wednesday evening; eschewing the shelter of the side terrace to be among the fifty diehards and Williams the Chant, whose voice seemed to carry even further in the night air.

We witnessed defeat clutched from the jaws of victory, dogged, shapeless draws and the occasional inspiring victory. We saw legs and noses broken and bleeding injuries tended by the pigeon-toed Spencer Evans and his famous magic sponge, capable, like Snake Oil of curing 'Whatever ails you'.

We abused referees with equal venom for blowing too early or extending the game too long. We harangued visiting goalkeepers and swayed in unison like cobras behind our custodian of the nets, Millington, whenever he had to face a penalty so as to put off the opposition spot kicker.

Witnessing the footballing melee at the Rhyl Ground was all well and good but it was no more than a small skirmish compared to what I really relished. I wanted, without much hope of it happening, to watch sport played on an altogether bigger scale—an international rugby match at the Cardiff Arms Park. I was to get my wish sooner than expected.

Chapter Eleven
PARK

Saturday, February 5th 1972 would turn out to be an unforgettable day. The excitement had begun three weeks before when Evans the Ball, our wiry P.E. teacher, announced that through his contacts with the Welsh Rugby Union he had managed to obtain fifty tickets for the international match between Wales and Scotland at the Arms Park in Cardiff.

We stood at rapt attention, hanging on his every word. He would select the lucky forty-five students to attend from a raffle. To be entered for the raffle, you needed to have attended ninety percent of training sessions and to have played in at least eight of the ten games played that season. Evans was a canny operator and he knew that this would ensure full attendance at training between now and the international. I did a quick mental calculation. I realised that I met the first criteria but fell short on the second on the basis of my trial and game for the County 15—I felt sure that this would qualify me—especially as Evans had picked me for the trial in Wrexham and had attended the County game himself. Nevertheless, I wanted verbal confirmation that my name would enter the hat. This was too good an opportunity to miss. This was duly confirmed and I, like forty-four others, went home to impart the exciting news.

My excitement was not shared at home. My mother merely stated that it might be nice to go to Cardiff. My father, who had denied that the newspaper reports of the County match referred to me, as there were so many people with my name in Wales, suggested whilst reading the paper that I shouldn't get my hopes up. This was not the reception I had expected.

Whether there was any jiggery-pokery in the draw I cannot say. However, all the first teams for the three years were selected to go to Cardiff. I was hardly going to argue with such a result.

I was in bed by 8.30 p.m. on Friday, February 4th. Never one to voluntarily miss my sleep, or to arise before dawn, this was the only hardship of the trip. Besides, I wanted to be sure that I was sufficiently awake and with all faculties working to take in fully the sensual experience of the game. As if it was a sixties' Christmas Eve, I slept fitfully, waking at intervals to consult the illuminated dial of my dad's alarm clock, which he had thoughtfully placed on my bedroom table. The mechanical tick of its clockwork mechanism was part of the reason I could not sleep. I seemed to sleep briefly, dream vividly and wake up with only another half an hour elapsed. This repeated pattern was deeply exasperating and I felt more tired each time I awoke. When I woke at 4 a.m., I just knew I would not sleep again and lay there willing myself senseless to retreat one more time into slumber.

At 4.30 a.m., my mother entered the room and shook me gently by the shoulder. I was surprised to be woken from my cat nap and took a while to register the significance of the time and the day.

"The immersion is on so you can have a good wash! I'll go and make your sandwiches."

The story of the immersion heater was a continuing saga in our household. If there was a coal fire burning, then adjusting a metal bar in the chimney opened a flue which directed hot air onto a boiler which provided hot water to the taps. In the middle of cold winter days with the fire blazing, there was sufficient hot water to power a fleet of steam engines. When the fire was out or low, there was need to supplement the flue with an electric immersion heater. This was controlled by a substantial red switch in the kitchen and we all touched it at our peril.

Anticipating global warming, and with a commendable regard for reducing carbon dioxide emissions, my dad was obsessional about ensuring this switch was not on for more than twenty minutes at a time. He patiently explained the efficiency of the heating system, the volume of water required for a bath and the optimum temperature of said water. On other days, he just shouted about the immersion being on, usually with the observation that we were simply trying to heat a small volume of water and not power Blackpool illuminations with the amount of electricity we were wasting. At the time we thought he was just bloody mean. It is only now, in the fullness of time, that we can recognise him as an early environmentalist.

The only time I had had the temerity to shout and swear at my dad was when I had been third to have a bath one winter's Sunday evening and had inherited the remains of a single tank of lukewarm water. I'd come down in my paisley dressing gown and threadbare slippers, cold and festering and sat shivering through *Sunday Night at the London Palladium*.

An hour later my dad had stood in the hearth to consult the octagonal mirror which hung over the mantelpiece. I continued to seethe as he tried to check a boil that was erupting on his neck. Clearly, he was unable, no matter how he turned, to get a clear view of the back of his neck. He looked like a dog with a flea, twisting and contorting.

"What's this on my neck, *Crid*?" he finally asked my mum.

Without thinking I exploded, "It's your bloody head, you fool!"

I knew instantly that I had overstepped the mark in the manner and choice of words I had used. It went ominously quiet as my mum and my dad turned to face me. To my relief they both burst out laughing and I considered I had had a lucky escape. I decided never to push my luck in such a confined space again.

Taking a deep breath, I pushed off the flannelette sheets, the eiderdown, the candlewick bedspread, my dressing gown and the coat that had kept my feet reasonably warm throughout the night. Donning the dressing gown as quickly as possible, I skip-hopped to the bathroom over the black and white chequered marley tiles and turned to face the electric heater on the wall. I pulled the white cord and it immediately glowed red as the electricity, possibly *not* enough to power Blackpool illuminations, surged through it. No doubt my Dad would not approve of this extravagance but he was not here. He was not having to wash in a bathroom with frost formed on the inside of the window.

The heater, with its silver parabola reflector, had the unusual property of concentrating the heat about six inches from the element. At this point, it was hotter than the sun but beyond that, as cold and forlorn as Pluto. I ran the tap to bring some heat from the hot water into the room. The mirrors and windows steamed up instantly. I did my minimalist all over wash with soapy flannel and quickly put my dressing gown back on. Wiping the mirror, I decided my sleep tousled hair needed a wash. This was an inconvenience and would keep me in this cold hole longer than I would wish but I wanted to look my best for the match.

Fixing a hand towel round my neck I soaked the flannel again and wet my hair, and then found, as I dripped across the bathroom floor, that I could not locate the open sachet of Vosene, lightly medicated, shampoo. I toyed with using my mum's sachet of Silvikrin luxury lady shampoo but thought better of it. Ten hours on a bus to Cardiff and back was no place to be confined wearing women's shampoo. I settled for some Palmolive soap and tried to work it into a creamy froth without success. It proved very resistant to being washed out and left my hair clumpy.

Standing under the heater with the top of my head on fire and the rest of my body freezing, I furiously massaged my scalp to dry it quickly. The Vosene immediately appeared, as if out of nowhere, in the soap dish, behind the Mum roll-on deodorant. I somehow knew that it would—just to mock me.

Then I went back to the bedroom, with hair half dry, to endure the ordeal of putting on my cold clothes. I wished at moments like this, that I had not seen Glyn's house with its central heating radiators and tomorrow's clothes neatly arranged to greet you, warm and welcoming in the morning. Had I not seen this vision of the future, which some of my new friends were living now, I would not have become disgruntled with the cold bedroom which had been my lot from birth. My father claimed to despise central heating as if it were the work of the devil.

"Think of the heating bills those idiots are paying. The body is meant to be cooled down overnight—it prevents the spread of disease," he had stated with conviction. I knew that my dad's concern for our health and the parsimonious nature of the council house development budget meant that central heating would not be for us.

I'd chosen my clothes for the day very carefully, trying to anticipate every combination of weather and, although it was difficult to imagine at this moment, not wanting to be too hot. I went with a white vest and underpants and thick sports socks as an under layer. My new Christmas present Ben Sherman shirt with button down collar in the national colours of red and black tartan check formed the next layer, together with jeans. I reviewed the tartan design, not wishing to be identified as a Scotland fan, and reasoned that it would be hidden over several other layers. On went my ubiquitous bell bottom jeans and a thick polo neck sweater in a tan colour. The latter itched like hell at my neck, but nothing in my limited wardrobe was warmer.

I came down to the kitchen to find my fish-tail Parka had been draped over the chair in front of the beginnings of a new day's fire 'to take the chill off'. My mother was completing my baps and had boiled some milk to pour over my cornflakes. I had said I'd get myself up and make my own sandwiches, but I'd been relieved when my mum had dismissed this suggestion, insisting that she saw me off.

I settled at the new breakfast bar my dad had made, all Dulux and formica. I drank in the available heat from the stove and ate up the warm cornflakes, burning my mouth in the process.

My baps complete, my mother was wrapping them in greaseproof paper on which she had already written in pencil, *F for fish paste, B for beef spread* and *H for ham and mustard*. This seemed strange to me as I was going to eat them all myself anyway. My mother was a stickler for this type of detail. She had even put off going to Williams the Grocers until after four in the afternoon the previous day to ensure she had the freshest rolls from the last baking.

I was never one for swapping food on such trips as I did not believe anyone could make baps with the finesse of my mother. I certainly did not want to enter some lunch lottery where one of my prime ham and mustards was exchanged for a renegade sandwich of marmite or, horror of horrors, peanut butter.

I hated fish in all its forms but two: chip shop bought battered cod, and sardine and tomato fish paste! The latter I reckoned, with its unholy reek, might mean that no-one would be prepared to sit next to me and I would have a seat to myself. This was a major consideration on such a long journey where the bus and coach builders conspired to always give me an inch and a half less legroom than I needed to sit upright and comfortable. I determined to eat one of these sardine and tomato anti-personnel baps once seated on the coach and save one for the journey home, thereby reserving myself, by quarantine, a double seat on which to stretch out.

The baps were placed in the duffle bag together with some Kia-Ora, the remains of a large plastic pint bottle diluted with water, three slices of heavily buttered bara brith, two shortcake Cadbury Snacks, a large bag of wine gums and a packet of TUC cheesy sandwich biscuits. A picnic fit for a king, or even a dynasty, come to that.

It was now five to five, ridiculously early to set out on the ten minute journey to the school gates, but I started out anyway, anxious to avoid any potential snags on the journey and keen to baggsy a good seat on the coach. My mum kissed me on the step as if I was setting out for war. I had all the usual warnings about crowds, and pickpockets, and getting lost and asking a policeman. I listened absently, with the arrogance of youth and nodded at the appropriate times. I recoiled when my mum moved forward with the look of someone who was about to reach for a cleaning hankie to wipe my mouth. I thanked her for my 'snap' and set off.

The streets were deserted and I proceeded like a worker, duffle bag over one shoulder, up the road and round the corner. Despite the excessive time margin I had built into the journey, I found myself walking faster and faster due to the excitement of the impending journey. I ended up the first to arrive and sought shelter up against the railings set in the red brick wall, with scant protection from an out of season chestnut tree to keep the drizzle off my head.

Most of my friends arrived on the stroke of five twenty-five, then again, each had the luxury of arriving in their mum's or dad's car. Evans arrived and parked his car in the school car park, bundling some papers and what appeared to be the tickets into a briefcase.

The coach had still not arrived and I felt anxious that it might have broken down and it would be too late to find a replacement. I was also somewhat miffed that my early arrival had not been rewarded with a choice of prime seat. Clearly the teachers were beginning to share my misgivings as Mr Morris, with his typical lope, set off down the road to the public telephone box to check on the errant coach.

Assuming that there would be someone in the coach office at this ungodly time of the morning seemed a tad ambitious to me. He needn't have worried though as out of the drizzle a cream and orange Voel Coaches Bedford passed him, distributing a puddle in his general direction. It pulled up rather asthmatically and exhaled diesel fumes around the vicinity. The door opened half way with a hiss of compressed air and then the driver was forced to come and wrestle it fully open.

Clearly, we had been given the pride of the fleet.

My initial misgivings proved unfounded though, as the coach gave sterling service that day, despite the fact that the gear change sounded like rocks being ground up in an industrial washing cleaner.

The older boys made a beeline for the back seat for some, no doubt, illicit activity. This never appealed to me. I allowed the coach to fill up and took up a seat in the aisle so that I could stretch my legs and close enough to the teachers in the front seats so that I could ask questions en route.

I failed initially in my attempt to secure a double seat to myself so fifteen minutes into the journey, as we negotiated the road through St Asaph, I put plan B into operation. I reached for my sardine and tomato bap. It seemed very strange eating savoury baps so early in the morning and the taste did not register properly on my slumbering taste buds. The smell had the desired effect though and my seating partner, John, quickly beat a hasty retreat to another seat. I spread out, wiped the condensation from the window to obtain a better view, only to be greeted by grey mist and drizzle.

The whole bus was animated now, as if we were the Welsh team scheduled to play this afternoon. Released from the thrall of sleep, people were becoming hyperactive. There were the usual rounds of *Green Bottles on Walls* and *Men going to Mow*, together with my favourite *Welsh coloured Goats*, but even I drew the line at the idiot who started banging the seat backs in time to the song and released dark, musty clouds of stale-smelling dust from the red flecked seat material into the air. Eventually, and inevitably, the teachers intervened, and Morris the Magnet simply stood up, faced down the aisle and threatened to glower. It was enough to still the coach, and most then settled into a fitful sleep, or talked in hushed tones, as we wound our way down the length of Wales to Cardiff.

To my surprise, I was one of those who nodded off and I awoke, an indeterminate time later, with a headache where my head, lodged against the window, had been vibrating in time to the engine. I momentarily prayed that I would not get a migraine today of all days. Then I thought better of it and willed myself to feel all right.

The journey passed largely uneventfully. I glimpsed signs to places I wished to visit by train—Shrewsbury, Oswestry and Hereford, even Birmingham got a distant mention on one road sign. By the time we reached Ludlow, the drizzle had made a tardy departure and there was bright sunlight. It was 10 a.m. and the market town was bustling. We drove down several Medieval or Tudor streets and suddenly turned to skirt a river that shone silver deep below us. A distant memory stirred of television interludes and 'the distant Wye, much beloved of the romantic poets.' In my haste for confirmation, I interrupted the teachers' conversation and asked, "Sirs, is that the silvern Wye?"

"No." said Morris the Magnet unhelpfully, without elaborating on his answer.

Leominster, Hereford and Monmouth were quickly passed as the teachers shared a flask of coffee between them. The driver drank his from the plastic cap of the flask whilst driving one-handed down the dual carriageway and holding an animated conversation with the teachers in the seat behind him.

Boredom and confined spaces always led to trouble, and like animals who can smell a victim, we turned our attention to David Royle. I'd been through primary school with David and he was a totally nondescript character. If asked to describe him, I think we all would have paused and struggled for adjectives beyond medium height, medium length hair of a mousey colour, no distinguishing features. David was on the coach only by virtue of having competed in the required number of games for the first team. How he managed that was a tale in itself.

In his uniform blank greyness, David had one outstanding asset. He could run quickly in a straight line. Morris had picked up on this in one games lesson and he had pencilled David into the team as a flying winger. Morris' team picking ability was legion. Whilst at college, he had played rugby for the fifth team of one of the big South Wales clubs and that had somehow invested him with coaching ability.

His team picking methods were hardly scientific. Robbins, with his thickset body and lack of a neck was secured for the hooker position. Martin, the smallest of those who trialled for the team was made scrum half. I coveted the number 10 shirt, Barry John's shirt, the creative inspiration of the team. I thought my height would intimidate the opposition and my speed would allow me to command the game, setting up try after try with deft kicks, explosive penetrating runs and fast recycled ball for my wingers. Morris listened with interest to my strategic nouse and tactical awareness and said two words by way of reply.

"Number 8."

I tried to elucidate my role as a creative dynamo, unshackled from the grunt and grind of the scrum to bound like Mercury across the open vistas of the opposition half, causing scintillating mayhem with my jinking runs and creative distribution. He looked me up and down as if digesting my passionate resolve and replied, "Second row."

I knew if I continued to pursue my case the next word I would hear was, 'Prop.'

So much for the beautiful game.

I would spend the next two years with my head sandwiched between the bum cheeks of our dubious front row having my ears chamfered and my creativity ground down. Whenever I got the opportunity, much to the disgust of Morris, I'd run like a stallion with the backs, moving the ball quickly, passing, jinking and distributing like a natural. Once every two or three games I'd score a try, much to Morris' disgust. With spittle foaming from the edge of his mouth, he'd castigate me from the sidelines for, 'dereliction of duty'. Had this been the Somme, I'm sure he would have had me shot.

"You are a forward, boy—your job is to win the ball, not to run with it—leave that to others more creative than you!"

In such ways is the soul of the enthusiastic teenager punctured.

Whilst I was grunting and grinding with the Neanderthals in the pack, Royle got to stand on the wing, conserving energy and losing concentration, his explosive speed nowhere in evidence. Over a number of weeks since his debut, he had developed a series of irritating habits which were trying the patience of the rest of the team.

He was delivered perfect passes in open ground with a ten yard unopposed jog to the line to score and he would fumble the catch, juggling it and knocking on all the way to the try line. On the occasions he took a pass cleanly, he seemed to have no directional awareness and set off in the direction he was pointing, admittedly at great speed, and ran into touch—and then continued running until the third blast of the whistle stopped him somewhere between the next pitch and the dressing rooms. There was no hint of irony or direction in his running.

His most irritating habit though was when going to pick up a ball from the ground. At first, I thought he was doing it for a laugh as he repeated it several times in one match. He would bend to pick up the ball and inadvertently kick it forward a few feet. He'd dash forward and bend again, only to kick it forward again. His worst case of rugby Tourette's was repeated five times until he finally got the ball under control, only to be sacked by the opposition's rampaging forwards and thereby conceding a try from our attacking position. Having been bloodied and bruised in the scrum, ruck and maul, I did not take kindly to his profligate stupidity and the coach trip provided the ideal opportunity for revenge.

When Royle finally reached into his duffle bag he produced a ripe banana for his elevenses. We let him eat it like a wary squirrel, taking nibbles and then looking around. As soon as he had finished, we broke into a conversation about the digestive system and the mush of the banana being masticated (good word that—resolved to work it into five conversations the following week) and the curdling of acids in the stomach. At first he feigned not to hear our treatise of food disintegration but the increasingly graphic nature of our description could not help but entrance him. Behind, in front and across the aisle from him people were describing the action of acids and bile and the mixing of the banana with yesterday's undigested food. Eventually, the power of auto-suggestion and all his neighbours feigning heaving had him rushing to the front of the bus, as we had been instructed, to request a sick stop, as being sick on the coach was a capital offence.

We took ample satisfaction at the sign of him bent double, heaving behind a small bush. I called out, "I'm shaking the tree boss, I'm still shaking the tree!" in the manner of Paul Newman in *Cool Hand Luke* and this got another laugh.

Royle re-entered the bus to a hearty cheer, his face a sort of ashen sepia and his eyes tearful from the heaving exertion. I felt he had paid in full for his inept play in previous games and would have been prepared to write him a receipt to that effect.

Baiting Royle had been a pleasant distraction on the tedious journey and by the time he was settled back in his seat the first road sign for Cardiff appeared, much to the appreciation of the weary coach inmates. It was greeted with a cheer, as was every road sign featuring Cardiff and a diminishing tally of miles from that point on.

It was the best part of an hour before we finally reached the outskirts of Cardiff and joined the throng of fans heading for the game. The fact that the opposition was Scotland meant that there was a general air of revelry and what BBC sports commentators would describe as 'lively banter' between the fans.

To be honest this was true of three of the four games in the Home Internationals. With Scotland, Ireland and France one was amongst family. Many purists could even stomach a Welsh defeat, just so long as the game was played with the right spirit, kicking was limited, precise and expansive, and open rugby was played. Only the game with England had a harder edge to it. Perhaps it was the fact that English rugby at the time was seen, rightly or wrongly, as a privileged game of the public schools, whereas Welsh rugby was a game of the Valleys and the working classes, or such was the perception.

For some, the English game brought back the memory of centuries of subjugation by the old enemy, of invasion and castle building, of Owain Glyndwr and the banning of the speaking of the Welsh language. I knew little of this as it had not appeared on the interludes on the television and apart from the tales of the *Mabinogi*, which Mr Ambrose read to us regularly, I was surprisingly ignorant of Welsh culture or language.

I was happy to forego a foundation of Welsh history. I much preferred our own century. But even I found myself suddenly seized by rampant Celtishness. I felt the need to sing and be part of this tribal experience. I imagined the Nazis, gathered at Nuremburg felt much the same way—being part of something bigger. I immediately felt uneasy and decided not to give myself completely to the moment but to try and understand it as an observer.

Our proximity to the ground was indicated by the growing density of the crowd, which occupied paths and roadway now and slowed the progress of the bus to a walk. Members of the constabulary, in their efforts to speed up the traffic flow by intervening with hand signals, as always, had the opposite effect, and we were brought to a standstill and forced to join in the revelry outside the coach, flashing scarves and rosettes and waving banners to the approbation of the passing fans of both teams. Someone spotted a banner from Rhyl Rugby Club and a cheer resounded round the coach.

To be honest, the magnanimity with which I described victory or defeat for Wales as immaterial was a little wide of the mark. The current Welsh team had the hand of greatness upon it. A backbone of forwards who were as cunning as they were strong formed the foundation for winning and stealing the ball from the opposition. The backs were magicians to a man—fast, beguiling and capable of individual initiative and group cohesion. Holding the whole edifice together were Gareth Edwards and Barry John, as great a combination of talents as ever graced a rugby field.

The Arms Park hove into view now and no sooner had this registered in a reverent silence on the coach than we made an abrupt left turn and began to head away from the hallowed ground. We found ourselves corralled with hundreds of other coaches in, if the signpost was to be believed, Sophia Gardens.

Evans the Ball rose slowly with the match tickets in his hands. He wafted them in front of his face and a hypnotic silence fell on the coach, all attention cast on those magical tickets.

"Right lads," he began, having gained our undivided attention.

His pep talk was short, but comprehensive—eat now as the food stalls closer to the ground were expensive. Do not, under any circumstances, try to pass yourself off as eighteen in order to visit a pub as, if arrested, the coach would be leaving without you at the appointed time. Make a mental note of where the coach was in the park and enjoy the game. Coach leaves at six thirty sharp, no excuses for being late.

Starting from the front, people were allowed off the coach having received their anointment by match ticket.

"In the name of Rugby, the country and the Arms Park I hereby bestow this ticket upon you."

It was all I could do to stop myself muttering Amen when my ticket was gently pressed into my sweaty hand.

Aged twelve, with £1.50 in my pocket and a duffle bag of food on my back I was now cast into the milling throng of fans churning the Sophia Gardens grass into thick glutinous mud as we made our way down to the road, across the Taff and to the ground. I had never felt safer or more part of a common purpose.

The Arms Park was hidden from view as we approached by a bevy of shops and other buildings and it was difficult to gain a feel of scale for the shrine of Welsh rugby. Certainly we saw the new stand, a gleaming precipice of ivory concrete which launched skyward at what seemed an impossible angle and immediately brought on feelings of vertigo. Together with John, David, Gareth, Glyn and Keith, I circled the ground, observing it from the Taff River end and waiting impatiently for the gates to open.

I had carried the ticket in my hand for the last half hour, frightened of losing it if I stashed it in my pocket or duffle bag. I noticed that all the others were doing the same thing. We must have looked like a troop of Neville Chamberlains, piece of paper in hand as we negotiated the streets of Cardiff with the promise of glorious rugby 'in our time'.

By the time we went through the turnstiles the ticket's lustre had begun to melt in our hot sweat. The stub was torn off and we carefully stowed the remains of the ticket; it would form pride of place on each and every bedroom wall in years to come.

We gathered just inside the turnstile and, common sense prevailing for once, headed to the toilets and waited for each other so that we could walk up the entrance tunnel together. We were almost alone in the ground except for a few other school parties. Any adults would be engaged in the pre-match lubrication of voice boxes or a lightning strike on the Cardiff shops.

As we crested some ancient steps we were confronted with the full majesty of the stadium. Across from our modest stand, which was seen as the haunt of the diehards, was the giant new stand arching skywards with precipitous red seating. We stood silently for some moments, staring in disbelief at the enormity of this cathedral to rugby and our good fortune to be there, until the build up of spectators behind us propelled us forward like a stream of red, viscous magma. We were forced to run down the steps and took our place in the front row behind the white hoop-topped railings about thirty feet from the try line towards the end that contained the scoreboard.

Across from us, the doors must now have opened, as a stream of red ant-like figures began to appear on the staircases and make their way to their seats high, high above the pitch.

As I looked around trying to take in and store, like a memory camera, all the sights and sounds, I saw every face smiling. Scots and Welsh were mingling and joshing. To a man, the Scots looked as I had imagined them, tall, sandy-haired and kilted. I imagined that if the team shared these characteristics they might be able to overwhelm the Welsh team and then I thought of David and Goliath and was reassured.

The stream of humanity trickling into the opposite stand had now turned into a torrent and the murmurings that had rippled through the growing crowd now began to give voice. To my surprise, the terraces behind me had filled to capacity as I had been observing the opposite stand and they now began to rehearse the full canon of Welsh hymns and arias as featured on my uncle's records of *Ten Thousand Welsh Voices from the Albert Hall*.

There was I, in the front row of this heavenly choir, fifty thousand Welsh voices and me, miming.

I mimed not because I did not know the words. Countless morning singing sessions in Emmanuel School had imprinted the words of *Calon Lan, Sanctiadd, Bread of Heaven* and even *Sospan Bach* in my mind. I mimed because in the previous year's audition for the school choir, which was populated by countless fit girls and a few of the more nerdy boys, the choir leader had encouraged all to listen to my audition piece. She swore that it was the first time in a generation that the choir had the possibility of containing someone who could sing exclusively in the key of H. My initial pride subsided when I realised, with each passing line, that the assembled choristers were suppressing laughter, but I was compelled to continue to the end of the song, Mrs Jenkins' strident piano playing urging me forward with gusto. It was a long way from the piano to the door that day and I wove a sorry path between the girls, their musical instruments, hockey sticks and mocking laughter.

Such was the searing impact of that humiliation that I had resolved never to sing publicly again.

I was, it seemed, the only tone-deaf Welshman in the land of song. But I did mime with passion on the terraces that day, all my words and phrasing perfectly formed, but silent. I was haunted by the prospect that the singing would abruptly cease as some fifty thousand voices 'screeched' or rather harmoniously ceased and a rich voice somewhere at the back of the terrace would boom out, 'Hang on a minute, there's some bugger at the front ruining it by singing off key!'

And one hundred thousand eyes would bore into me for committing such a heresy in the Holy of Holies.

Several generations of commentators have robbed the language of sufficient hyperbole to do the moment justice. The roar that greeted the emergence of the teams, I felt, would do structural damage to the stand opposite. I felt myself unceremoniously pressed against the railings as the crowd surged forward and then the pressure was relieved as people regained their composure. It was as if we were breathing as one. As Bill MacLaren might have observed with his fruity accent, "That roar will be echoing around the Welsh Valleys for the next hour!"

From where we stood, the national anthem reverberated off the opposing stand and returned to us amplified, inspiring the crowd to greater volume and me to even greater silent mouthing. The clapping that followed the anthems echoed like massed rifle fire around the stadium and at last we were away.

From our standpoint, the forwards looked bigger and the backs smaller than on television. When the action finally started, there was a melee of skirmishing that sent water and mud spewing but no great shape to the game. An attacking Scottish winger was sent careering across the turf towards us, launching a cascade of sandy mud in our direction. I couldn't say for certain who he or the tackler were as the kits, so pristine and proud at kick off, were now reduced to heavy, sodden greyness.

As one, the crowd watched as the ball was punted aloft to gain ground on this treacherous surface only to be returned by the opposing team, often with interest. There was bumpage and grindage, slippage and slideage as maestros were reduced to mortality by conditions underfoot.

Incredulously, as the half time whistle blew I consulted the scoreboard to see that the Welsh team were twelve points to ten down. All I had indicated previously about not being too concerned about losing to the Scots was abandoned. I had not come this far, consumed so many baps and slept so badly on the coach, to endure a Welsh defeat. The sense of urgency was, in part, accelerated by a desperate need to go to the loo. I'd made a hearty inroad into my Kia-Ora orange squash and the pressure of the crowd on my back and the drink in my bladder made the pilgrimage to the toilets an urgent necessity.

While I debated the journey and the chances of getting through this crowd to the toilet block and finding my way back to the front row of the terrace, the time ticked away. The decision was made for me when I'd finally decided to risk the journey only to find the teams re-emerging from the tunnel.

I was now condemned to forty minutes of bladder control at the front row of ten thousand supporters eagerly pressing forward to encourage the team onward, and my bladder to evacuate. I contemplated the old standby of relieving myself in my programme and rejected it out of hand. This programme was too valuable and the insistent, pressing crowd gave me no space to manoeuvre. So, the surrounding spectators gained the impression that I was a particularly excitable teenager, hopping from foot to foot whatever the action on the pitch.

My decision not to lose my place in a trek to the toilets was quickly vindicated as I had a grandstand view of what many consider to be the finest half of Welsh rugby ever. It was as if the team collectively transcended the conditions and ran on the turf of the Gods. Barry John disposed of his training boots and replaced them with those of Mercury. He flew across the pitch and every kick landed no more than a yard from touch and then obligingly headed out of play, having taunted a Scottish hand to claim it first. The crowd, if possible, became even more animated, the singing more heavenly. More taxed than the Scottish defence were the scorekeepers who constantly adjusted the scoreboard as Wales began to rack up the points.

With an hour gone and from deep in his own half, Gareth Edwards, our saintly scrum half, received a nothing ball and set off towards the Scottish line. The jink he made past the first Scottish defender, given the conditions, was the work of an artist. As the mere mortals shuffled about the pitch, Edwards, seemingly with all the time in the world, looked up and saw the Scottish full back advancing towards him. In an instant, he kicked into the remnants of grass and mud behind him. The full back instantly realised he was undone as he tried to stop his forward advance and find reverse gear.

Several Scottish defenders now moved to plug the gap and it appeared that the ball would roll out of play. Edwards was having none of this and he sprinted over the sodden ground and carefully kicked the ball forward with a degree of control he had no right to expect, given the conditions.

Edwards, in the muddiest part of the pitch, was now sprinting directly past us and the crowd appeared to be blowing him forward with screams of encouragement. He was no more than twenty feet away from us as he dived after the skidding ball, grounded it behind the try line and continued to slide off the pitch and into the cinders that formed the outside of the greyhound track.

All that had gone before had been a mere whisper compared to the eruption of celebration that greeted this miraculous try. I was there and I was twenty odd feet away from the epicentre of possibly the greatest try in rugby history.

I looked around to capture the scene as indelibly as possible and found Scots as well as Welsh applauding the audacity of the try. Gareth passed by us much more slowly on his way back to the half way line. At least I think it was Gareth, he was one of many pebble-dashed with the red mud which formed a perimeter to the pitch. They looked like miners on their way home—only the whites of their eyes giving an indication of their identity.

This turning point demoralised the Scots and energised the Welsh who ran in two more tries and King Barry added conversions and a spot kick to the tally that finally read: *Wales 35, Scotland 12*. If only I could have bottled that moment, it would be the antidote for any moment of self-doubt and depression for several lifetimes.

When the final whistle went, we all clapped and sang with hoarse voices, or in my case, mimed. Whether it was hysterical reaction I don't know, but my voice was worn raw despite never having uttered a note.

The revelries continued as the crowd dissipated and there was no feeling of returning to normality as we patiently waited to exit the ground. The sheer volume of happy humanity meant that I was soon wrestled away from my friends and found myself bobbing along the open area outside the main gates. It felt like a red and blue ocean swell and, like a spectating Peter Pan, I found myself with my feet lifted off the ground and flying with the flow of the masses. For more than a hundred yards, my feet did not touch the ground and I relived those vivid dreams from the distant past when I dreamt with conviction that I could fly.

Eventually, the crowd began to thin out and my feet gently made contact with the pavement. The further away I moved from the ground, the more the rush subsided and the tsunami was now a stream as I reached the Taff Bridge.

I washed up at the coach, parked with thousands of others in Sophia Gardens, and resolved, like every young spectator that day, to play for my country at the Arms Park.

It was unlikely to happen of course. So many seeds of ambition which began to germinate on that day would wither on the barren ground of a lack of ability or the herbicide of a mis-spent youth and the discovery of girls during those critical years.

I would like to think it was the latter rather than the former that put paid to my ambition, but the truth was probably a bit of both. Losing the curse of excessive height in my teenage years as others caught me up also lost me a vital physical edge. A series of injuries meant that I went no further than representing my county and being picked for a North Wales fixture which was subsequently cancelled. In such banal ways, dreams are turned to dust.

Chapter Twelve
DOSH

Having got by with relatively little money when we lived on the Reso, I was surprised how quickly the need for money crept up on me once I entered my teenage years.

The idea of anything taking me away from spending long summers playing with my mates, planning to play with my mates or being someone else, somewhere else in the shed, did not rest easily with me.

I also took the idea of employment far too seriously. I had seen the fathers departing the estate in their grey clothes with grey expressions and I, if I had to become a wage slave, wanted a fulfilling and well paid job before I'd trade in my freedom.

Despite these principles, the pressure was mounting.

I had always considered myself fortunate that Christmas, Easter and my birthday were equally spaced on the calendar and my coffers, such as they were, could be replenished at equal points throughout the year, unlike Brian, whose birthday fell on Christmas Day and for whom I always felt sorry as his family combined Christmas and birthday presents. I was never more than a few months away from a cash top up. However, this easy cash was being squeezed by reciprocal arrangements that my mum had worked out with family members. Once we reached teenage years, the presents for all the cousins would stop. I was not consulted on this and would have played merry Hell had I been. Unfortunately, my voice counted for nothing in this negotiation.

That left pocket money. Since the unfortunate incident of the tea caddy, where I had been spiriting away threepenny bits from my Dad's little green banking bags, leaving him light and embarrassed when the bags were weighed at the Trustee Savings Bank, I had been promised pocket money every week. For the first few months, one shilling was delivered every Saturday morning. Then the shilling became intermittent as parents forgot and once I got to ten years of age, there seemed a determined campaign to put me under financial pressure, much as a parent bird pushes the untried fledgling from the nest. No doubt, my parents thought they were being cruel to be kind. I just felt they were being cruel.

The shilling-a-week pocket money had once been more than adequate and, with decimal currency and inflation, this had now doubled to what we were still calling ten new pence. Delivered before ten a.m. on a Saturday morning, it allowed the fulfilment of all my dreams before twelve thirty. By ten o'clock, I'd be in the queue for the Mickey Mouse Club at the local Odeon, taking a seat in the stalls for sixpence and miming the club anthem like a good 'un.

So here we go on Saturday morning…

Greeting everybody with a smile!.

Having seen the cartoons which finished with, "That's All Folks!", we'd watch an ancient Buck Rogers in black and white with hardboard sets and cardboard acting, and a spaceship that looked like it was powered by a small economy firework.

Come the intermission, I'd jostle with the other clubbers and irritate the usherette who would threaten us with, "knowing our Dads!" and would finally scream for Mr Golightly, the cinema manager. Mr Golightly knew enough about massed groups of youngsters on a Saturday morning to ensure that he was always in the projectionist's office at this time, out of harm's way. The full house lights would be turned on and the whole cinema would suddenly go quiet and compliant. The melee at the ice cream queue would suddenly resolve itself into an orderly queue. It reminded me of those thirties American prison films where the escaping convicts had to cross the prison yard under the trigger happy view of the guards high up on towers. The lights would be turned off again and Mr Golightly's high powered torch would be shone from the projectionist's window, scanning the cinema for trouble, which always managed to be out of his electric prying gaze.

Emotions in the queue were not helped by the presence of George, a scruffy boy who wore what looked suspiciously like his school uniform cast offs on a Saturday morning. He really didn't help himself by carrying his sixpence in a small coral coloured purse. Had I been George, I wouldn't have drawn attention to myself but he seemed to take delight every Saturday in being at the front of the queue and gazing into the tray the usherette was carrying as if he had never seen its contents before.

He was clearly doing this to annoy, as we had all memorised the contents of the tray that was suspended around the usherette's neck in crystal clear detail. Back left, large stack of tubs of vanilla ice cream. Back centre, small light on a stalk which illuminated a square cash tray with partitions for the bronze half pennies, pennies and two penny coins, the silver five pence, ten pence and fifty pence coins. The partition at the back for pound notes was always empty on a Saturday morning. This section also held wooden spoons for scooping the ice cream. Front left, Zoom lollies. Front centre, single colour suckers in orange flavour wrapped in cheap paper sleeves that stuck uncompromisingly to the lolly. Front right, Strawberry Mivvis and Orange Mivvis with golden Cornish ice cream filling.

George would rub his chin and even scratch his improbably Brylcreemed hair as he agonised over his choice. He'd take off and rub his round National Health spectacles with the metal rims on the bottom of his pullover, then replace them. He'd decisively pick up a tub of chocolate ice cream and would be ready to hand over his money before shaking his head and equally decisively returning it to the appropriate partition and starting the thought process again. When he finally decided, spurred on by a weekly punch to the back of his head, he would insist on handing over his money one penny at a time counting it slowly and methodically into the impatient usherette's hand as the queue bayed behind him.

My preference would have been for an Orange Mivvi but, at five pence, it would blow my careful spending plan. So I'd purchase a three coloured Zoom ice lolly for three pennies. This I'd suck until all the colour was drained, leaving an insipid block of spaceship shaped ice and then I'd crunch it loudly and slurp my way through the earnest British Children's Film Foundation Film.

This was usually about children with clipped accents called Julian and Cassandra wearing grey shorts and red spotted neckerchieves becoming embroiled in an adventure on the heath involving foreign spies with sinister bald heads, planning to steal designs for the latest British experimental fighter 'plane.

I liked the shots of the 'plane which looked like a De Haviland Vampire, but thought the rest of the plot was a bit improbable.

Certainly such things did not happen in the Rhyl I knew—neither, in my experience, did children wear neckerchieves. Although Rhyl did have the world's first hovercraft operating from our beach for a brief time in 1962. It operated a service to Wallesey on the Wirral—although why anyone would feel the need to travel at high speed between Rhyl and Wallesey was beyond me. Perhaps its demise in the September gales of that year was a cover for sabotage…no doubt the first I'd get to hear of it was when the Children's Film Foundation made a film about it. Although they'd be hard pressed to find anyone wearing neckerchieves in Rhyl and certainly there was nobody called Julian and Cassandra.

At the end of the film, the National Anthem would be played, accompanied by pictures of the Queen on horseback reviewing the soldiers at the Trooping the Colour ceremony. The words were imprinted over the pageant and a more effective way of clearing the cinema has not been devised. The invitation to God to save the gracious Queen in the first line would be accompanied by an unholy dash for the red lit EXIT signs indicating the nearest point of departure. By the time that God was commended a second time to Save the Queen in the third line, the cinema would be completely empty save for some Mivvi wrappers, assorted discarded ice cream tubs and the odd coat that had fallen down the seats as the impatient audience had vacated the rows in an indecent rush.

On the journey home, I'd join another queue of boys who were determined to climb up the twenty feet of stone wall of the Vale Road Bridge rather than walk up the perfectly serviceable steps that led to the pavement over the bridge. This was truly a 'rites of passage' thing, like the Zulu boys I'd seen on the Horizon TV programme, hunting a lion with only an assegai and a loin cloth. In Rhyl, you showed you had reached maturity by climbing up the wall of the steps of the Vale Road Bridge and I was proud to be part of the generations who had made this Climb of Death, or more realistically this Climb of Minor Bruises and Potential Concussion.

This only left the purchase of a Beano for the bargain sum of three pennies to make the Saturday morning complete, assuming I'd managed to purloin an extra penny from somewhere.

Whilst my tastes remained simple, ten pence was adequate pocket money. However, the call of manhood was ringing insistently in my ears and I had discovered the Airfix kit, Series One, for the princely sum of eleven pence. My heart desired one every week. I was like Hitler re-arming in the mid-thirties, creating an air force at breakneck speed, one 'plane a week. One 'plane a fortnight simply did not satisfy my craving. It was this, more than the insistent encouragement of my parents, who compared me to cousin Tim, who at two years my junior, was already gainfully employed on a number of jobs, that drove me to find paid employment for the first time.

The obvious first choice of a summer job in the town was 'casing' at the station. This involved constructing a cart from an old pram and offering to carry the cases of the holidaymakers to their digs and caravans when they arrived, tired and excited, at Rhyl railway station. I liked the idea of this as it kept me close to the railway. Even if the last of the steam engines had now departed, this was still a place of excitement and expectation.

However, the changing winds of the economy were catching up with the one week seaside holiday and the casing boys who relied on it. There was an oversupply of boys with ramshackle carts and an undersupply of arriving holidaymakers.

The best organised casers timed their arrival at the station to coincide with the most likely holidaymaker trains—the 09.17 from Manchester, the 10.40 from Birmingham and the 11.21 from Nottingham and Derby. I just turned up and hoped for the best.

The best casers had painted their carts and named them: *Lion, Speedy* and *Caradoc's Casing Carts*. The latter was a stroke of genius as it immediately immersed the holidaymaker in the feel of a foreign holiday—who in England was ever named Caradoc?

I had a ramshackle cart with a split plywood carrying area and rusted Silver Cross pram wheels. My cart had an unerring knack of deciding its own path rather than responding to my steering in much the same way as the new trolleys introduced by Albert Gubay, Mr Kwik Save, at his cut-price food emporium across the tracks on the wasteland next to the railway marshalling yard.

I took my turn in the queue to service the holiday makers and was regularly bumped backwards by the older and more experienced boys who resented the newcomers with their amateur attitude and conveyances. I was also bitterly resented and abused by the taxi drivers who shuffled in line outside the station and made for their cream and maroon cabin with the telephone bell on the outside. As we placed ourselves between the station exit and their rank, they considered we were stealing bread from their table. In truth, most of the holiday-makers, on a tight budget, would not have countenanced the expense of a taxi fare when, cooped up on the train for several hours, all the family required was, according to the parents, "some bracing sea air and to stretch your legs!" Thus they combined physical health with economy, to the total satisfaction of the dads. I could picture, in my mind's eye, my dad saying this to us had we had the good fortune to be going to a seaside resort for our holidays.

I was also mildly rebuked by the Crosville conductors who loitered near their drivers' windows of the all-over green and cream striped Bristol Lodekkas and older single deckers. These serviced the more exotic destinations like Llansannan via Abergele Chest Hospital in the bus bay across from the station. It was from here that the open topped bus, called locally the Toast Rack, departed for a tour of the coast from the Pontins Holiday Resort at Prestatyn to the Winkups Caravan Park beyond Towyn. This was definitely in direct competition with us on the casing trucks. We sometimes had to discourage the holiday-makers, particularly those with children, from taking the Toast Rack, with tales of horrendous expense or children toppling from the open top deck, thus ruining such a promising holiday.

If I was lucky enough to secure a punter with cases to lug, we had to navigate crowded streets of holidaymakers walking slowly and randomly in various directions as well as the locals clogging up the pavements. If you had a choice, and you seldom did, you never chose a couple with walking toddlers as they would inevitably slow you down and get distracted, thereby prolonging your return for your next fare. The more wily casing operators would check where the fare wanted to go and would reject the long haul to Winkups and Pontins in favour of shorter, quick fares.

You might think it would also be obvious to negotiate a fare before the journey, but I was so embarrassed by the whole 'asking for money' thing that I seldom did this. This resulted in me taking fares on long journeys of over an hour for two pennies.

The worst fare ever was a bluff Yorkshire man with a crisp, white shirt and grey flannel trousers pulled up too high, who had me take him the three miles to Winkups Camp with his wife and five children. Their luggage collapsed the springs on my casing truck. He offered me his hand, shook mine and thanked me for being so helpful before wheeling away into his caravan and shutting his door. I knew better than to knock and demand my money.

The final straw was a Birmingham couple with two children, all of whom wore the same pattern National Health tortoiseshell glasses, spoke too loud and approached the journey to their Bed and Breakfast like some intrepid Antarctic Expedition. The father informed me that he had been to Rhyl two decades earlier and the town was imprinted on his memory from that happy time. He refused to give me a destination but proceeded up Bodfor Street giving a running commentary of his previous holiday and what the family would see when they turned the next corner. His descriptions animated the children, who became increasingly sullen as they turned the corner only for the father's predictions to be habitually wrong. Unperturbed by this, we spent the next hour and a half on what should have been no more than a half mile journey.

When the father, after so many anti-climaxes, finally admitted defeat and reached into his pocket to produce the booking confirmation with the address emblazoned on the top, we ended up retracing our steps for two thirds of the previous journey, much to the irritation of his wife whose white, stiletto-heeled sandals, bought especially for the holiday, had now chafed her bunions to raw meat and stained the plastic with blood.

I had thought that my rescuing of the situation might have earned me a bonus but, so engrossed in placating his wife was the directionless Brummie that he simply thrust an old three penny bit into my hand and disappeared into the guest house, leaving me to decant the cases alone. I left them on the pavement by way of revenge and hoped a miscreant was doing his rounds at that instant.

Taken together, these experiences turned me against casing. The Silver Cross casing truck, which had once transported me as a baby, was shunted behind the shed to continue its rusty demise.

The call of the Airfix kit however was loud and insistent.

My second foray into employment was at the other staple of the Rhyl youngster craving summer employment, the Fun Fair.

The fair was such a great place to visit, I wrongly supposed that to work there would be great fun. I was not old enough or plausible enough to join the big lads on the rides but, a friend of a friend suggested I turn up at his uncle's stall and get stuck in. So, at nine in the morning of the second week of the summer holidays, I duly turned up at Ray's Pots of Gold.

The stall was on the long drag of amusements leading from the Marine Lake to the Ocean Beach Fair on the promenade, opposite the Foryd harbour mouth.

Having crossed from the little train station of the Marine Lake, I made my way up the hill to the stall. On my left, was a concrete built Café in garish cream stucco which was the first port of call for the day trippers as they alighted in the cinder covered coach park behind it and searched for the nearest toilets. On my right, were a couple of lavishly painted wooden sheds, one of which sold fruit and sweets, whilst the other housed the *World Famous* Gypsy Rose Petrulengro, Fortune Teller to the Stars.

The front wall of the shed was decorated with photographs of Gypsy Rose shaking hands and gazing into the camera with a *host of Stars*, none of which I could identify clearly, although Frank Ifield (of *I Remember You* fame) and Laurel and Hardy were mentioned. I wondered if Frank Ifield would remember meeting Gypsy Rose? If he did he could sing his song to her, I thought.

I never saw Gypsy Rose enter or leave the hut, but a succession of females, some old and serious, some young and giggling, certainly did enter there. They all came out with a look of surprise and bewilderment on their face. Whether this was down to some knowledge imparted by the said Gypsy or a result of the cost of a ten minute consultation, I never found out.

Back on the arcade side of the row was a Donkey Derby where people purchased balls which they rolled through holes to propel their wooden horses forward, the winning horse earning their owner a 'Star Prize'. This was usually a cuddly toy of some description which expanded in size and garishness depending on the number of wins. Why people would want to exchange money, which could be used to buy useful things (like Airfix kits) for nothing more than the prospect of winning some garish pink monstrosity that looked vaguely like a bloated hippo was beyond me, but such is the human condition.

The next stall was a rifle range where sixpence would buy you ten rounds with which to knock down five metal targets. As these were air rifles and the targets were no more than ten feet away it would seem to be implausibly simple, unless the rifle barrels had been bent out of true or the targets were fixed so that the pellets merely ricocheted off them. Not that I had any evidence for either of my cynical propositions.

Operating on a similar principle was the darts stall next along, on which you received a prize if you could hit three playing cards to the value of twenty-one or higher for sixpence. I'll say no more than the regularity with which a winning throw hit, then fell out of the ace might lead a suspicious person to believe that there was a piece of metal behind the baize designed to achieve this effect.

Bizarrely, the prize for success here was a goldfish, slowly losing consciousness in a plastic bag. Why anyone would want to invest in a pet on the basis of their darts prowess was beyond me. What you did if you were a holidaymaker winning such a prize did not bear thinking about. Had the bleach used in the disinfected toilets of the guest houses not got them, contact with salt water would have finished off the poor fish once they had completed their dark journey down the sewage system. For a goldfish, perhaps this was preferable to a life in a plastic bag surrounded by noise and garish lights.

At the top of the ascending walk, just before you turned left past the Ghost Train into the fair proper, there was a mobile candy floss and toffee apple stall made out of red and gold fibreglass which went nowhere. Here sweet alchemy was performed as sugary powder was turned into fluorescent pink candy floss before your eyes and once succulent apples were coated in a treacly coat of thick red goo with the consistency of industrial strength lubricants.

This stall, as all the donut, hot dog and burger stalls, was manned by a girl or woman with a poor attitude and pimply complexion. I never saw any of them eat produce from their own stalls so, on both counts, I avoided such food totally.

The last stall before you turned left, nestled underneath the Big Dipper roller coaster, was Uncle Ray's. This was to be my place of work for the summer.

The stall was ingenious in its simplicity. The punters stood in front of the arcade behind a waist high decorated, wooden and metal wall and purchased six table tennis balls for ten pence. They then proceeded to throw these into the 'in' area which was painted green, so that they bounced and hopefully landed into the mouths of a selection of coloured pots.

Your prize was determined by the colour of the pots they landed in. There were umpteen red pots which gave you an extra go and reducing numbers of other coloured pots, each with an increasingly valuable prize.

I'm using the term 'prize' very loosely here as they rose in value from a plastic troll to place on top of a pencil to four plastic toy soldiers which looked like they had had a recent encounter with a flame thrower. There was a comb that doubled as a pen knife and near the top of the list, a Rhyl souvenir flower vase which was as tasteless as it was clumsy.

The gold pot brought forth the top prize. These flitted enticingly in the back of the stall, literally, for the top prize was a budgerigar. About twenty of them in exotic hues were incarcerated in a bird cage that stretched the length of the stall. On the plus side, there was room for the birds to fly in a space twenty feet by two feet wide by four feet tall. On the negative side, the back of the cage was made up of a mirrored wall so the budgies would always believe that they were flying with a twin. Some of the more anti-social birds perched all day looking suspiciously and with menace at their mirror image. I believed they would have felt at home on the Reso.

I'd initially been appalled that my job would involve me in this sordid animal trade and was relieved when I was told that the birds were Ray's prize collection and he would rather lose a hand than part with any of them. Thankfully, even the bird that was kept in the collapsible plastic bird cage, ready for the 'first prize winner of the day!' was only there in quarantine and never left the stall. It was moulting badly and Ray suspected some lurgy which might transmit to the other birds.

My job, Ray grudgingly informed me, was to stand in front of the stall with a selection of prizes, including the mangy budgie, convincing others that they were easily winnable. Every so often, and not more than twice in two hours I was to shout "Gold!" and Ray would, with great ceremony, pick the gold pot nearest to me and magically remove a table tennis ball from it and announce like some Master of Ceremonies, "Ladies and Gentlemen. We have a Lucky Winner. Choose your budgie, son!"

In all the time I worked throwing balls at the pots, no ball every entered a gold pot and it was only Ray's sleight of hand that made one appear on my call. Ray's budgies were indeed safe.

I was both appalled by, and admiring of, Ray with his shifty eyes and dirty sheepskin coat. His greased back hair marked him out as a real spiv, as did the way he secreted a lighted cigarette in his cupped hand and drank strong black coffee with six spoons of sugar in it. Despite this, he had managed, in twenty feet of space, with some paint and mirrors and numerous pots and table tennis balls, to earn a living for himself and provide a Las Vegas style home for his budgie collection.

Ray and the birds worked, like me now, from ten in the morning until ten at night throughout the season that lasted from Whit Bank Holiday to the first week of September when the call of school and the increasingly bitter wind would mark the end of that tourist season.

From then until the following May, Ray would be away somewhere and, whenever you saw him in the town, he would be driving not the clapped out Morris Van he parked in the road opposite the Fair, but a tidy if dated, electric blue Jaguar saloon. He must have been doing something right and he was his own boss, working to his own rules.

Keen fool that I was, I arrived early on the first day and was there before Ray. When he finally arrived, I introduced myself and he just grunted and gestured for me to help him remove and store the wooden front shutters that had protected the stall from ten thirty the last evening. Ray resisted any attempt of mine to engage him in conversation, merely grunting in a way that could equally have meant yes or no. He poured himself the first coffee of the day from his thermos and did not invite me to share any. Mistake number one had been not to bring any food or water. He thrust the plastic bird cage in my hand and told me to look excited and not to let the budgie get a chill. How I was to achieve the latter task when standing no more than a hundred yards from the beach and with a stiff sea breeze blowing through the bird's open cage was beyond me.

He gestured for me to empty my pockets and, seeing that they were empty, he gave me five shillings worth of change to give him back as payment for my goes on the stall.

At first, I thought this was a pretty good deal. Spending my time doing for nothing what others paid to do, and then getting wages at the end of the week seemed pretty satisfactory.

An hour later the grinding monotony of this task, the worries about being held responsible for the budgie's health, for now the budgie appeared to be wheezing, and the insistent hum of the candy floss stall's diesel generator combined to dull my initial enthusiasm.

I'd always been a moving target in the fair before, a mere punter. The klaxon sounds of the rides' starts and finishes, the flashing lights and neon and the incomparable smell of caramelising onions were intoxicating, in a good way. Standing still for hour after hour, with an aching back and all senses assaulted, I was almost delirious—and not in a good way.

In four hours, I'd memorised every click as the Big Dipper above the stall rode up its chain to the start of the ride. From that point, I knew every turn and scream on the ride, when it clattered by and when it went quiet as it breasted another wooden summit. I knew from the Vincent Price full-bodied manic laugh to the first, second, third and final girl's screams on the Ghost Train that whisked along on rails directly behind the budgies' mirror on the back wall of our stall. I knew the precise round of records played. In the past, it had seemed random and exciting, now it was boring and predictable—Classic Hits of the Sixties on K-Tel, no doubt.

The air of mystery and excitement that always attended the fair wore off and I was left to think about the banal and mechanical life of the rides and the people who ran them, day in and day out. I'd made up my mind, in my twenty minute dinner hour, whilst hastily eating the beans on toast for seven and a half pence, the cheapest thing on the menu at the little café in the street parallel the fair, that I didn't want to go back in the afternoon. Despite this, back I went and stayed until the end of the shift at ten in the evening, running home in tiredness and hunger.

I got no sympathy at home either.

"Welcome to the world of work, son. Now you see what I have to put up with on a daily basis."

I realised that I could not simply give up and have my parents think that I thought that work was beneath me, that I was too good for the drudgery of manual labour. So I determined to see it out, at least for a week or so.

I was cruelly mistaken if I thought that Ray was testing my resolve on my first day. He was equally uncommunicative on the second day and took delight in helping himself to the food that my mum had prepared for me and placed in a Tupperware box in a Marks and Spencer *St Michael's* paper bag. My chocolate-covered Penguin biscuit went with his first cup of coffee. My Tuc biscuits and Smith's Cheese and Onion crisps went with his early lunch. I was expecting a crafty smile or wink to acknowledge the hilarious joke of eating my food. I got neither. This was simply someone higher up the pecking order taking advantage of their position.

Ray spoke to me for the first time half way through the third day. He told me to go and get change for a pound note at the slot machine amusements at the top of the fair which acted like a kind of bank for all the stalls. I was tempted to simply do a runner with his quid. I reckoned it would be poor reward for three days work but I'd be free of this serfdom. Then I realised that my mum's Tupperware box was behind the counter in the Marks and Spencer bag. When Ray had turned his nose up with disdain at my Shippams Sardine and Tomato paste sandwiches, I'd insisted on having my mum make them every day, safe in the knowledge that they were the one thing Ray would not pilfer from my lunch box. Had I returned home without the treasured Tupperware box, questions would be asked and my mum would be, "up that fair faster than a dose of salts!"

So the week wore on and I became more desperate to get out of this horrendous situation. A though occurred on the fourth day that I could not extinguish. What if, on the following Monday when I was due to be paid, Ray denied all knowledge of employing me? We certainly had not discussed a contract and no promises had been made. As far as Ray was concerned, he could simply say that I was an annoying and persistent punter who had spent much of the last week just standing at his stall making a nuisance of myself. The lack of a break in the sequence of punters and Ray's reluctance to speak to me at any time meant that we did not have the time, and he did not have the inclination, to discuss pay.

The tipping point came at two o'clock on a wet Sunday afternoon. In a just world, I would now be at home eating roast beef and Yorkshire pudding with crisp but yielding roast potatoes, carrots and cauliflower. All this would be followed by the prospect of either banana custard or the house speciality, buttery rice pudding with a skin of nutmeg and cream. Instead, I was cowering under the canopy of the stall, edging myself towards the middle to avoid the worst of the rain. I'd managed to reduce the rain damage to the length of my jeans below my knees. This was compounded by the torrents of water now racing down the incline off the promenade.

Ray saw me edging towards the middle of the stall and hissed in my ear with bad breathe and attitude, "Shift your arse to the end of the stall and keep the rain off the paying punters!"

I saw out the end of that day's shift and sullenly walked home to find a rather shrivelled Sunday lunch waiting for me under a plate. I determined at that point never to return to the Pots of Gold stall.

I was disappointed that my resolve had cracked. I wondered if I would ever be ready to get a job, if this was what it entailed. I was relieved to be away from the fair and the seediness that had, up to a week before, appeared as glamour.

Unfortunately, I did not have the resolve to confront "Uncle" Ray and demand my pay for the six days from ten in the morning until ten at night that I had worked. By the time it was brought up by my parents, two weeks had passed. Any thought I had that my mum or dad would redeem the situation and my wages by a determined trip to the fair that involved the pace of a 'dose of salts' was wishful thinking on my part. I was told to put it down to experience. Experience, in my humble experience, buttered no parsnips nor bought any Airfix kits.

Chapter Thirteen
EMPLOYMENT

Events at the Fair had left me with a growing worry that the whole world of employment was equally squalid and I worried that my life was to be a long grind of meaningless, manual labour of the sort that I suspected my dad endured.

Luckily, the following summer provided a happier situation.

I'd long been used to being able to lie about my age. Suddenly, being inordinately tall was getting to be an advantage. It was harder for me, at six feet tall, to convince people I was still twelve, than it was for them to believe that I was sixteen. Most of the time, I could stroll into 'A' rated films at the cinema without fearing a challenge from some officious usherette. On one occasion, my mate from the Reso, Mikey, who was the same age, but half the height of me, used me as a way to get into an adult disco at the Queen's on the Rhyl promenade. We were still at primary school, yet in my best blue striped shirt I confidently offered my money as Mikey scampered in on his knees under the eye of the lady at the counter.

We spent the next three hours listening to the booming Rock and Roll Psychedelia of a band called the Purple Chapter. Working my way through the swathes of adolescent girls wearing tan suede boots, brown cord skirts and long hair made me feel like a zebra in a herd of wildebeest. I perched myself in front of the speakers as this was the first time I'd seen or heard live electric guitar music and it was mesmeric. Mikey, all front in a four foot six inch frame, actually tried to chat up some of the girls, and appeared to be pulling! It was amazing what confidence and the gift of the gab could do, I thought. Then again, Mikey had sisters and knew about the mysteries of women and I was not yet privy to such information.

I even managed to buy a coke and a lemonade from the bar without challenge. The bored girl with a complicated hairstyle and too much eye shadow was more interested in chewing her nails than asking me my age. She took my money, gave me my change and returned to biting her black nails.

One thing that was abundantly clear about this evening was that getting access to this illicit world was going to require a regular supply of money and that would require a Saturday job.

You had to be fifteen to work in Currys but the manager took one look at me, after a recommendation from my cousin, and hired me on the spot. He explained that my duties, he was afraid, would not give me much opportunity to be in the shop working with the customers. He obviously saw this as the cutting edge of the operation but I was indifferent to being nice to people all day. The core of my work, he explained from the safety of his brown suit and spectacles, was to support Roger, delivering fridges, televisions and washing machines in the van to expectant homes all over the North Wales coast.

I could hardly believe my luck. I would be spending my days being driven around a twenty five mile radius from the shop in a nearly new, but well scratched, dark blue Bedford CF Van. I would be paid for this. I would in fact be paid £2.50 for a Saturday shift from nine until five thirty. The manager went on to suggest that whatever money was made in tips for the delivery of what was known in the trade as 'sets and white goods' was up to Roger to sort out with me.

In my mind's eye, I saw lazy Saturday morning mooching disappear, together with watching Rhyl play football or slumping on the settee to watch the late afternoon wrestling before the results came on.

The first few days with Roger proved a little awkward. Standing five foot six in his platform boots and shoulder length brown hair, Roger possibly felt a little put out by this six foot streak who had been taken on to help him. As the days passed and he realised that I was no threat to him, and could possibly prove useful on all the jobs he did not enjoy, like rewiring plugs, he warmed to me.

At twenty-three, Roger made it very clear to me, if not to the manager, that the job was what he did to earn the money to live his life. The job was not a consuming passion and it was to be done efficiently and with the minimum of fuss to conserve energy for a hectic night life which involved visits to night clubs from the Club Seventy Degrees at Colwyn Bay to the night spots of Chester and as far afield as the Northern Soul scene of Wigan Casino.

I'd heard of the latter, as some of the older lads at school spoke about their dream of going there. I was familiar with the Club Seventy Degrees, but only from the outside, as we passed it on the way to Colwyn Bay and marvelled at the exotic nightclub perched on the steep cliff which sloped away at an angle of seventy degrees. This was as sophisticated as North Wales got in the seventies and I envied him his hedonistic lifestyle.

Many weekday mornings and every Saturday morning, Rog, as I now called him, would arrive at work with tired eyes and ruffled hair, his best brown pin-stripe flared trousers and multicoloured tank top over a round collared, plum coloured shirt. Frankly, he looked a mess and was quick to don a Currys' overall to hide his inappropriate attire.

"What did you get up to last night?" I'd always enquire, fascinated to find out.

"Don't ask!" would be the habitual reply and I knew that until he had been lubricated by strong coffee and a pasty from the baker's next door, he'd say nothing.

He'd leave me to select the deliveries for the day from the upstairs warehouse and enjoy the treat of having to crane them down on the platform that swung out from the roof to the entry below. How I loved this responsibility.

What was a chore to him was a novelty to me, never having been left responsible for industrial machinery before. I toyed with the idea of holding the yellow control box in my hand whilst travelling down on the crane platform. I knew it would take my weight but I also knew that the wire for the controls was too short to reach the bottom of the alleyway and I'd be unable to control it. I could be left stranded and without a plausible excuse.

When I finally plucked up courage to try it, the cable was prised from my fingers as the crane platform descended and I was indeed left dangling twelve foot off the ground like a medieval miscreant on the city walls, without a plausible excuse.

If the manager came out now I was done for. Luckily Rog was the first to turn up and after some good natured teasing he lowered me to the ground, declaring me to be the silliest bugger he'd come across in a long time.

Meanwhile, Rog was off yet again on one of his urgent errands which he was unable to share with me. I learnt to cover for him with aplomb. He was always, "Here a second ago!". I made to look in the front and the back of the van as if I expected to find him, before venturing that he was probably in the front of the shop, "He mentioned getting some extra fuses," or upstairs in the spartan, paint-flaking restroom with the whistling wall heater as he had a gippy stomach or, even better, was 'feeling bilious' but was 'pressing on' as he didn't want to let the customers down.

This always seemed to placate the manager and I'd then move on to talking about fishing and sailing, about which I knew nothing, but which were passions of the manager, in order to buy Rog a little more time to complete his errands.

Rog arrived as I was delaying the manager in the back alleyway once and, out of eyeshot of the manager, I gestured to him to go round the front of the shop and appear at the back door as if by magic. This he did, muttering something about five amp fuses as he arrived nonchalantly.

Rog had been so impressed by my tactics that once out of town he pulled the van up on a grass verge, took out a wad of bank notes, peeled off a pound and gave it to me.

"You did well today, our kid," he winked. "Keep up the good work."

It felt good to be 'our kid' and I resolved to keep *schtum* or speak out on Rog's behalf whenever the occasion called for it. Rog knew I would as well, which was fair enough by me. I think Rog was one of the few adults who appreciated my presence at this time and I didn't want to let him down.

The wad of money suggested afterwards, but not at the time, that Rog was lining his pockets in some way on his various excursions. I did not ask, and he did not tell me, what the game was and that suited us both just fine. He didn't need someone knowing his business and I didn't want the burden on my conscience of having to keep a secret about something in which he, and now I, may have been implicated.

I was always keen, like a Labrador puppy, to prove my worth to Rog and he had to take me to one side on a regular basis to put me straight. He explained that there was a bible that governed how the job was to be approached and that the commandments for delivering appliances had been brought down the mountain by Moses. At this point, he asked me what Moses' favourite car was. I had no idea, and was about to demonstrate my book learning by suggesting that he'd find that the characters in the Bible predated the internal combustion engine by several millennia, when he replied that Moses drove a Triumph as it said in the Bible that, "Moses came down from the mountain in his Triumph!".

"It's like those ice cream wars in the Bible, isn't it?" he continued.

"What ice cream wars?" said I, adding with some conviction, "They couldn't have made ice cream then."

"That's where you are wrong, isn't it! You don't want to listen to them teachers you know, they'll mess with your mind. There were two ice cream sellers mentioned in the Bible and they were always at each other's throats!"

I was clearly dumbfounded and stared quizzically at him. He savoured the moment before adding, "Yeah, Walls of Jericho and Lyons of Judaea. In the end, it was the cornets of Lyons that brought down the Walls of Jericho."

"Trumpets!" I insisted loudly.

"Pardon you," he replied. "You need to go easy on the beans when we are in the van!"

And so I was initiated into the commandments of the delivery van man:

1. Never refuse a cup of tea and a biscuit.
2. However light an object like a fridge or a cooker was, always make out that it was a real struggle. That was the way to maximise the tip.
3. Anything that required carrying appliances up steps would mean that one or other of us would put on the 'pulled muscle' scam, which always brought out sympathy, possible a back massage from a young housewife and a suitable tip.
4. Always ask how they were going to dispose of their old fridge, cooker or TV and remind them that the Council would do it for a fee. Let them know that your company did it for a quid but, as a favour, you'd do it for fifty pence. Then take it directly to your friendly scrap yard and cop another quid for it.
5. Never refuse a cup of tea and a biscuit.
6. If told to go and sit in the van for fifteen minutes at the end of a delivery, just do it and ask no questions.
7. Always put the newspaper on top of the dashboard.

I asked Rog about the last commandment, trying to work out what the ulterior motive was for putting the Sun newspaper there. Was it some secret code or to obscure the tax disc? He replied that I was to put it there so that he knew where it was when he wanted to read it, or more accurately, read the sport results and as he put it, look at the progress of Bristol City on page 3. I asked him if he supported Bristol City as it seemed an obscure team to support from North Wales. He said he certainly did support them on every conceivable occasion, particularly at weekends and evening matches.

So my summer was spent humping and shunting white goods and televisions into households across North Wales. Amply fed and watered by wives, old and young, and tutored by Rog in the ways of his world.

The work dried up by the time September came and I was left to return to school with a host of stories and memories of being treated as a grown up for the summer season.

What I did not have was the mellow sun tan of those of my friends who had managed to wangle a job from the Council and had spent their summer distributing or collecting deckchairs or wading in the boating pool and rescuing people such as my cousin who could not walk past the pool without falling in.

Chapter Fourteen
SPARKS

I had hoped to resume my delivery responsibilities at the time of the Christmas rush. I looked forward to the banter and the deliveries of Christmas televisions and Zoppas Italian fridges which smelt inside of freshly minted plastic. Mostly, I hoped to show Rog how I had put his teaching to good effect in school. But, without my knowledge, they took on a school leaver in October and that was the end of my time on the delivery van.

The following Easter, dressed in my best shirt and new school blazer and with a regulation short haircut, I attended an interview at Marks and Spencer's on the High Street.

Marks and Spencer's was the premium summer employment in Rhyl. It was the job to aspire to with its good pay and additional benefits such as subsidised lunches. Whereas it seemed that every Rhyl girl had worked there at some time or another, and a fair proportion of their mothers, the opportunities for boys in M and S were strictly limited. There were dozens of girls employed on the shop floor in the summers and on Saturdays, but no more than three boys taken on in the warehouse.

The turnover of boys was small as it tended to be the call of higher education that weeded out the older boys and presented an opportunity for the next vetted candidate on the list.

I was in an unusual position in applying for this job as I already knew the majority of the managers who worked at the store and included them in the myriad aunties and uncles I'd inherited. This was due to the fact that my Auntie Margaret had been staff manageress at the store and had worked there for over forty years. Auntie Margaret was a small dynamo of a woman who, quite clearly, took no messing from anyone. I had not dared apply whilst she had still been in post, but her retirement, a few months previously, had given me an opportunity.

I still resented losing my free Saturdays but the money proved enticing in my financially straitened circumstances.

It felt like being in a successful stage production working behind the scenes of Marks and Spencer. I was now part of a cast which was revered throughout the nation. I'd grown up in a household where the mantra, 'you pay a little more but it is wonderful quality at Marks!' was deeply ingrained and my mum would not think to buy my socks or underpants from anywhere else. She'd delight in telling me of the green 'cavalry twill' slacks that she had seen on offer and suggest I should hotfoot it to the store before they were all sold out. I was not about to foot it anywhere, hot or cold, for a pair of green trousers recommended by my mum. I knew an evangelical Christian who might be tempted though.

I'd shop at the Army and Navy Stores and the connected Mr. Pauls, with their Ben Sherman shirts, round-collared shirts with plum and deep green colours and parallel light blue jeans with coconut trees embroidered on the backside, thank you very much. Unlike me, my mum knew nothing about fashion.

Although Marks and Spencer's fashion items were slightly suspect, representing what your parents would want you to wear, their food was always impeccable. When she had been working, Auntie Margaret would often drop in on us on a Friday evening and deliver a range of goodies which were disposed of to staff at cut price rates if they were even idling towards their sell by date.

For my dad, there would be his favourite Battenburg cake with its distinctive yellow marzipan outer layer and harlequin ends of yellow and pink. For my mum, there would be chocolate éclairs of the lightest choux pastry held, dark chocolate side up, by prongs in the white plastic tray. For my brother and I, beef paste for our teatime sandwiches and butter and cream rich double Devon toffees in blue wrappers which stuck to the roof of your mouth and oozed butter like nectar.

Now I was part of this emporium. I felt very proud to be part of it as well. I was even happier on the first morning when I was introduced to the full-time team of Ronald, Gareth and Peter to find that the other Saturday boy, Howie, would be joining us later. Sure enough, Howie arrived later with a beaming smile and a look of mischief about him and I warmed to my new work.

To be fair, at £6 for a Saturday shift, the job was very rewarding. Coupled to this was the two and a half pence subsidised lunch. Braised beef and mash, fish in a sauce other than parsley, beef stew and dumplings and a steamed pudding were all available for this token payment. However, the work was often monotonous and tasks like washing the large plastic trays with scourer until they gleamed while bent over a steaming sink at the end of the shift were not to be looked forward to with keen anticipation.

Like all successful operations on this scale, Marks and Spencer's was a well oiled machine with rules, more rules and a strict hierarchy which defined who did what, when and how. I was firmly at the bottom of this hierarchy, at the beck and call of all, even the Saturday girls who summoned me on the telephone on a regular basis to remove sick or dog poo from the shop floor. There was also a procedure for this to ensure, as the Staff Manageress informed me in her precise and pedantic tones, that the, "offending discharge is removed discreetly whilst maintaining the highest standards of customer health and safety by quarantining the area and ensuring that a moist free environment was left on completion of the extraction of the offensive material".

She spoke like a manual and Gareth reassured me she was like this with everyone, not just me. This was the first time I heard the words 'health' and 'safety' in the same sentence and, in that respect, she was before her time.

"Imagine going out with her—remove outer packaging and insert grommet A into recess B!" Gareth had said.

I'd laughed out loud with him, but didn't really have much idea what he was talking about.

For the fast track graduate who now held the post of Staff Manageress, the Rhyl post was an inconvenient stopping off place on her meteoric rise to being manager of her own store and eventually a big cheese in H.Q.

She had hoped for a placement in the flagship Marble Arch store or at the headquarters of the Marks and Spencer Empire and had been seriously miffed to find herself shunted from all she knew and loved in London to the provincial backwater in a foreign land that was Rhyl.

"Even Llandudno would have been better!" she had been heard to say.

Consequently, she had determined to shake things up a bit in this backwater. She had no intention of staying a minute beyond her allotted placement. Her social life was on hold and her friends were all in the metropolis and connected by 'phone so she had no need to worry about offending the despicable local staff. She clearly intended to be a 'force to be reckoned with' and would pick up every shortcoming of the staff and chastise them in front of customers which caused considerable resentment and demoralisation. And so the legend of the Dragon Lady was created.

On one day, she criticised me for not responding quickly enough to her summons and for pushing the trolleys too fast. I was exasperated with her and I only saw her one day in seven. For those on full-time work, she was a constant drain on their enthusiasm. The worst thing I saw her do was lie that she had instructed an older and much valued member of staff to do certain duties and then claim that the staff member was incompetent.

I could reduce my exposure to her by volunteering for the early morning shift, which involved the unloading of the delivery lorries, a free breakfast, a late lunch and a four thirty departure from the store. This meant that I would avoid both extended contact with her and the irritation of the underpants and sock ditherers who would slow down the closing of the shop at six p.m. with their incessant inspection of each of the extensive range of socks or underpants in terms of colour, size and style before deciding to, "Leave them and come back in on Monday to have a better look."

A prompt four thirty finish meant I'd miss Kent Walton presenting the wrestling to 'grappling fans across the nation' from provincial town halls like Bolton or Hanley, but, if I ran, I could be home in time to hear the Final Scores being read out, hot from the teleprinter.

Eventually the Dragon Lady was recalled early from her placement at the Rhyl store. She claimed loudly in the staff room that she was urgently needed at Head Office, but the suspicion was that the Store Manager had pleaded to have her removed as she was having such a detrimental effect on both staff and customers at the store. Unfortunately, this was not before I had to suffer several run-ins with her.

The pattern of the Saturday shift started with a frenetic hullabaloo to unload the lorries that backed up to the warehouse at seven thirty. I turned this into a race to exceed my personal best time and trolleys full of fresh vegetables, salads and frozen and chilled foodstuffs would be trundled off the unloading ramp and past Ronald who would check them off the printed list with military precision using the knife sharpened pencil kept in a clip in his breast pocket.

Only when satisfied that the order tallied with what had been unloaded would he reach officiously for his biro and sign the form with a flourish which ended with a full stop. The driver, anxious to get off to his next drop in the Llandudno store, would have to wait impatiently for Ronald to sign off and would be smiling through gritted teeth and slyly looking at his wristwatch, wondering how he was going to make up the time lost in this daily ritual.

The food supervisor would intercept me now and direct certain of the trolleys straight into the store to restock shelves (ensuring that the newest stock went to the back of the chilled cabinets and the older stock was moved forward in the time honoured tradition. Her uniform would be immaculate, as would be her make-up. As a concession to the cold of the loading bay and refrigerated areas, she'd be wearing a short jacket with no arms and warm gloves. The higher ups in the management hierarchy would refer to these jackets as Gilets, but, not seeing the relationship between them and the manufacturers of razor blades, they were always jackets without sleeves to me.

As with everything about Marks and Spencer, the trolleys ran with a silky precision and were clearly over-engineered for the task. They had obviously, 'paid a little more for them, but they were of undoubted quality'.

Following the unloading of the produce lorries, I would be released for a free breakfast by nine o'clock. A full breakfast with golden fried bread, bacon, eggs, tomato and mushroom would be served up with a large mug of tea. The mug always looked like it had been plucked that morning from the stock on the shop floor, so clean and pristine was it. It was good to be two hours into my shift and unavailable for the rumpus that was the opening of the store doors.

The rest of the morning was spent responding to the calls of the food and clothes sections for additional stock.

The store produced copious amounts of cardboard each day from the boxes in which stock was delivered. A white painted, pre-fabricated garage in the back yard of the store contained a baling machine which dealt with all this waste by compacting it in a giant press. Once under full pressure, two metal bands were placed round the bale and secured using a pair of pliers. The pressure was then released and the metal bands took up the strain as the cardboard expanded. The bale would then be manhandled out of the front of the machine and stacked outside ready for collection.

This was a big boy's machine and I would happily spend hours in the baling shed methodically turning cardboard boxes into uniform bales and thinking that this was work as my dad would know it. The monotony of this task was relieved by a hidden bonus. Some of the boxes that had contained sweets had the remains of any burst bags in them and that might reveal a bonanza of midget gems, allsorts, wine gums or dolly mixtures.

We had been solemnly warned not to eat any produce whilst on duty, particularly if it came from broken packaging, but I was hardly going to condemn free sweets to the baling machines and I was occasionally able to pig out and thank the Lord for faulty packaging or someone's carelessness.

This feasting came to a rapid end when, haven eaten a handful of sweets, I came across the tell tale signs of sawdust in the bottom of a box. Sawdust in the store meant only one thing, a nasty spillage on the sales floor and either form of nasty spillage mixed with my bonus jelly beans did not bode well…

The general pace and the fact that they probably knew there would be mischief if we were not kept apart, meant that I usually saw little of Howie in the course of the day. Whenever our paths did cross, we would look to pull some stunt on each other. Habitually, he would ensure that I would be called to clear up some mess on the shop floor and I was carefully thinking through how to get him back when he hit me with his knock-out blow.

Across the yard from the baling shed was the old concrete and brick air raid shelter which had been refurbished as the vegetable store. Its substantial white painted walls ensured that whatever the temperature outside, inside was significantly cooler. A series of open vents at the top and bottom of the building maintained an almost refrigerated temperature in winter and a refreshingly cool one in the summer.

On a hot Saturday afternoon, I had returned to the shelter for the umpteenth load of spring onions and lettuces when I, and my loaded trolley, were met at the door by Howie with the water hose that had been used for the fire fighting practice that morning. Looking as unreadable as Lee Van Cleef in a spaghetti western, he dared me to push past him and across the expanse of open yard. To challenge me further, he opened the valve of the fire hose a little and made a neat circle of water splash that outlined the heavy green doorway in which I was standing and the concrete floor inches in front of me.

My first thought was that he was bluffing and I moved forward smiling. In a smooth action, Howie opened the valve fully and a jet of water crossed the space between us effortlessly. It hit the lower tray of the trolley, dislodging lettuces which scuttled across the concrete like green hedgehogs in raincoats. The water jet then ricocheted onto my shins with the impact of a cricket ball.

I looked at Howie hoping for some sign that the joke was over but his face was full of fun and steely resolution which, granted, is a difficult look to pull off. I thought to appeal to his better nature. "Don't mess about Howie, the Dragon Lady sent me to get these salad vegetables and I'll be in trouble if they are not on display, like yesterday!"

I thought mention of our common enemy, the Dragon Lady Store Manageress, would put an end to the ordeal. It was a wasted effort. Howie's better nature had clearly 'phoned in that morning, claimed to be sick and had gone off on a junket somewhere. Drenched with the power of the hose, he was now laughing in the style of a maniac in a horror film.

He proceeded to let off three short bursts of water which had me retreating into the storehouse. He had me well cornered and I made to move the trolley out of the way and secure the door, but I had no hope of outpacing Howie and his roaring hose.

Realising my position was hopeless. I retreated inside hoping to buy some time in which a senior manager might appear to chastise the rampant Howie. In his current mood, I though he might not be beyond soaking a senior manager. I reasoned, somewhat forlornly, that the prospect of damaging stock would bring him to his senses so I looked to shelter in the area with the most valuable consumables. The punnets of strawberries seemed the best bet so I barricaded myself between the strawberries and the raspberries with a last tray of blackberries as a further impediment. It was hardly the defences of Stalingrad, but it would have to do.

My predicament reminded me of a film I'd seen the previous Sunday in which some Czech patriots had audaciously assassinated Reinhardt Heydrich and had holed up in the crypt of a church. The Germans had proceeded to flood the crypt until the Czechs were forced to surrender. A vision of Howie feeding the hose through one of the vents and the water level climbing until I, the soft fruit and the salad vegetables, were occupying a diminishing air space just below the ceiling played on my internal cinema for a few seconds until I realised this was an unlikely scenario as the door was still open.

Blocking the door space like a malevolent stormtrooper was a smiling Howie. It was clear that having tasted the power that the hose had conferred on him, he was not going to relent.

He offered me his terms.

I could get soaked inside and also have to explain the damage to the fruit and vegetables or he would give me a three second start from the door to leg it across the concrete yard and into the store.

I chose the latter option as I could offer no plausible explanation to the Dragon Lady for water-damaged stock in the middle of a heat wave. I squeezed past Howie at the door and he started his count.

I quickly calculated that, whilst I could not get out of range of the hose in three seconds, with a lightning sprint I could be a fair way across the yard to the sanctuary of the door into the store. I would then have the problem of why I had arrived soaking in view of the public on the main shop floor—a short, sharp, summer shower I reasoned against the logic of the drought.

Howie began his count, "One!"

I inhaled hard to power my muscles across the yard and was immediately drenched in the powerful spray. Howie was clearly not playing by the rules. To be fair to him, in his position, I would not have been able to resist dousing my victim either. He now had me trapped against a wall and he gave me a long ten seconds of a powerful soaking.

There was no point in complaining and I soon gave up trying to cover my vitals. The nylon overall I was wearing ensured that my clothes underneath retained the water and it spread evenly across my skin and pooled in my neatly polished shoes. In different circumstances it would have been refreshing, but not at this time.

I was only saved by Beryl, one of the Food Section staff, coming out to let me know that the Dragon Lady was on the warpath, demanding melons and bananas like some vengeful tropical island goddess threatening all with her terrible wrath. Beryl removed her ornate glasses, surveyed the scene and offered the comment, "You silly buggers!" and turned on her heel, laughing.

I thought this was unfair as Howie was having the fun and I was the innocent victim in the matter. There should not be equal blame. No doubt the affair would now ripple across the shop floor and I would be held up to ridicule.

Howie finally relented and relished his final comment, "I wouldn't like to be you if the Dragon Lady catches you in this state." He then disappeared to secure the hose in its locked cupboard so that I would have no prospect of exacting a similar revenge.

I was now torn between delivering the fruit and drying off. I did neither particularly well and explained away my dripping presence by a combination of a hard afternoon's work in the baling shed and a short and intense rain shower. It wasn't plausible, but luckily the Dragon Lady had other fish to fry and gave me no more than her usual contemptuous look. That just left Howie to sort out.

Revenge, it is said, is best served cold. As no opportunities presented themselves for a number of weeks, my revenge was refrigerated when delivered.

As the summer drew on, I brooded on how to get Howie back. The return of some overripe tomatoes finally gave me some ammunition.

I secreted them away upstairs near the sink where I would spend a backbreaking two hours trying to clean the food trays at the end of my shift. At some time, Howie would have to cross the yard below and I would be able to pelt him from the perch of the steel staircase. With any luck or justice, he would not see what was about to hit him.

The Gods did shine on me that afternoon as Howie emerged from the store carrying a load of cardboard stacked so high that he could hardly walk or see to left or right. From thirty feet above him I took aim. Never had I wanted to make my throw more accurate. Luckily Howie was ambling with difficulty to the baling shed and I had time to line up and release a first shot.

To my relief, it made contact on his collar and there was a red explosion of overripe tomato across his shirt, overall and face.

Howie was torn between dropping his load and trying to identify what had hit him and he froze for a couple of seconds. I could almost hear his brain computing the size and impact of the tomato with possible scenarios; a seagull with diarrhoea, something nasty expelled at height from an aircraft, an egg, a sniper's bullet, each one unlikelier than the last.

I fluffed my second shot as in my excitement. I grabbed the tomato too hard and it exploded like an anti-personnel device in my hand. My third shot was the largest tomato of all. It impacted on the back of Howie's neck sending him forward a couple of paces. It struck as he was feeling his shoulder and taking in the red gooey liquid that appeared to be oozing from a deep wound—seemingly the sniper theory was not so far fetched.

Dropping the cardboard, he spun round in time to see rounds four and five arrive on and around his person.

He went to speak and then thought better of it, turning instead and running into the baling shed. I made to run back into the building from my bombing position, letting him think I was scared of his retaliation. I skulked behind the door and waited for him to emerge from the security of the shed. I was about to give up my vigil when he emerged from the shed still trying to clear the mess from his overall. He had taken it off and was dabbing the recalcitrant tomato juice from patches on his shoulders. He was so engrossed that I was able to get my last tomato off unnoticed. Having recovered sufficiently from my laughing fit, I caught him in the middle of his white shirt with an impact that Dirty Harry would have been proud.

What had been a glorious summer rolled into Autumn and, in an effort to spend more time with a significant person who had come into my life, I reluctantly gave up my job in Marks. I cited my desire to spend more time on my GCE examination studies as my excuse, one which I knew would sound plausible and positive. In truth, my new girlfriend and I spent as much of the gained time as possible mooching up and down the beach frozen stiff, or sitting very quietly in each other's houses wishing to be older and somewhere else together. At the time, I thought this was a fair trade off for the loss of a free breakfast and six pounds a week.

Chapter Fifteen
WALLOW

June 15th, 1975 was the day my life changed for the better.

It started hopelessly enough, a bright summer's day full of verdant promise and tennis, ruined by being scheduled as a day for summer examinations. This took us out of our regular routine and always made us crotchety. In a piece of logistical organisation of which Albert Speer would have been proud, Mr Williams the Timetable, had relocated me and half a dozen of my classmates to room C2.

Room C2 was the most inhospitable room in the whole school. It formed part of the school frontage of red brick and, to accommodate the fine architectural features of the public face of the Old Grammar School, the usual squareness of the room was compromised with metal supporting bars and unusually shaped brickwork. To prevent distraction, the windows of the room were set six feet up the walls and enabled only the movement of the clouds to be observed in between academic toil. The lights, of which there were few, had cream plastic shades which I always associated with hospitals.

To reach C2 meant ascending a meandering and uneven wooden staircase on which the plastic linoleum had been worn away. The narrowness of the corridor and the fact that the inhospitality of C2 meant that pupils were inclined to cascade out of the room at the end of lessons made the journey upwards hazardous. A flurry of knees, elbows and satchels descended like a river in torrent.

Not today though. The examinations had cowed the natural spirit in us and we moved mopishly to our next timetabled room and examination, anxious to be neither early nor late. To be the former would be seen to be too keen and also to be the mug that got the job of giving out the examination papers and other assorted paraphernalia for that particular examination. The worst examinations were Maths and Physics when, to the usual detritus of rulers, rubbers, pencils and cheap biros would be added protractors, compasses, log books and those little green pieces of string with metal clasps at the end that I later discovered were called treasury tags.

All these accoutrements were counted out and counted back in to the stationery boxes to be delivered back to the examination cupboard at the end of the day. Had they been distributing live ammunition, the accounting process could not have been more stringent. I suppose in the case of the rulers and compasses it really was live ammunition for those of us with a short attention span and no affinity for Maths or Physical Science.

Whichever examination it was, you could take as a given that the distribution of this academic tat would be accompanied by an impatient homily from the teacher which would include the phrases, "In my day", "How will you cope in the real world?", "Personal responsibility" and "Forgot your pen indeed!", but not necessarily in that order. The homily would be rounded off with a rebuke to an individual child which, depending on the teacher present, would range from, "Thoughtless, thoughtless child" from Ma Bullen, the ancient R.E. teacher to, "But for the fact you move laddy, I'd have assumed you were low quality fertiliser!" from the belligerent Rural Studies teacher.

I took a deep breath and sighed loudly on entering the room as it was always airless and heavily laden with the sweat of previous generations of scholars. The battleship grey upper walls and lower dark wooden panels seemed to sap both spirits and sound. It was so difficult to move furniture up the staircase that the room still held the ancient individual wooden desks with inkwells and tip up seats.

It had been in one of these traditional desks that the previous October, Capper the Nutter had planted a firework rocket. He'd lit it and patiently put up his hand. Williams the Strap had impatiently asked him why he had his hand up. Capper had stated that his desk was on fire. Williams, sensing Capper's habitual baiting, had risen from his desk in a rage and advanced on Capper, intent on doing him grievous harm when a fountain of fire and sparks had erupted out of the inkwell.

The volcano plumed upwards at an angle, making contact with a wall display about Mother Theresa who, after a brief hiatus, reached a critical temperature and was slowly consumed by the demonic flames. The whole class did not move a muscle such was the bizarre nature of the spectacle.

By now, the firework has subsided and a small yellow flame emanated from the inkwell fuelled by the paper Capper had secreted in the desk. The wood around the inkwell had now received sufficient encouragement to ignite. Williams the Strap, oblivious to the fact that the wall and the desk were now on fire, had taken to beating Capper about the head with a series of syncopated slaps which were accompanied by a torrent of rhythmic invective. The words 'moron', 'imbecile', 'idiot' and one that I'd only ever heard used by Lord Snooty in the Beano, 'dunderhead' were used. It appeared that Capper was being assaulted by a raging thesaurus. Perhaps Williams would turn on us in a minute and ask, "Am I using homonyms or synonyms?" I knew Theresa would say, "Cinnamons", because she couldn't say synonyms and we would try on every occasion to get her to attempt to say it. The truth of the matter was that Williams was using neither, he had graduated to clenched fists now and the tell tale trail of spittle from the left hand corner of his mouth indicated a teacher fully out of control.

This was of little comfort to those of us who realised that the one exit from the burning room was past Williams, Capper having chosen the desk nearest the door for his fiery escapade.

Girls were becoming hysterical now and some were encouraging others to scream. I helped shepherd them out of the room, past the flailing arms of Williams, in what I assumed was a noble and titanic gesture. Other lads made their way down the stairs to the landing where a fire hose reel was located.

The prospect of using the fire hose in anger far outweighed any fear of the fire. Luckily, wiser counsel prevailed and Glyn, sensible, organised Glyn, had located a cone-shaped fire extinguisher from behind the desk, read the instructions twice, struck the knob on the floor and pointed the sharp end of the cone at the fire and had it extinguished in no more than three seconds, soaking Williams and Capper in the process. Leaping up the stairs, Mally and James entered the room with pious enthusiasm with the snaking hose, only to find the crisis over. They stood there with a limp drip emanating from the hose, the opportunity to nobly serve the school and soak Williams in the process having dried up, so to speak.

But that had been last year. The desks would only perform their traditional function this afternoon, more was the pity.

Whilst others received the varied instructions about their particular examination papers, I glanced around the room at the assembled pupils. Generally, we bitterly resented being put together with pupils from the year below us but relished being assembled with those from the year above. Such is the rigid hierarchy of a school.

We had been assembled with pupils from the year below and I sighed in disappointment. There would be few distractions from the treasury tags and the endless sheets of writing paper this afternoon.

As I turned to face the front of the class, my eye fell on a girl sitting parallel to me and five desks away. I felt sure that I could not have seen her before in my life as the effect she had on my physiology in the next seconds was like being touched by the electric hand of God. I felt unable to look away from her upturned face, taking in every word of the teacher's instructions with wide innocent eyes and a perfect, lightly tanned complexion. I had the horrible feeling that my tongue was hanging limply from my mouth and I was dribbling like an imbecile. My main worry at this moment was that she would turn, conscious of someone staring at her and see me, drooling like some cartoon dog, in her general direction.

I'd experienced mild attraction, heavy attraction and even lust in the near past but this was of a different order all together.

Algebra was a foreign country to me at the best of times and for the next ninety minutes the 4xs and 7ys simply mocked me. God knows I'd asked time and time again what the Xs and Ys were. Had they been egg cartons or the dimensions of a lawn, I'd have been in with a chance. I'd have seen the problem and had a stab at it. I'd never owned an x or a y for that matter, never felt the need to multiply or subtract them and was hugely indifferent to their fate.

This was my normal relationship with algebra, but this afternoon the primal need to glance at the enchanting girl every ten seconds meant that my efforts at solving the equations were even more random. My latest answer had resolved that x equalled the improbable sum of 14,728,361.757 and I moved to the next equation without any great confidence. I was on the edge of simply randomly guessing or putting the same answer to every question. The latter strategy was not so fanciful as it seemed. It came about because the maths teacher had insisted that a watch that is broken is twice as accurate as one that is five minutes slow because at least it was correct at two points in every twenty-four hours.

With an hour gone, I gave up the pretence of completing the exam paper and slumped with my head supported by my arms on the desk so that I could stare at the serene beauty undetected. From nowhere an old, and by now deeply unfashionable, Beatles song slipped onto my mind's jukebox and the words perfectly complemented the occasion. The song preceded the psychedelic days, the acrimonious personality clashes and even the foray into animation. In my head, four fresh-faced lads from Liverpool, well suited and booted and earnest were singing about a face and a place and a girl who was just for me.

I was clearly out of my depth here and the beautiful girl sitting five desks away from me was looking immaculate and writing with purpose on her examination paper.

Falling, the song was repeating, and falling I definitely was, in much the way that you sometimes have the sensation of uncontrolled falling when sitting quietly in a chair.

I didn't even know where this song lyric had come from. It was not a favourite track of mine. Yet it seemed to capture the spirit of the moment. The guitars lilted like waves lapping a shore and the drums shimmied like a breeze in the background. My brain had turned to sentimental mush.

It felt that for the first moment of my life, I knew what all the fuss was about. Love. Falling, I most assuredly was. Until now, it had just been a word with a thousand connotations but now every muscle in my body seemed charged with energy and all I wanted to do was to drink in the image of her.

I was suddenly conscious that with ten minutes to go, the chance scratching of the examiner's pen that had placed us together in this room would tear us asunder, perhaps never to meet again. Apart from loving her ardently, I knew nothing of this girl, not even her name, and a panic swept over me. I needed a plan to get me from this point to the point where we were married and she had borne my children and we lived life happily ever after. Unhelpfully, the Beatles chipped in with, *When I'm Sixty Four* on the old mind's-eye jukebox.

I now had less than ten minutes to affect an introduction to the one person whom, I was now convinced, would play the seminal role in my life. To call the plan I came up with 'a plan' was perhaps over-egging it.

It was a crass ploy which bypassed subtlety and accelerated past intelligence without a second glance.

Granted, I was not acting rationally at this point. I assumed that everyone could view a transparent me and could see the emotional maelstrom I had entered. I was caught knowing that my first introduction to the mystery girl needed to allow her to reciprocate my feelings, if only in a small way. I needed to make a good or memorable impression.

Yet my good impression-making tools had deserted me and my mind could not find the key to access them, what with the Beatles track playing incessantly and my eyes absorbing every detail of her silky skin, dark brown eyes and jet black hair. Throwing caution, common sense and dignity to the winds I executed The Plan.

At the end of the examination, I took the unprecedented course of volunteering to collect in the completed papers. This action was greeted mainly with disbelief from my peers who suspected some false motive. I casually suggested that I wanted them collected efficiently so that we could get out of the room in a timely fashion and on to the park to play football. This seemed to placate them. For once, I didn't give the proverbial monkeys what they thought—which was symptomatic of my current euphoric state.

I conspired to collect them in a very methodical and fast fashion and then ended up collating them slowly on the desk of the angelic vision. This accomplished two objectives. Firstly, I got to see her name written on her paper, *Victoria Roberts*. Secondly, with what I thought was impish audacity, it gave me the opportunity to actually speak to her in a contrived, but legitimate way. I declared as casually as I could manage, "That was easy if you'd done the revision, Victoria."

I thought this gambit would give me two openings. Firstly, I could give her the impression from those words that I was clever and well prepared, which might appeal to her in a life partner. Did I say life partner? What was I thinking? It was as if my brain and my common sense had parted company, and I was relishing the sensation. I'd never felt the way I felt in this moment. It was the essence of joy. I could taste Christmas, see fireworks and smell steam engines in a single sensation. It felt warm, glowing and energising. Past and future counted for nothing in this second.

Alternatively, I could be implying that I was one of those devil may care individuals who some girls could not resist and who would not take the easy path by revising. Either way would yield a result, I thought.

It has always been my experience that when you use people's name when they are not expecting it, they are always disarmed.

I was now hoping she'd say, "How do you know my name?", and ignore the obvious conclusion that I had simply read it off the top of her exam paper.

To which I had a number of replies ready and loaded. There was the enigmatic, "You'd be surprised what I know about you!" which would always open up a conversation, establishing a teasing nature to the relationship. This was particularly useful as it suggested further conversations where the beautiful Victoria would quiz me about what, precisely, I knew about her.

There was the riskier, "I make a mental note of the names of all the best-looking girls in the school." Useful for establishing the terms of engagement, but a little too glib and shallow to do justice to the golden electricity now coursing through my veins. This ploy smelt heavily of cheese. Not the solid, crumbly Cheshire cheese we had at home but foreign, runny, smelly stuff with blue veins like an old auntie's legs.

In all honesty, I could have settled for, "I love you and want to spend the rest of my life with you." I was feeling so earnest at this moment that had I said the words I knew I could not retract them as a joke. The effect they would have on her might be a little disturbing for a first conversation though.

I hoped she was thinking words beginning with G about me. 'Gorgeous' would be a solid start, but on first acquaintanceship I would settle for 'Good-looking'. In my heart of hearts, I had the misgiving that she was probably thinking of words with P. 'Psycho', 'Pervert' and 'Prat' came to mind too quickly for comfort. I'd never had to think and act so quickly to make and sustain an impression and I seemed to doubt instantly the quality and sincerity of any of my thoughts and actions. It felt like a three dimensional sensual examination in which I had done no revision.

As luck would have it, she said nothing but looked at me with coy, smiling eyes. I was lost and stood there gazing back at her for what seemed an uncomfortable lifetime before realising that I could shuffle the examination papers and use that as my cue to disengage. The problem was that there seemed to be an interminable time and distance between the thought and the action.

In my mind's eye I could see my nervous system like a crash diving U boat, all alarms, red lights, bells, shouted orders and urgency, but everything happening in slow motion. Amidst random scenes from my past life, I thought of the episode of *Star Trek* I'd seen the night before, with Scotty, the Engineering Officer declaring, as he did on an episode by episode basis, "It's no good Captain, the engines won't take any more!"

My conscious and unconscious minds collided and I heard me mouth the words, "The engines won't take any more!"

I'd *actually* said that aloud. Victoria looked at me and screwed up her nose rather quizzically, which was even more appealing, and smiled again. I tried to muster a smile of my own to countermand the order from my central nervous system to flush my face with blood by opening the embarrassment cocks. My attempted smile was not altogether successful but I turned on my heel and scuttled off to place the assembled exam papers on the teacher's desk.

Internally, I could hear a continuing conversation. A voice that sounded like Woody Allen was saying, in what I assumed was a New York, Jewish accent, "I cannot believe you just said that, I'd fed you a brilliant opening line and had readied a reply that would have sorted you out with the most beautiful girl you have ever seen and you say, 'The engines won't take any more!' Words with P? Forget words with P, she's moved on, she's thinking a word with M now—Moron! That's it! I resign as your inner voice. I'm too embarrassed to be associated with you—even in your unconscious mind—we're finished, I'm out of here!"

And Woody Allen, whom I'd seen in a film for the first time a few weeks before, was gone. I was waiting to hear the voice of my mother, that sounded like my conscience, chip in but she was strangely silent at this critical moment.

In this instant, I realised I was alone.

This, in all probability, was the moment in which I grew up, stopped hearing my mum's voice as my conscience and had to sort things out by myself. It was terrifying. It was also recklessly exciting.

I made a mental note to watch less television, particularly *Star Trek* and Woody Allen films shown late at night when I was particularly susceptible.

In the next weeks, Victoria was never far from my thoughts. I replayed the image of her bathed in light in the musty examination room over and over again and tried desperately to engineer encounters when our paths would cross in school. On these occasions, I had a repertoire of witty sentences ready but as soon as I saw her, I was always struck dumb by her beauty and movement. I was even happy if she did not notice me and I could just add to the images of her in my mind's eye. Crossing the courtyard, queuing for lunch, sitting with her friends in a tight circle on the field, she seemed to do everything perfectly and with effortless grace.

By contrast, I felt so ungainly near her. I'd try football skills that simply didn't come off, walk into things, like teachers, whilst craning my neck to follow her down a crowded corridor.

This was not how it was meant to be. After all I was in the year above her in school. She should be fawning over me and I should be playing it cool.

The normal, timeless protocol for resolving such affairs was that I'd get my friend to talk to her friend, to gather some information and then make her an offer she could not refuse—a trip to the swimming baths, a walk on the promenade, a bag of chips on the High Street. This approach had several major flaws.

First, the use of a friend as a go-between usually meant that I could deny all knowledge of the actions of my friend. But failure was not an option I wanted to consider here—the prospect was too painful.

Second, the friend in question would be none other than Brian, and I'd seriously hacked him off with the liberties I'd taken the previous month when performing a similar service for him with the girl with plaits in the year below. It was only now that I realised that Brian was probably feeling about the plait girl the way I was now feeling about Victoria. It was too late to recant and apologise to Brian for the distasteful things I'd said to the girl and, had I been Brian, I would have relished the opportunity for revenge that I would have served up on a plate for him.

I decided, against all previous experience, that I'd have to ask her out myself and not, under any circumstances, tell any of my pals how I felt about her.

In the event, lack of confidence and fear of failure meant that I mounted a long campaign to bring me into her orbit. I would habitually be at the school gates when she left for home and graduated from saying, "hello", in an off-hand and overly casual manner to having a snatched conversation.

I'd engineer reasons to walk into town with her on some pretext of an urgent purchase from the shops and managed to graduate to walking her all the way home which was several miles past the journey to my own house. The pretext of going to the shops was abandoned and insofar as I was now walking many miles to and from her house to escort her to school, we were an item.

It would be agony walking with her and trying to think of things to say. I'd constantly revolve thoughts to say in my head, and then reject them, just as I was about to say them. How boring I must have seemed.

It turned out that our families all knew each other and that provided some light relief and conversation. We'd talk banalities, television, music, friends, endlessly. Even her voice had a sweetly musical quality. Several months were spent in this way. The desire to make physical contact with Victoria grew daily. Unfortunately, my shyness had to date outstripped this passion.

Eventually, after two months one week and three days, I reached out and held her hand. To have felt her delicate, cool, exquisite hand in mine that week had, in all honesty felt like the highlight of my life to date. I'd been planning the move for over a month. Given that I had first seen Victoria in the exam room over four months now, I suppose you could hardly call me a fast worker.

I'd worried that she would shrug off my advances and was heartily relieved when I'd reached out and grasped her hand at the traffic lights at the bottom of the Vale Road bridge.

If she recoiled in horror, I'd already prepared a fallback position which was that I'd worried that an errant cyclist might jump the lights and run into her and I'd needed to be prepared to avoid the accident.

To my relief, she looked up at me and smiled and flicked her hair. She delicately squeezed my hand and said nothing, with what appeared to be enviable self-assurance. I could not understand how she could seem so quietly confident whilst I, despite being older than her, was always so awkward.

By now, I knew every paving stone along the route and as autumn turned to winter, we braved the wind the rain and the blown sand sleeting in off the promenade and into the recessed doorway of the abandoned shop where we would stop and talk and cuddle for hours before Victoria ran across the road and into her house for her tea and emergency treatment for hypothermia.

I would always stand and watch her as she ran across the road and turned to wave at the entrance to her house. She'd shoo me away so that I could get home and in the warm and dry. I'd shoo her back and we'd both stand gormlessly shooing until her mother called her in for a tea that was getting cold on the table.

Hopefully no-one saw us there gesturing like mime artists. In truth, it was highly unlikely that anyone other than a fool would have ventured out in the stiletto wind and torrential rain. Our intimate partings would be known only to the two of us.

The coming of spring brought new passion. As we said goodbye, having held hands on the way home for the past week, I reached out and kissed her.

And suddenly it wasn't funny anymore. It was deeply serious.

I lived to be in her presence and grew bored and irritable with the time spent away from her, be it with friends or playing football or rugby. I would happily spend hours sitting in our front room with Victoria, gazing at each other. I hoped she felt the same as it must have been horribly boring and repetitive if she didn't.

The novelty of her beauty didn't wear off.

I found myself doing bizarre things to lessen the time spent apart from her. For the first time, I had cause to use the telephone. As my parents were still debating whether to have one installed, I would nip to the telephone box at the end of the road to 'phone and irritate her parents by asking to speak to her.

Sometimes, it was enough to know that the electric umbilical cord was linking us through time and space and I happily disposed of a pile of ten pence pieces simply to hear her breathing.

Using my Christmas present Binatone cassette recorder, I'd try and record the Radio One top forty on a Sunday evening, hoping to capture a tune which I felt encapsulated my feelings for the Divine Victoria. The process of recording from radiogram to recorder was difficult enough itself but there was always the inane prattle of the resident DJ, usually Tony Blackburn in my case, talking over the intro and the chorus and completely ruining the effect.

On the previous Thursdays, I'd tried recording David Bowie on *Top of the Pops*. My first attempt was ruined by a jammed tape and my second, which was going suspiciously well, fell foul of some particularly noisy interference. The interference was none other than my dad volunteering the unhelpful opinion that, "A bloody good haircut and a spell of National Service would sort out Mr Bowie. Do they call that singing? Can't make out a single word of it! Sounds like a rooster being throttled."

I reached for the Stop button which cancelled the Record and Play buttons. In time honoured fashion, my Dad tapped his head and said, "Am I right lad? I'm not wrong! Up here you want it (and pointing to his feet he continued) and down there for dancing."

Catching his breath from this tirade, he studied the new smoky plastic digital clock on the mantelpiece. Through the heat haze emanating from the Belling gas fire, which had recently been installed against his better judgment, he announced, as was his nightly habit, "Right Crid! It's seven forty-eight and fifty two seconds and I'm off to bed." The novelty of the digital clock radio which counted off seconds as well as minutes had not worn off yet. Clearly, he was on the morning shift which meant he'd be up by two in the morning making a cooked breakfast. I'd often hear him coughing profusely as he made for the door with his snap tin in hand to catch the lift to the factory in Greenfield, some fifteen miles away.

There was nothing else for it but to buy a tape to play to Victoria over the 'phone. I browsed endlessly at the new record and tape emporium that had opened on the promenade. It had to be something timeless and significant which captured my feelings for her. I toyed with *Layla* by Derek and the Dominoes with its strident guitar solo that oozed raging passion, before moving into the Sixties Rock and Pop section and finding the perfect solution.

In a cassette case with a dark blue moonlit scene was the answer: *The Greatest Hits of the Moody Blues, Volumes 1 and 2*. I scanned the tracks to make sure it was there and sure enough, *Nights in White Satin*, shone out at me.

That night in the drizzle, I stood outside the telephone box to wait my turn. I had to leave the queue twice because there were people behind me and I didn't want them listening to my intimate musical moments. Finally, I found the box vacant and 'phoned the well pressed digits of my girlfriend's number.

Having fended off her irritated father who resented me hogging his telephone line to whisper sweet nothings to his daughter, I was finally put through to Victoria who whispered quietly down the 'phone. I said I had something special for her and pressed the fast forward button by mistake. I talked like an incontinent DJ to give me time to rewind to the beginning.

I then played six minutes twenty seconds of *Nights in White Satin* to her. I hoped the intensity of the experience was as great for her as it was to me. Suddenly, I was enveloped in the sensation of insistent sound; the experience was almost religious and certainly painful. The epicentre of this sensation was a raincoated man rapping on the glass of the telephone booth next to my ear. He had heard enough and I had been oblivious to him as I was lost in the musical moment. I only had time to whisper, "I love you Victoria," as I was propelled backwards from the telephone box, Binatone cassette recorder in hand, by a large fist which had attached itself to my collar.

I thought myself quite the heroic lover in this moment, standing in the rain like Humphrey Bogart in *Casablanca*, parted from the one I loved. Then, the Binatone slipped from my grasp in the rain and fractured on the paving slab, rendering the Moody Blues mute forever.

For once, this misfortune did not seem to matter in the intensity of the moment and my inner voice did not even register the usual, "Bugger!" to sum up the situation.

Chapter Sixteen
RESULT

The weather set the tone for the day. The fourth week of August, and leaden clouds were raining stair rods almost horizontally down our street. Gusts of wind ensured that for even those well protected by raincoats, the rain would find a way to infiltrate even the best protected areas.

I recalled other occasions when the rain had left me a dishevelled and freezing wreck. I could feel the dampness seeping through my trousers above my knee and shuddered at the bleakness of the sensation.

I pulled the curtain closed and resolved to venture up to school a little later to avoid the rush.

"It's ten past nine, David", my mother announced with a mixture of urgency and irritation.

"I know," I replied by way of bland acknowledgement.

It wasn't as if I had slept well over the previous days. I really did need this lie-in. I'd spent most of my life to date demanding instant gratification, the presents opened at the earliest opportunity on Christmas days past, nagging to open my Easter Eggs on Easter Saturday against all sense and tradition. I'd questioned the religious tradition of chocolate egg giving and the appropriate day to remove the sensuous dark blue foil around the Cadbury eggs and the garish harlequin foil around the inferior Smartie egg with its surface cast like a tortoise's shell. Today, I was in no hurry to receive news of the result of my handiwork in the O level examinations.

The careless days of the summer holiday had contained the persistent seeds of fear and alarm. I'd pictured this day as a rampant success and a dismal failure. Unfortunately, the former day of celebrations seemed utterly unconvincing and I was left with a haunted feeling that today was when there would be much roosting involving returning pigeons.

I lay for the next twenty minutes with the eiderdown pressed under my chin held with clenched fists, willing myself back to sleep with such energy that there was no way I could relax into slumber.

Downstairs, no doubt my mother was picturing me as the embodiment of coolness, indifferent to what the monumental day offered. How wrong she was! In my turmoil, I was turning over every combination of excuse to cover my indifferent results. Even my 'hope for the best' attitude, like the joker they played in *It's a Knockout* had deserted me. There would be no Hungarians or Ukrainians coming to my aid today, no excuses or stories, no artifice or sleight of hand. A little piece of typed paper headed solemnly, *Welsh Joint Education Committee*, would tell its undeniable truth with crystal clarity.

I had no alternative but to expect the worst and try to weather the storm. There had been an unspoken weight of expectation on me. Nothing was said to my face, but my results up until the time I had left primary school five short years ago had given the family some confidence in my academic ability.

I finally decided that there was no alternative to getting up and made my way in my underpants to the bathroom. In some forlorn attempt to manipulate the day, I pussy footed across the black and white Marley tiles in the same way I'd avoided the cracks in the pavement when younger. If I can get to the sink without stepping on a black tile then it will be a good day. Despite my absolute belief in such dogma when I was little, it sounded utterly unconvincing today.

As I was moving diagonally, like a chessboard bishop, across the bathroom floor, my mother appeared at the bathroom door and in a blinding statement of the obvious, uttered, "You're up!" Taken by surprise, I spun round and my left foot landed on a black square. There really was no hope for this day or for me.

Securing the bathroom door, I now stared blankly into the mirror and saw a self portrait of failure and misery stare back at me. The best I could hope for was damage limitation. If I could only muster the five O levels required to enter the sixth form, then I would be home and dry. I could brazen it out for a few weeks until the results of this day no longer had any bearing on the future.

Pleased to be turning the grey matter to some more useful purpose, I calculated the odds of five magic results. I thought I could count on the old staples of geography, history, English language and literature so that would be four in the bag. I simply needed one more from biology, chemistry, French, physics or maths. One good result from five chances looked like a sound bet on paper.

However, I had no expectations from maths or physics and, although I'd really enjoyed the practical chemistry experiments with their colour changes, explosions and acidic ability to dissolve school uniforms, it seemed indecent to reduce such wondrous alchemy to a series of rational chemical equations.

The number of electrons in the orbits of elements had been the final straw for me. In an attempt to visualise what I was being asked to believe, I'd asked the flame-haired Roberts the Atom, to show me an atom with the electrons whizzing round it. He'd started off explaining that they were very small. I'd asked how small. He'd countered by saying something about ten to the minus something. I'd insisted he show me one to prove that what he was saying was true. Things had degenerated quite quickly from this point.

He'd shown me a picture in the text book, I'd countered that we had learnt in history that we should not believe everything we read in books as much of it was from secondary sources and we should look to examine the primary sources, which was why I wanted to see an atom. He asserted that I was denying the veracity of scientific principles which formed the basis of human knowledge and the fabric of the universe. I acknowledged his point but stated that science in the Middle Ages had put forward the view that the sun moved around the Earth which had subsequently been found to be incorrect so that perhaps his view of the atom was misguided.

Hurtful words were exchanged and I found myself standing alone in the corridor whilst the lesson proceeded without me. I had little hope that chemistry would prove my salvation today.

The same could be said of physics in which the teacher considered me to be an imbecile whose main role was to entertain those who had more than a cat in hell's chance of passing the examination.

Biology held out more hope but the examination had been littered with questions on sexual reproduction and this was not my strong suit due to an unfortunate incident almost two years before. In truth, biology had not been my first choice of option. I'd plumped for German. Why I'd done this was a mystery. I'd shown no great aptitude for languages and had found French alien, so why I'd chosen German could only be explained by the fact that I had a passing familiarity with the language from my plastic modelling exploits. It was unlikely that I could support two years of study and an examination on the basis of Focke-Wulf Panzerkampfwagen, Fallschirmjager, and Jagdgeshwader, gleaned from my model building activities.

Even my extended work reading *Victor* and *Commando* magazines at the weekend had only added *Kamerad*, *Hande Hoch* and Aaaarrrgghhh!!!! (the sound of a German shot by a bren gun—not to be confused by Aaaaaiiiieeee!, the sound of a Japanese shot with a sten gun).

Unless a translation was called for involving a squadron of fighter bombers supporting tanks and paratroopers or an unfortunate gun related incident in the central platz, I did not have much hope. What were the chances of a Blitzkrieg based translation exercise? Extremely remote, I reckoned given the sensitivities of mentioning the war in German.

I had been invited to join another subject after only a few weeks of mauling the German language. I say invited but perhaps advised would be a better description of the German teacher's emphasis on me leaving her class. When I say advised, I mean it in the sense of veering towards insisted. Anyway, within three weeks of the start of term, I was in the biology group.

Being in the biology group actually suited me well. The only sticking point was that in the three weeks in which I had been insulting the German language, the biologists had covered human reproduction and had produced some natty models out of layered card which had been coloured and annotated and stuck in the exercise books. They had also seen some graphic films which illustrated the salient points of human and animal reproduction.

I was resigned to having missed the films, reckoning that a private screening was probably out of the question, but I was keen to cut out, colour and illustrate my own reproductive system models so that I was up to date with the work.

I asked the teacher, a genius of a man with a dishevelled lab coat and hair that looked as if he had just stepped off a yacht in a gale, for copies of the models in question.

Unfortunately, Mr Hastings had moved on to photosynthesis and was preoccupied boiling up grass in flasks and adding various chemicals. He asked me to see him at the end of the lesson, which I did. At the end of the lesson, he was too busy and suggested I see him the following week. This I did, when he gave me two sheets and asked me to stop bothering him. Unfortunately, the sheets showed the digestive and circulatory system so I returned with my original request which I repeated, at least once a week for the term.

Mr Hastings eyed me as some sort of apprentice sexual deviant as my requests for models of the reproductive system became more insistent and he took to shooing me away in exasperation before I could even make my request. I never did get to make those models and the wonder of the human reproductive system was lost to me in annotated form.

It came as no surprise in the examination when the compulsory question featured a diagram of the male and female reproductive system and the invitation to label the parts. I moved on quickly.

Mr Collins was reckoned to be a mathematical genius but he could not even explain to me what X and Y stood for. Were they eggs or house bricks? If so, I'd have been in with a chance. I could calculate how many of the former would be needed to cater for a school kitchen making egg salad for 120 children, three of whom were vegetarians and one of which had a food allergy based on albumen intolerance. If it was the latter, I could calculate the number required to make a tessellated surface to a walled garden of perimeter 17 feet by 9 feet.

I'd been able to amaze Mr Collins with my trigonometrical skills but that was because I reduced every problem to that of a pilot navigating an aircraft. Unfortunately, trigonometry counted for no more than five percent of the O level paper's marks and I was beyond knowing where I could find the extra thirty five marks, or should that be forty five, to register a pass mark.

Unfortunately, the paper had been loaded with algebra. Algebra always sounded like a back complaint to me, like sciatica from which my dad suffered. It certainly was a pain in the arse not knowing whether I had the right answer or not.

The answer to one of the questions on the paper: $2X^2+4X-30=0$ seemed unlikely at 17, 681,666.66 but, you never knew. If an inability to find the right answer would hamper me, the meanderings that constituted my workings out would surely be my downfall. Things had clearly not moved on in this field since the events of the previous summer.

Show your workings out! was a regular comment in my maths exercise book in a rather manic red script which indicated an otherwise pleasant evening's marking for my teacher ruined by my mathematical ineptitude. It all seemed a lot of energy expended when they had given us the fact at the beginning that the answer was nothing. Why worry? I certainly had no illusions that maths would provide the fifth element of my magic O level tally.

It was, therefore, with a heavy heart and a sense of grave foreboding that I arrived, rain-drenched and crestfallen, outside the main assembly hall to await my turn to be given my results. I stood at the heavy wooden door with its frosted glass panes and put my foot on the circular brass door stop on the floor which could hold the door in an open position. I revved away on it as if I was in a getaway car at the scene of a crime, which, in a way, it was.

On reflection, it had been a mistake to suggest extended revision sessions with Victoria, but I had reached the point where it ached with the insistence of an inner ear infection not to be near her.

I had spent hours sitting opposite her over mounds of text and exercise books at our dining room table. I watched the slow, steady rise and fall of her bosom in her white blouse, the light flecking through her black silky hair and her radiant perfect skin. I saw her eyes screw up in concentration and then those perfect almonds would glance upwards, conscious that someone was staring at her and that someone was me. I'd immediately glance down as if enthralled in some particularly delicate equation before looking up to gaze upon the very grail of feminine beauty.

I'd spent hours like this just admiring the space Victoria occupied so graciously. Her beauty and serenity held me transfixed and at no point in these extended sessions was I able to spare any time or energy to actually do any revision. What was the point? I could never emulate in my studies a result more perfect than the vision that sat opposite me.

I mock revised so hard that Victoria and I had no problem in convincing my parents that we needed some fresh air to balance out our concentration. We would habitually end up running hand in hand on the sun-lit beach like the lead characters in *Love Story*, or messing around on bicycles like Paul Newman and the actress everyone has forgotten with the long hair and the patterned dress in *Butch Cassidy*. It was only afterwards that I recalled that both films ended badly for the lead characters.

Unfortunately, the time spent on bogus revision sessions merely raised the expectations of my parents. I caught the tail end of a conversation between my mum and my Auntie Glad in the kitchen during her habitual Tuesday visit. My mum was saying that she was so pleased that I was devoting so much time to revision and that they had high hopes for the results' day in August.

The day of the results was the day that the word 'responsibility' caught up with me, introduced itself in a curt manner, and punched me in the mouth.

The words 'gobsmacked' and 'double take' were not in common currency at the time but they came close to describing my reaction to the reading out of my results. The full gravity of my failure now caught up with me. My banker, English literature, in which I was predicted a 1 had failed me completely and I had achieved a 9 which was considered an 'irredeemable failure'. I had scraped five passes with physics and biology coming to the rescue, but the chances of being considered for A levels in geography, history and English now hung by a thread.

That meant leaving school, being parted from Victoria who still had her fifth year to complete, and finding a job. This was turning into the worst day of my life to date and I passed the throng of my classmates celebrating in the corridors, stormed home with the weather catching the tone of my mood, and went back to bed to plan my way out of this hole of my own making.

Chapter Seventeen
EXAM

An intense period of grovelling ensued to ensure that I secured a place in the sixth form. My teachers were canvassed as to my suitability as an A level student, and with a uniform and unbecoming relish, shared their reservations about my application, ability or both.

Like a penitent, I had to foreswear my previous hedonistic life and commit to the world of learning, of British History from 1760 and European History from 1815, Shakespeare, Milton and Chaucer, and re-sits in Maths and English Literature and new subjects like Geology. Without a plan B, I was prepared to meet all these demands and more and settled into work again after a period of humiliation. The lower sixth year passed quickly and finally the re-sits were achieved and I was taken off academic probation.

I was preparing in the coming year for the A level examinations and believed this to be the major hurdle to be attempted. As things turned out, there was a far more fierce and personal examination to overcome.

"This is Kay dissecting a rat," I announced to my Dad as we entered the laboratory on Parents' Evening. "The rat is the one on the table with its insides hanging out," I added helpfully.

Kay exhaled violently, and I wondered if I had gone too far. Recovering her good humour she beamed at my Dad and said, "You must be very proud, Mr Hughes. We are all so pleased with David's progress. We think he might master a knife and fork for eating before he leaves the sixth form."

This went down extremely well with my Dad. "Really? That's a bit ambitious—we are pinning our hopes on him being out of nappies by the end of the year."

Touché! Out-joked by my own dad—the humiliation! This was not the way the final parents' open evening of my school career was meant to go. We were now days away from our A level examinations and taking my previous examination humiliation into account, I should now be reduced to a state of panic. Instead, I felt calm and in relative control. The nightmare of the last six months was hopefully put to rest. In that time, I had lost Victoria, had left home and had become a virtual recluse surrounded by revision books.

These three related events only become clear if considered chronologically. In my own mind, the last six months had simply been a chaotic hole from which I had struggled to free myself.

The O level debacle had had a profound effect on me. I was determined to arrive at the A levels in better form and prepare properly for the examinations. I was concerned that leaving school would also, I hoped, involve me applying for, and being accepted by, a university. It seemed such a massive step, leaving home and starting again with a clean slate, having to make friends with people who I suspected would have nothing in common with me.

I was also concerned about how my leaving for university would impact on my relationship with Victoria. The prospect of her parents allowing her to come over to stay the weekend with me was a great incentive to study. We'd be able to sell it to them as her preparation for applying to university but to be legitimately together for the whole weekend would be beyond heaven.

All in all, my final academic year looked to be both frightening and exciting and I made a series of resolutions in a diary in my lower sixth year, laying out my plan for the future and the milestones I needed to achieve to reach this goal. It was most unlike me to plan so meticulously and I was quite proud of my foresight. I looked forward to showing my plan to Victoria once all the waypoints had been achieved.

I might have known that fate would intervene to thwart my new, earnest self.

From nowhere, a calamity struck the family and threatened the foundations of what, in my seventeen years, had been the bedrock of my life. In our efforts to deal with the crisis, we compounded the problems and all of us lost something in the struggle. We all hoped that what was lost would only be temporary, but none of us knew for a fact if we would ever experience normality again.

The crisis did not overwhelm us suddenly but approached like a distant thunderstorm. Until the last moment, we hoped it would pass us by but, by the time we had been mesmerised by its strident approach, it was too late to take shelter.

It became clear, slowly at first, and then increasingly rapidly, that my brother was ill and getting worse. He was not physically ill insofar as his only symptom was a reluctance to eat his meals fully. This was totally uncharacteristic as, despite his thin frame, he ate heartily. He progressed to absenting himself from family meals and retreating to his bedroom to play his record collection on the enormous wooden radiogram which had almost given my dad and me a hernia when we had lifted it up the stairs to his bedroom.

What started as erratic behaviour and changes in the routines that governed his life, led to hours of absence when he was in the room but not part of it. Then, the whispering began, the halves of conversations with the wall, the door and the invisible presence outside the front window which was egging him on to mischief.

We fought the symptoms with rationality. I would open the door to show that there was no-one outside and John would scuttle into the back kitchen pursued by some malevolent spirit which only he could see.

Despite it being clear that we could not go on covering up like this for John's increasingly erratic and agitated behaviour, we laboured on. Nothing was said but I knew that this was something that was not to go outside the walls of our house and I said nothing to anybody. My mum had worked so hard from his birth to ensure that John had as normal a life as possible and all her efforts were now in jeopardy.

It is incredible how secretive a family can become when stretched to the limit. The house, which was usually filled with light and mostly laughter, now took on a sombre and nervous hue. We battened down the hatches and made our excuses and tried to dampen down the drama unfolding in our living room.

I began to realise our efforts were in vain as John retreated further into his own private world of torment, spending more time there than with us as we all sat together desperately trying to weave normality around him. My parents kept trying with kindness and reassurance, applied like antibiotics to a fever, to bring John back. But he was too deep into the mental fog to have the ability to exercise any choice about the matter anymore. Despite this, we pressed on with our normal routine, waiting patiently for him to become less agitated and more himself again.

We must have lived like thousands of families who had been visited by the taboo of mental illness. All four of us, Mum, Dad, John and I, had not felt so alone and vulnerable before.

For me, the most difficult part was in dealing with my relationship with Victoria. We had by now developed a cosy domesticity and, at the beginning and end of every school day, she called at our house and we'd walk to school together. Then, after tea and biscuits, we'd wander across town to her house to stand in the abandoned shop door for hours until she was called in to tea.

I bluffed it for a couple of weeks, explaining away John's behaviour and then we stopped calling for tea and biscuits and I'd meet her outside our house in the morning. As the problem intensified, I realised that I was left with only two choices, to tell her everything or to make a pretext and finish with her.

With the summer holiday looming, I knew it would be impossible to impose a quarantine at the door of my house, where she had previously been so welcome. I told her I thought we should not go out with each other anymore. I didn't elaborate on the whys or wherefores and she looked as shocked as I felt devastated. I moved off from our shop doorway as gutless as I had ever felt.

It was truly awful finishing with Victoria and having so little to look forward to outside our family unravelling inside the confines of our house. This was the last summer of school. A long hot summer beckoned and I would have no part in what should have been a last, golden holiday.

We received some respite a week later when, with sleep virtually banished from the house, my mum had 'phoned the family doctor. He came quickly, knowing that our family, over thirty years, had only once asked him to make a house call. He was quickly onto John's symptoms and gave him an injection and some powerful tablets after a hushed conversation with my parents from which I'd felt relieved to have been excluded.

We had been here only once before, some years previously, when eventually the same family doctor had arrived. He'd examined John and seeing the exhaustion of my parents, had arranged for an ambulance to pick up my brother.

He had been whisked away into the night and up the valley to the local psychiatric hospital. No-one had spoken for the best part of the week as we tried to come to terms with this and the worry that the separation would be permanent.

It looked like this would be a repeat of that horrific experience until my mum had managed to convince the doctor to try and give him a chance with medication at home. For more than a week, my brother sat, zombie-like, in his slippers near the hearth, only his eyes darting and weaving. He answered any question with a 'yes' or 'no' but could be drawn no further into conversation or engagement with the world. Even the cat, his constant companion, was ignored and took up residence in the kitchen rather than on his lap, just as frightened as we all were of his agitation and melancholy.

Perhaps the effects of the medication wore off over time or the voice in his head grew used to the medicine and was able to shout above its comatosing effect. Maybe it was a combination of both, but after a week of peace John was off to his hellish place once more and this time the symptoms were even more pronounced. The doctor was called again, and this time there were no alternatives.

This was clearly something that we could not share with anyone, and even close family were unaware of the drama unfolding in our house. The truth came out in dribs and drabs, first that John was ill, then that he had been hospitalised. It took some probing before we let it be known which hospital and even more before we let out the most acceptable form of words to cover his condition, nervous exhaustion.

This seemed a strange choice of words as John was anything but exhausted. He was, on the day he was hospitalised, highly animated, pursued from room to room by some malevolent spirit who alternately whispered and shouted in his ear, telling him what to say, do and think.

The ambulance duly arrived and I said my goodbye to John who shuffled out bent over in his slippers with a blanket around his shoulders and all the worries of the world in his eyes. My mum went with him in the ambulance talking quietly and reassuringly and my dad followed in the car, ready to bring mum home when he had been settled into his closed ward.

I was left alone in the house which had been my place of quarantine for the past months. It had become a desolate place over the past weeks with desperate moments of gloom and anger I'd never associated with my home. I wanted to 'phone Victoria but knew, from the embarrassed way our eyes met in the corridor at school, that she probably would not appreciate the opportunity to speak to me again after the way I'd ended things with her so cruelly and without explanation.

I ran the ancient Hoover around the room and made a half hearted attempt to tidy up generally. I washed the surprisingly small amount of plates and knives and forks we had used in the past few days and thought how effective mental illness in the family was as a suppressant of appetite. I pictured a character from a technicolour advert explaining with all the mock sincerity of Hughie Green how, "Mental illness in the family really will have you shedding those pounds. And I really do mean that most..."

I abandoned the thought halfway, not wishing to give up any headroom to anything other than my own voice, given recent events.

Gathering up some change from the metal sugar jug in the living room cupboard, I ventured outside into the drizzle to get a fresh uncut loaf and some soup for when my parents returned. I walked between the amber smudges of the sodium lights along Vale Road to the grocer's. The rain had penetrated my T-shirt and I was now thoroughly soaked, something I'd normally do anything to avoid. Today, I'd at least felt the sensation of the rain which was an improvement on the last three months when we had all felt nothing positive at all.

"How's your family? Haven't seen your mum for a few weeks," asked Anthony from behind the bacon slicer where he moistened the tip of his pencil and did a quick calculation of the amount I owed on the pile of white paper in which the purchased uncut loaves were wrapped.

"Fine," I said with a finality which bordered on rudeness.

Anthony took the hint and neither ventured further on this line of questioning nor asked me why I had ventured out in such miserable conditions without a coat.

When my parents arrived home ashen faced a couple of hours later, I was able to entice them with fresh bread and chicken soup. The soup had been a standard pick you up from a hard day. I associated it with having a tooth out, breaking my arm playing rugby and the grazed knees from long forgotten accidents.

Clearly, the palliative qualities of chicken soup didn't extend to days such as today. Whilst my mum thanked me for the thought, she felt she couldn't eat anything in her current state. It was left to my dad and I to eat it up with copious amounts of dark-crusted fresh bread and butter. This was the first time I'd felt hungry in almost a month.

Visiting John in hospital was another trauma to be faced. I'd remembered it from the previous episode and it seemed worse now than then as I had grown up more and perhaps realised how far from what I regarded as normal these patients had strayed in their various illnesses and conditions.

The hospital was set in large wooded grounds and was a substantial series of Victorian or Edwardian buildings which looked like a collection of expensive country house hotels. Although now branded at the gate as the North Wales Psychiatric Hospital, it was known far and wide as the Denbigh Mental Asylum. On the Reso, even the name Denbigh was sufficient as a term of abuse. 'Mental' was habitually used as an adjective rather than a noun and Asylum conjured up images of a bedlam of lost souls rather than a place to rest from the troubles of the world.

This was where my brother would spend many months in a drug-induced semi-comatose state whilst his brain decelerated from its current frantic state and took the slip road leading back to the place most of us think of as normality. There were no shortcuts, no miracle cures, just a retreat from madness and the hope he would see in advance the sign that could lead him off this motorway of despair.

John's ward was full of large, white-shirted male nurses with Welsh names who were kind and supportive and were keen to show how well they had bonded with John. The strangest thing about the ward was not the elaborate security measures to enter, nor the bars on the window. It was the fact that the ward was a mixture of kindergarten and old peoples' home.

Sixty year old women ran about with rag dolls under their arm and thick cast-me-down skirts in inappropriately pastel shades. Men with hollow faces were gathered in leatherette high chairs studiously avoiding the gaze of nurses, patients or visitors. The chairs were either too heavy to lift or were screwed to the floor. The spirit of most patients was so broken that they could not work together on any act of rebellion. They were like asteroids randomly occupying a piece of space with no purpose.

A man in an ill-fitting grey suit stood at one window as if admiring the tree lined avenue. But his eyes focussed no further than the bars with whom he was involved in a vast circular argument that was alternatively whispered or bellowed.

Some patients averted their eyes from us, the visitors, like beaten dogs. Whilst others were over-familiar, grasping our hands and explaining to us in minute detail who they used to be and asking, like one lost at sea, if we recognised any of the places or people they mentioned.

"Do you know her?", "Have you seen him?", "Have you been there?", all attached, with desperation, to the end of each sentence. Like the past, normality was a foreign land to them and many would retain refugee status for the rest of their lives.

For some of these poor souls, these wards and this hospital had cared for them since childhood when cruel names like 'idiot' and 'moron' had been applied to them with some sinister medical precision. Although I felt sorry for them, and the terrible condition of their existence, I did not want my brother to be among them. I feared that like fairies, they might spirit him away permanently to their world.

I realised, in that moment, that I did not consider these creatures to be real people. Fifteen miles from the comfort of my own home, in a psychiatric hospital, set in rolling countryside was as far as I needed to travel to rob these people of their humanity. They were uncomfortable and inconvenient in their existence and they were in my presence. In that moment, I realised how easily right-thinking citizens could be galvanised from thought to action and how pogroms and genocides took place.

They were alarmingly different from us and our normality. In their infantile state, they were beyond usefulness and reason. They were a mockery of all that we stood for. They were a drain on our physical and emotional resources, a virus of insanity in our midst. How much kinder it would be for them to be released from this mental torment and, in the matter of a few sentences, I had arrived at a similar conclusion to the Nazis—my own 'final solution', borne out of fear and false concern.

Christmas was now almost upon us. Unable to concentrate or devote the appropriate time to them, my mock A level examinations had gone by in a blur with the inevitable consequences. I had not mentioned at school what would be called by the Head of Year my 'family circumstances'. In the first place, it was none of their business and I wanted to try and quarantine the problem within the confines of my home. Secondly, family circumstances or not, there was no insulating me from the dispassionate A level examinations which were now less than six months away.

There was no doubt that decisive action needed to be taken to propel me from my current performance to achieving the sorts of grades needed to start a course in the Humanities at university. My friends, studying Sciences, were being offered unconditional grades or three Es. I had not received less than three Cs as a provisional offer, so there was considerable ground to make up.

After a very subdued Christmas, I announced that I was going to stay at my Auntie Margaret's for the duration of the revision period. I thought my parents would be glad to see me knuckling down to work but I could not have been further from the truth. My mum in particular, in her exhausted state, saw this as an act of betrayal, of leaving a sinking family in their hour of need. It was a measure of how desperate things had come that I'd never had words with my mum like this before. Indeed, I was hard pressed to remember a cross word between us to that night, which was pretty good going over an eighteen year period. She finished in uncharacteristic mood saying that if I left the house, I could not be sure of a welcome back.

I was shocked that what I thought had been a constructive suggestion had been greeted with such hostility. Clearly, I was thinking this through from a selfish perspective of what I needed to do, rather than the bigger picture that my mum saw.

Nevertheless, I found myself packing a suitcase and lumbering off with it down Prince Edward Avenue and over the crossroads to the railway bridge that led to my auntie's bungalow.

I did not know if I had done the wrong thing. I felt my judgment, and that of all the family was less than sound at present. I'd finished with Victoria for what I'd thought were the best of reasons and it had brought nothing but misery and bad feeling. It looked like I was making a similar mistake now.

It was on this night that I finally grew up and realised that sometimes there is not a right and a wrong answer, just two difficult alternatives from which the best you could achieve was to limit the damage to yourself and others.

The best I could do now was to succeed in the examinations.

Chapter Eighteen
GRAFT

My revision regime, given that I had nothing else to do with my time, was extended and thorough.

Buoyed by a diet of yeast extract, Mackeson stout and Marks and Spencer food to build me up, I set to arriving in the examination room in prime condition.

In an uncharacteristic flurry of activity which did not abate for six months, I managed to drown out most thoughts of the mess I'd left at home. I also managed to keep at arm's length, most days, the continuing pain of not having Victoria around. She had moved on and she was a stranger to me when we passed at school. I hoped the estrangement from my mum would prove to be temporary but I knew I was now invisible to Victoria. What had proved to be the happiest chapter of my life was now, without doubt, at an end. Thoughts of a life together beyond school, when we would have access to a car and funds and a shared future, were shattered.

It had been the most difficult year of my life to date and the only thing that could partly redeem it would be my success in the examinations which would hopefully restore me in the eyes of my family. Examination success would also be my ticket out of Rhyl and away from the torture of seeing Victoria on a daily basis in school and in the least expected moments in town.

The only respite from revision was the morning or evening jog on the beach. That, along with the toffee tasting yeast extract and Makesons, had recovered the stone and a half of weight I'd lost in the preceding months and had left me fitter than I'd been for some time.

The beach was always my favourite retreat. Running along the sea wall between Rhyl and Prestatyn gave a solid, concrete roadway beneath you and the ability to lose yourself in the warm sun and gentle sea breeze. I always warmed down on the beach, looking at the vast expanse of sea and sky spreading to the horizon and trying desperately to put the last year into perspective as being insignificant in the wider scheme of things.

On good days, I managed it and found myself thinking of nothing at all, staring blankly at a sunset, which was a welcome relief from the incessant thinking I had been doing.

The ring binders full of tightly written notes on A4 paper copied and condensed over two years study, looked like unpromising material at first. Only the geography notes, punctuated with maps and diagrams seemed to make any impression on my memory and they provided me with the template for rewriting all my notes in a different format. This had to be better than simply reading undifferentiated notes whilst falling asleep which had been my previous and uniformly unsuccessful method.

Each subject was divided into topics and the notes for each topic had been summarised on a single sheet of A4 paper in the form of an illustrated diagram with connexions and relationships highlighted. Each A4 sheet had been stapled to the appropriate section of the file. From each A4 sheet, a colour coded postcard had been made containing only keywords in a precise order. Each postcard had been written in proper ink with a professional quality Rotring mapping pen that I had purchased at great expense from Hughes the Stationers. Apparently , if the notice was to be believed, this was 'The Home of the Finest Pens'!

It was the most extensive and complete revision procedure known to man and I had absolutely no idea if it would work or not.

However, on the day of the of the English essay examination, I reaped a golden harvest for my revision. This had been the paper I'd anticipated to be the most difficult and I'd given it my best attention in the preceding months.

The paper consisted of seventeen essay questions on the texts we had studied, of which I needed to answer any three in the allocated three hours. I turned the paper over on the cue and read the questions quickly. I put a mark beside those questions that showed some promise, marking the first and then the second. I then went on to mark all seventeen as I had used my colour coded revision system on all the presented questions. I took a deep breath and smiled inwardly and picked three questions at random, such was my confidence.

I looked round the room where at least thirty of my friends were engaged in the same exam. Some were scratching their heads or chewing their pens trying to summon up three questions.

I'd never felt so relaxed in an exam and casually undid the cuff buttons of my lucky yellow shirt and set to in workmanlike, no artistic, fashion to weave my magic on the answer sheet.

My mind was working so quickly, pulling out the requisite model answer from my brain, visualising the layout of the answer and the related quotes. The only problem was ensuring that my hand kept up with the speed of my brain.

The only time I stopped in the three hours was to flex my hand which was developing an annoying cramp as I wrote faster than I ever had before. The inside of the longest finger of my left hand had developed a dent and a swelling where it cradled my lucky pen. I finished with ten minutes to spare, put my pen down, flexed my fingers and put my head on the table for thirty seconds and thought of somewhere else.

I chose a holiday beach and water running through my toes as I dug them into the soft sand. As I relaxed into the scene, I saw Victoria in my mind's eye, walking towards me, smiling, and I quickly snapped out of this favourite place and checked my answers.

To my surprise, there was nothing to add so I sat flexing my muscles and rotating my shoulders to relax them from the stress of the last three hours.

It felt good, it felt very good. As all the tortured examinees gathered in the sixth form lounge for the usual post-mortem of opportunities missed and questions misunderstood, I sipped my tea and kept my own counsel.

It was only on the way home that a pang of doubt set in and I wondered if I'd really been fooling myself that I had done so well. Perhaps it was the fact that I had spent so much time in the preparation that the possibility of failure was so bitter. Six months of living my life like a recluse might just amount to a copious pile of postcards and ink which were worthless. I'd have just over nine weeks to find out.

All the exams continued in this vein and once they were complete, I took the opportunity to move home as quickly as possible and mend broken bridges. I filled in my days working full shifts behind the bar at the Labour Club and trying to save as much as possible for a triumphant or inglorious exit from my home town.

On the day of the results, in contrast to my O levels, it was brilliant sunshine. I was at school as soon as it opened so as to know one way or another what fate had in store for me.

I was second in to see the results posted on the wall of the administration block. Someone was even more determined than me to end the agony, or perhaps they had work to go to.

Whether my eyes were welled up with tears or tiredness from a restless night's sleep, in which I seem to have dreamt about every eventuality, I could not say, but I had inordinate difficulty focussing on the sheet of paper and the results that seemed to be swaying against my name.

I checked and double-checked until it registered that the two As and a C were indeed my reward for the last six months. The results exceeded my own expectations and vaulted over the offer that York University had made to me. Having written down the result in colour coded script, I turned on my heel and ran home to let my mum and my auntie Margaret, who had sponsored my efforts most generously over the last months, know the good news. We drank tea and ate *bara brith* in celebration and I 'phoned York to let them know I had the grades, just in case they allocated my place to someone else. They assured me not to worry as I only needed to inform them had I not met my grades.

An hour later, as we were still talking excitedly in the kitchen, I felt a pang of doubt strike with the intensity of a stroke. What if I had made a mistake and the grades lined against my name represented no more than wishful thinking on my part. I made my apologies and ran back to school to recheck the results.

The entrance hall was now cluttered with my fellow students, friends with whom I had shared the last seven years. Some were ecstatic while others were crestfallen. Some patted me on the back as I moved through them to the significant paper on the wall and congratulated me.

Before I was able to reach the board, my English teacher flew at me and embraced me with more passion than I'd felt in the last six months. She gave me what I still registered as an inappropriate hug and a kiss before holding my face in her hands and whispering, "The future is yours—I never doubted you!"

It was now official. I had managed to gain the grades to leave Rhyl, the Reso and the last year behind.

Chapter Nineteen
BLOCK

As I entered the room, I had the sensation of a generation of National Service squaddies or even of a lout (if that is the collective word) of miscreants in Borstal.

This is it, away from home, committed to an indefinite sentence, and no time off for good behaviour. I had to remind myself that I was here as reward for meritorious brain service rather than as punishment or civic duty. I was here for me.

The architecture of the particular block which was to be my home for the next year hardly reassured me. It had been sold to me as more substantial and newer than the other blocks in my college. The sixties' dream building material, CLASP, a concrete and metal Lego building set, characterised blocks A, B and D but C Block had a contemporary breeze block, minimalist construction. Whereas blocks A through D, excluding C had a particularly distinctly bouncy sprung floor which made all attempts at moving through corridors reminiscent of a springer spaniel with an over-active thyroid, C Block echoed to a dull, concrete thud.

This was leading edge, seventies' architecture and was to be my first acquaintance with the colours terracotta and beige. The closest I had been to such shades had been when my dad, after a cursory discussion about redecorating the living room had, due to his shift pattern, gone from discussion to execution of the painting of the wainscoting and full height panelled cupboard in a shade described in the Valspar Superior range as Wild Mushroom. It had been a bold step, made bolder by the fact that he had chosen, as always, the Full Gloss version. He had remained more circumspect in the choice of wall colour, defaulting to the standard of Brilliant White Vinyl Silk Emulsion over hastily applied woodchip.

My mother said nothing but I could tell she was livid. No doubt, from her flushed face colour, as livid as Valspar's Full Gloss Wild Tomato shade. I noticed that when she sat in her habitual seat to watch television her eye was constantly being pulled right to the reflection of the screen on the Full Gloss Wild Mushroom sheen on the built-in cupboards. The narrowing of her eyes and slight curl of her lip suggested she was troubled by a ringing in her head like the buzzing of the television when the programmes finished at midnight and you couldn't be arsed to rise from your gas fire induced slumbers to turn off the television. I imagined my mother's frequent migraine headaches faithfully reproduced this shade of wild mushroom and the tang of wet paint as sensations.

In a middle class household, she would have put up a volley of objection. I could imagine her, echoing the sentiments of the female inhabitants of the TV sit-coms,

"But Jack, I simply can't live with it!" and with Wildean turn of phrase, "Either the Wild Mushroom goes or I do!"

But this was our house and my mum would have to lump it for twelve months until their smoking habit had tanned the walls Cancerous Tobacco—not one of the Valspar Superior range. Coupled to this would be my incessant nagging, "If that's what it does to the walls, imagine what it is doing to the inside of your lungs".

Finally, nagged and shamed, my dad would be sent into another spasm of redecorating. In this manner, the frail woodchip paper, in successive coats, attained the thickness of the bulkiest anaglypta.

Yet here I was, in the foreign world of terracotta and beige, in my self -contained room. I lay on the bed for twenty minutes to take in my surroundings. I felt that if I could know the room like I had known the inside of the over the stairs cupboard in the Reso box room from childhood, I could tame its foreign harshness.

I'd known the box room cupboard like a womb and chose to hide there on more than one occasion when the going got sticky and I'd run out of foreign scapegoats. I'd sat there for hours holding Airfix kits, like the diminutive blue Grumman Wildcat. Contemplating it from all angles and flying it in my imagination. My backside had picked up the corrugations of the wooden slats and I could feel the dimensions of the room to the inch. The coldness of the exterior wall and the warm throb of the wall behind which hid the immersion heater were hard-etched onto my memory. Not in an electronic way, like a computer circuit, for such things were only fleetingly contemplated in the half hour that was Tomorrow's World. In an industrial way of acids on metal, I knew that space.

I hoped to know this university room as intimately, and, in knowing it, tame it.

The walls had a rough unyielding texture which was urban, but not chic. Mortar lumps which had dried on the breeze block work had simply been over-painted. They produced a distinctively contoured map over which I would run my finger in a strangely compulsive way as I drifted off to sleep on subsequent nights.

There was an eight foot by three foot notice board which had been screwed to the wall straight from the factory and the determined greyness of its colour and texture reminded me of something I'd prefer to forget. On the otherwise pristine board, someone had drawn a Mr Chad and underneath had written, *Wot no servants?* I hoped this to be an ironic quip and not a statement of revulsion at the egalitarian world to which I aspired and, no doubt, he deplored. I knew it was a male's comment by the structure of the handwriting and the fact that the ground floor of C Block was a male bastion at the beginning of the term, so as to afford greater security to the females confined to the upper floors.

It reminded me uncomfortably of the exchange I had at York station earlier, where a decrepit porter in pristine British Rail uniform had witnessed me, a strapping nineteen year old, manhandling my 'bought for the occasion' fawn leatherette case and had rushed to my assistance. Straining his back, he had yanked the case from my hand and placed it on his ancient trolley before whisking me away to the platform lift.

"Are you coming up for the new term, Sir?"

He addressed me in a way that made me intensely uncomfortable. For the first time in my life, I was being deferred to. I did not enjoy the experience. I wanted to tell him I lived in a council house like him and that I was here to smash the system, not to join it. I wanted to say that I did not deserve his regard, and that his age and efforts deserved my respect. But I did not say anything as it dawned on me that he believed in me and what I now represented.

I had left a cold, rainy Manchester Victoria station two and a half hours before, waving nonchalantly to a crying mum as a working class lad. I was now being shepherded across the grand concourse of York station to a waiting Number 5 bus as a bona fide student.

Until the A level results had been published, I had not been a bona fide anything. This was my rite of passage. As with all rites of passage, it was painful and melancholic and the transparency and certainty of what I had been before was lost forever.

As I and my fellow and anonymous students got to the bus, we reached the awful moment when I realised I would need to give him a tip. I'd never been in a situation that required a tip before—except when I had received one for carting cases from Rhyl station to the holiday camps. How much to give? Too little would be insulting, too much would make a serious inroad into my first week's contingency fund. I was still having trouble coming to terms with the idea that in a couple of day's time I would be given a cheque for the princely sum of two hundred and forty pounds from my local authority. They were going to invest that money in me as a student. I needed to economise in case that cheque failed to materialise, substituted by an official note on headed paper tersely typed, *Only Joking!!!*

The time between the limbo of waiting for results which could make or break my plans, and leaving home for the beginning of term had been too short a time to accommodate the magnitude of changes that had occurred and I was in constant fear that some official or other would snatch my place away from me as an administrative error or some horrible lesson in not getting ideas above my station.

I'd fingered the change in my pocket as we'd navigated the station. My delight at being in the railway station, where I had hoped to linger for an hour to catch my first glimpse of the Deltic locomotives I'd previously read so much about, was now ruined as this functionary propelled me to my bus with studied stride, or rather, sciatic limp. We'd smiled at each other but said nothing in the confines of the lifts that had taken us below the main tracks and back up. I had had no more than a cursory look back over my left shoulder to an explosion of exhausted diesel and the throaty roar of the Deltic's Napier engine as an indistinct blue engine accelerated its train northwards to Newcastle.

Working blind, I proffered a ten pence piece as he bustled me onto the red number 5 bus to Badger Hill. I tried to do it in the discreet manner of the veteran tippers I'd seen in the Sunday afternoon films. My effort felt more Ealing than Broadway. He caught my hand in his horny one and declined my offer of a tip with a quietly dismissive gesture whilst squeezing my hand firmly. At first, I thought that the volume of my largesse had insulted him, but his words and his face were sincere when he said, "You save your funds for the new term, Sir."

In a single movement, he was away across the concourse but before he disappeared into the melee of arriving students he turned and waved, just like my mother had done and he seemed a significant other in that moment. Perhaps he was a figment of my conscience, reminding me in metaphorical terms, to remember my station. Rhyl Station and the town where I had grown up on the Reso were now light years away.

I determined to cover up the febrile doodling of this chinless Rupert as quickly as possible and arranged the timetable that had been posted to me and a selection of the contents of my welcome pack on the board in a frighteningly officious manner. This was the first time I had properly had a room of my own and I was aspiring to a tidy, functional look. I did not do student squalor. Why make a mess which you would have to tidy up when, with a little care, you could keep the room pristine?

It was only many weeks later when I had visited sufficient rooms of my fellow students that I realised that the tidiness of their rooms was proportionate to the lowliness of their origins and that this formed a universal and immutable rule.

York seemed to be the second choice of all those scions of the upper classes who had aspired to, and failed, to obtain a place at Oxbridge and the large numbers of Sangsters and De Veres treated their rooms with hearty contempt, as if anticipating the imminent arrival of the family retainers to do a weekly spring clean. I noted, with particular contempt, the way they treated the cleaners who did a daily clean up during the week.

I had managed to endear myself to the cleaners who had been meticulously washing the Marley tiled floor in the narrow corridor as I burst out of my door on my way to my first lecture on the third morning. I'd noticed that they had kept themselves to themselves, talking raucously and animatedly to each other along the distance of the corridor but seemingly oblivious to the gangling students who interrupted their progress.

Unlike the Ruperts, who blundered unconcerned through their floor cleaning, I immediately turned on my heel and apologised for my blue crepe shoes making contact with their newly cleaned and wet floor.

"Sorry!" I exclaimed almost involuntarily.

Three of them stopped at their squeegees and gazed at me. "No problem," I said, " I can climb out of the window". I thought no more of it but, when I returned in the afternoon, there was an extra pillow on the bed and the next morning they put a fresh brew of tea on my desk as they hoovered through.

By the end of the week, we were on first name terms and I was pleased to have some anchors in these turbulent and uncertain times — they could almost have been aunties. But not quite. Although we shared anecdotes and they knew my background, I remained a student and this seemed to trump my working class credentials and always kept a slight distance between us.

They certainly liked the tidy basis on which I maintained my room and rewarded me with little extras on intermittent occasions.

Behind the door of the room was a wash hand basin with a buzzing shaving light and mirror. Next to that was a built in, full length wardrobe into which I had decanted the contents of my suitcase, arranging socks and underpants on the shelves in meticulous order and ensuring that each shirt was neatly hung on its hanger.

On the night before I'd left home, my mum had summoned me to the front room and bade me sit down. She'd only done this on three occasions previously.

Once had been when my nain had died.

Once had been when the police had arrived at our door to arrest a tall, swarthy lad who had been nicking money from the machines in the promenade arcade. I was cleared when the man from the arcade arrived and confirmed my story by telling the police officer it definitely was not me and I realised some bugger from the estate, out of malice, or desperation, had given my name and address when he had been collared.

The third occasion was when she had ushered my Dad into the room to give me a talk about the birds and the bees and, in the embarrassed silence that lasted all of five minutes, we had both resolved to tell my mum that the birds and the bees had been fully covered from a variety of angles. We then sidled into the back room to watch a European Cup football match where Liverpool were playing some eastern European team called Red Star or Gornik or Partisan something or other.

The prospect of the front room was not one I entertained with any great glee and I was expecting my mum to impart some news of great moment. Instead, clearly out of her depth as to give me any advice on my new situation, she defaulted to the old standard of making sure I changed my underpants and socks every day (in case I was involved in an accident!) and how to fold my shirts after ironing them.

I realised that this piece of advice had accompanied generations of lads away from home for the first time. I could fail miserably at academia, be found cheating in my exams but I could uphold the family honour so long as my underwear was beyond reproach.

Having imparted her moral gem, my mum reached into her purse and conspiratorially handed me a ten pound note to, "tide me over until my cheque arrived."

I protested perfunctorily but accepted the money with gratitude as I had lingering doubts about that cheque arriving. I did the same early the next morning as my Dad loaded my suitcase into the car and slipped me another tenner whilst my mum found her coat to accompany me part way on my journey as far as Manchester, "to do some shopping." I mentioned that my Mum had already done the honours but he was strangely insistent. Perhaps he was of the same opinion—that the bubble would burst when the cheque failed to arrive. He was certainly dismissive of my mum accompanying me to Manchester—saying that mothers had not generally accompanied their sons when they had gone to join their regiments if his memory of the Second World War served him right!

In truth, there had been some angst when the euphoria of my results had died down. My parents suddenly realised they had spawned a student and were unsure of what the possible financial implications might be.

I had entered into a lengthy correspondence with County Hall in Mold. I had to ask my parents embarrassing questions about their annual income—areas which they barely shared with each other and which they reluctantly shared with me in order to fulfil the paperwork. It felt like a terrible intrusion on their privacy particularly as, despite their hard work and long hours, the combined meagreness of their income finally warranted me receiving a full grant.

Indeed, the previous year my dad had been laid off for the best part of six months so, administratively, there was never any doubt that I would qualify for a full grant of £740 for the academic year. He was able to console his pride by saying that the previous year had been an anomaly caused by short working but, in truth, I received a full grant for the subsequent two years. It seemed my Dad could accept the full grant adjudication or have his pride but he certainly couldn't have both.

I knew this means testing brought back bitter memories for both my parents.

My nain had told me of the bitter years of the 1930s' depression when my taid was on short working at the gasworks and had to apply for assistance. A man with a suit and clipboard had come round and made 'an assessment'. He calculated that the family had two more chairs than there were family members and that the family had no need of a piano in the household. Both items needed to be disposed of before they qualified for assistance. Such a systematic abuse of the family went a long way to explaining all my family's socialist fervour.

On my father's part, his father's unemployment as a floor layer during the depression had cost him his hard won place at grammar school and he was forced out, unable to afford the books and uniform and, more pressingly, needed to work to supplement the family income. My entrance to university had stirred worrying nightmares of history repeating itself and I am sure this was why he had as many misgivings about the fabled cheque arriving as I did.

However, until the cheque failed to arrive in five days time, I was a bona fide student and I determined, from the privacy of my over tidy room, with its buzzing shaving light, beige and terracotta paintwork, red angle-poise reading light and industrial capacity notice board, to make the most of it.

I was genuinely physically and emotionally tired by the day's journey, the sleepless night previously and the overly drawn out goodbyes on the grubby, litter strewn platform at Manchester Victoria station when neither my mum nor I wanted to be the first one to break away from waving.

Lying on the scratchy, brown chequered top cover of my bed, I wondered whether I was really that tired or if tiredness was simply a useful excuse for not having the confidence to confront my new environment. It was 4 p.m. now and I determined that I would go out in fifteen minutes to explore the college. My resolve was broken when I thought I would be so conspicuous if I merely wandered aimlessly around the college and loitered too long at the porter's lodge looking for the sixth time for any mail, internal or external, that had arrived for me.

When I had arrived, the porter had been quite short with me, demanding my signature in return for a key to my room and warning me of the dire consequences of losing the key. He read a script of do's and don'ts, handed me the sheet with the University crest emblazoned at the top and demanded a second signature. I was not sure if his animosity was personal or general. I hoped that it was brought on by the prospect of over two hundred fresh-faced lost sheep passing before his eyes in the next three days.

I was to find that his demeanour was general and that he was in a peculiar sort of job for one who clearly despised higher education and students in particular. But in all walks of life, I was subsequently to find, there are people who loathe their work with venom but prefer to stay in it and moan until a pension beckons, rather than move on and find something more fulfilling.

"*Chaqu'un a son gout,*" I may have mustered up had I not parted company with the French language at O level on particularly bad terms. Suffice to say we were not on speaking terms, nor had we been for the previous five years, at least not on my part. I settled for, "Bastard."

Not for the first time, my first impression was erroneous. I had completely misjudged the porter, with whom I would subsequently spend many an hour exchanging jokes and putting a mad world to rights.

On my second recce, I'd purposefully skirted past the porter's lodge and made my way into the Junior Common Room. It had a pool table and dartboard which were promising. I carefully positioned myself in one corner and surveyed the room and beyond to the views of the enormous artificial lake and the striking fountain in its middle.

The fountain that plumed from the centre of the lake reminded me of the one at Lake Geneva. Not that I knew anything of the fountain at Lake Geneva except second-hand, from the opening titles of the television series, *The Champions*. It suddenly struck me that so much of my knowledge was gained in similar fashion. Too much of my knowledge came with a commercial sound track.

Our urbane English teacher had once commented that you could tell an educated person from the fact that when they heard the William Tell overture they didn't immediately think of the Lone Ranger. I'd laughed with the others in the class in what I had come to know as a 'conceit'. But I would confess to a little confusion as I did know the theme to the Lone Ranger and did not know it was the William Tell Overture. I also knew the theme tune to the early sixties televison series *William Tell* and could whistle that theme tune as well as name Conrad Philips as the eponymous Swiss hero and Willoughby Goddard as the villainous Austrian Landburgher Gessler, full of sneers and too much food.

It seemed much of my televisually acquired learning was now redundant. I hoped I would have the brain capacity and time to acquire some more valuable information, particularly of a kind that would enable me to survive the next three years.

From my perch in the JCR, I could survey the lake and its cacophony of wildfowl, the giant space ship of Central Hall hovering beyond it, and pretend to be studiously reading one of the broadsheet newspapers which were carefully distributed around the low coffee tables in the room. I'd made the mistake of choosing a low chair with most of the springs removed at my first attempt and had had to recover from this Clouseau-esque moment and retrieve my dignity by shuffling on to another chair. Nobody in the room seemed to give me any attention so I assumed I'd got away with it. I made a mental note to avoid that chair in future and settled into my Guardian in a studious manner.

The print on the paper was something of a blur as I was more interested in the occupants of the room. I was aware that the people with whom I was able to strike up a conversation might well form lasting relationships which would extend through university and beyond and I did not want to make any mistakes.

On my preliminary visit to the university on informal interview, at which it had won my affection, I had met up with a number of other students. One, who had the great good fortune to have the use of his father's car, had offered four of his would-be student friends a lift to the station to catch our trains. It had seemed a generous and worthy offer, particularly as the lad making it was Yorkshire 'born and bred' and assured us he would have us back at the station in time for our train in a fraction of the time it would take the bus as he knew York, "like the back of his hand".

What he did not share with us was that he had passed his test only that week and was of a particularly nervous disposition. He had indeed visited York many times as a young lad, but never as a driver, and the one way system completely flummoxed him. The extended tour of the medieval sites of York would have been both exhilarating and educational had a waiting train not beckoned. We passed the station twice to the best of my knowledge, it may have been more, but the vagaries of the one-way system meant that we could not enter the forecourt.

The Minster loomed up several times as did a number of one way cobbled streets that we traversed in more than one direction. Had it not been a two door car I would have decamped much earlier at one of the interminable traffic light queues but a large, silent guy occupied the front seat. He neither spoke nor moved for the whole of the journey.

I was confined to the middle seat in the back, over the transmission tunnel, with a limp, languid, blonde-haired girl with a pale complexion who giggled and mumbled to herself on my left and a dapper-dan on my right with a floral scarf and an incessant line in chat about which Shakepeare plays he had studied. He asked lots of questions but left no gaps in the conversations for replies. "I'm a great fan of the bard's historical plays. Are you?" he'd venture only to move on breathlessly to another statement suffixed by a question which demanded no answer. This felt like Bedlam on wheels and I resolved not to be taken in so easily again.

At this point, with all hope of catching the 17.30 train abandoned, our automotive host reneged on his promise and suggested we get out of the car and make our own way to the station. He blamed recent changes in the one-way system for his inability to deliver us to one of the most blatantly signposted sites in the city of York.

I moved too quickly to take our driver up on his suggestion which I sensed seemed rude and ungrateful, but quite frankly, I was beyond caring. The lump on the front seat moved with indecent slowness to vacate his seat and allow us escape to the street. He informed us as he moved slowly from his seat that he was in no great rush as his train did not leave until seven and he was quite enjoying the company and the tour of York. I resisted the wholly justifiable desire to punch him in the back of the neck only on the grounds that his unconsciousness would delay our departure from the car even further.

My fellow back seat inmates joined me in the headlong run to the station which was no more than a quarter of a mile away. It transpired that we were all looking to board the same train for Chester from where our routes would diverge. There was no time to feign a Geordie accent and make out that I was catching a northbound train to escape their company and we ended up sharing a table in the Open Second Mark 2 BR carriage.

What should have been a pleasurable travelling experience for me, punctuated by train spotting through the winter gloom at Leeds, Huddersfield and Manchester was marred by the incessant chatter about Shakespeare and his plays to my right and the continuous sniffing of the thin, greasy girl opposite who insisted on emptying the contents of her bag on the table in a manner that was both obsessive and compulsive and accompanied by a running commentary about what she was doing.

But that had been in the dark days of January and since then I'd lived as a hermit and revised myself to oblivion, sat my exams, received my results on a tumultuous day and counted off the days until I could leave Rhyl. This was the start of my new life.

To whom I spoke to in these first days and what I said was going to have a profound impact on my time at university. I was determined to choose my friends carefully.

I was busily thinking up some legitimate and entertaining lines with which to engage someone in conversation when a striking girl entered the room. The first thing that stood out was that she clearly belonged; she moved with self-assurance and purpose. Clearly, she was not a Fresher.

She was at least a second year and a very self confident one at that. She was dressed in autumnal shades, a green tweedy skirt which did not signify frump on her, a brown roll neck sweater and expensive looking brown, knee length, leather boots. Her face was tanned and healthy and framed by shoulder length dark brown, lightly curled hair.

I suddenly realised, as no doubt Pol Pot was realising at the same time in the far away Khmer Republic, that for me, this was day zero of year zero.

I could write my own history from this point forward and be anything I wanted to be.

About Kings Hart Books

Kings Hart Books is a small, independent publisher, based in Oxfordshire, England.

<u>Our other fiction titles:</u>

The Invisible Worm by Eileen O'Conor
ISBN 978-1-906154-00-4
The Reso by Ambrose Conway
ISBN 978-1-906154-01-1
Meeting Coty by Ruth Estevez
ISBN 978-1906154-03-5
Apartment C by Ruth Learner
ISBN 978-1-906-154-06-6
The Price by Tony Macnabb
ISBN 978-1-906-154-08-0
St Anthony's Fire by Rod Sproson
ISBN 978-1-906-154-10-3
Nyabinghi by Shamarley Fontaine
ISBN 978-1-906-154-09-7
The Jewel Keepers – Book One: Albion by E.J. Bousfield
ISBN 978-1-906-154-14-1

<u>Coming Soon:</u>

Leaving Coty by Ruth Estevez
ISBN 978-1-906-154-04-2

Please visit our website at **www.kingshart.co.uk** for extracts and further information.

Available to order at all bookshops or through online retailers worldwide